ALL THE WAYS THE WORLD CAN END

ABBY SHER

ALL THE WAYS THE WORLD CAN END

SQUARE
FISH

Farrar Straus Giroux

New York

SQUARE
FISH

An imprint of Macmillan Publishing Group, LLC
120 Broadway, New York, NY 10271
fiercereads.com

Square Fish and the Square Fish logo are trademarks of Macmillan and
are used by Farrar Straus Giroux under license from Macmillan.

Our books may be purchased in bulk for promotional, educational, or business use. Please
contact your local bookseller or the Macmillan Corporate and Premium Sales Department
at (800) 221-7945 ext. 5442 or by email at MacmillanSpecialMarkets@macmillan.com.

Library of Congress Cataloging-in-Publication Data

Names: Sher, Abby, author.
Title: All the ways the world can end / Abby Sher.
Description: New York : Farrar, Straus, Giroux, 2017. | Summary: Lenny, sixteen,
    struggles to cope with her father's cancer, her best friend moving across the country,
    and more but in a sea of uncertainty, dreams of romance may become her anchor. |
    Description based on print version record and CIP data provided by publisher;
    resource not viewed.
Identifiers: LCCN 2016038107 (print) | LCCN 2017017716 (ebook) |
    ISBN 978-1-250-15847-5 (paperback) | ISBN 978-0-374-30427-0 (ebook)
Subjects: | CYAC: Cancer—Fiction. | Medical care—Fiction. | Best friends—Fiction. |
    Friendship—Fiction. | Family life—Fiction. | Anxiety—Fiction. | BISAC:
    JUVENILE FICTION / Family / Parents. | JUVENILE FICTION / Social Issues /
    Adolescence. | JUVENILE FICTION / Health & Daily Living / Diseases,
    Illnesses & Injuries.
Classification: LCC PZ7.S54418 (ebook) | LCC PZ7.S54418 All 2017 (print) |
    DDC [Fic]—dc23
LC record available at https://lccn.loc.gov/2016038107

Originally published in the United States by Farrar Straus Giroux
First Square Fish edition, 2020
Book designed by Andrew Arnold
Square Fish logo designed by Filomena Tuosto

1 3 5 7 9 10 8 6 4 2

LEXILE: 820L

For my dad, Roger Evan Sher,
and everyone lucky enough to hear him sing

CONTENTS

I wanted a perfect ending . . . Now I've learned, the hard way, that some poems don't rhyme, and some stories don't have a clear beginning, middle, and end.

—*Gilda Radner*

All the Ways the World Can End

vacuum decay

mass extinction

earthquakes

nanotechnology

pandemics

climate change

bioterrorism

artificial intelligence

nuclear proliferation

blood moons

supervolcanoes

coronal mass ejections (sun storms)

asteroids

megatsunamis

Not as Deadly, but Definitely Will Make It Suck to Be Alive

totalitarian dystopia (drones, surveillance)

psychological manipulation pharmaceuticals

Mayan contemplation apocalypse

zombie invasion*

* See the Centers for Disease Control and Prevention's guide on zombie preparedness.

Chapter 1

WAKE UP, WORLD!

My dad had turned into a nocturnal creature. Some rare half-owl, half-lemur, with a majestic wingspan but blood-shot eyes, shedding gray wisps of himself everywhere.

"Fancy meeting you here," he said when I walked into my parents' bedroom with his morning coffee. No matter how many hours he'd been up staring at the shadowy walls, Dad never let on how lonely or exhausted he felt. Only his slow, red-rimmed blinks gave him away.

"Are you really watching this?" I asked.

Dad shrugged. The prehistoric twelve-inch TV on the dresser usually served as a shelf for Mom's dry-cleaning pile. But today it was cleared off and actually showing signs of staticky life. Dad had on some morning talk show with three ladies discussing their *aha!* moments while perched on hot-pink stools.

"Apparently, peach pits are the new drug of choice," Dad said. "Orders from the Sergeant," he added, nodding toward his night table. On it was a stack of political biographies, a ziplock baggy full of trail mix, and a take-out menu for Peking Moun-tainside. Mom (aka Sergeant Nutbags) had left for work extra early that morning, but had jotted down in the margins between noodle dishes:

> saline rinse
> sprouted almonds with acai
> must watch <u>Wake Up, World! with Wendy Wackerling</u>
>   (special on naturopathic remedies!)

Coming up next was Chelsea Diamond, slightly renowned guru and author of *Cancer-Free and Fearless, Thanks to My Peaches*. I instinctually groaned. Not that I wanted Chelsea Diamond, slightly renowned guru and author, to contract more cancer or fear. But I was officially done with Mom's theories about how to outsmart uncontrollable cell replication with pits and seeds.

My older sister, Emma, was actually the one to crown Mom "Sergeant Nutbags," and I think Mom took pride in her sergeanthood. She carried around these little baggies of walnuts, almonds, and chickpea-flaxseed-macadamia-cacao kibble, telling us we had to eat them because they could make us live forever or grow new skin or some other miraculous nutty trick. And because Mom was always doing ten things at once and ran around like a wind-up toy on steroids, she tended to bark orders like a drill sergeant and talk in a storm of words instead of pausing for useless things like air.

"I've definitely learned a lot already," Dad said with a wink.

Leading into Chelsea Diamond's segment, there was now a string of commercials about finding freedom in feminine hygiene products. "How about we get this over with, huh?" Dad handed me another bag, which the good sergeant had filled with four alcohol swabs, two pairs of latex gloves, and a preloaded saline syringe.

"Woo-hoo," I answered weakly.

"Yeah," Dad said. "Sorry, kiddo." Which made this whole thing even worse.

I hated that Mom had left this for me. I'd never done the saline flush solo before. Everyone else my age was comparing hickeys or posting sweet sixteen dance videos, not injecting their dads while watching floating douches.

Dad had just hit the year mark since he was diagnosed with metastatic rectal cancer. It was exactly as ugly as it sounded. In the past 365 days, a team of surgeons had pulled out pieces of his abdomen, rewired his colon, and closed up his butt. Then they outfitted him with lots of tubes and a colostomy bag that he hid from me at all costs.

For the first few months, Dad acted like the whole cancer thing was just a bad-hangnail kind of annoyance. He took some sort of chemo that came in pill form and popped it in his mouth like a gumdrop, then chased it with toast and coffee and headed to his usual 7:23 commuter train for work—he was a partner at a patent law firm. A few times he went in on the 8:05. Once he skipped going in completely, but he said that was because he had a lot of conference calls and they were easier to do from home. I chose to believe him.

Things got more complicated after his first operation. They opened him up the Tuesday before Thanksgiving and then announced that Dad was banned from turkey and all other solid foods until further notice. Which led to a second operation just a month later. After that, he started carrying around the bag I was supposed to not see and he couldn't sit for very long without a special butt pillow packed with ice.

Once he was mobile, he started taking the train into New York City again—the 9:03 or the 10:38. I don't know how he managed the trek to his midtown office or what he actually got done at work without his ice pillow. His dark hair never fell out. Instead it just clung to his head in damp, tired clumps.

Mom, Dad, Emma, and I celebrated New Year's Eve in the emergency room because he was in so much pain he couldn't talk. That's when the doctors found new metastases in his lymph nodes. They started a supersonic blitzkrieg of chemo, pumping him with miracle venoms every two weeks and then giving him a couple of days to catch his breath before starting all over again. Everything fell out then, including his eyelashes. He didn't even have to get his parking validated at the hospital because the guard saw him so often.

Two months ago, on his last overnight chez Urgent Ambulatory Care, Dad got a chest catheter installed so he could do more of his treatments at home. It took me three weeks to get up the guts to glance at it, even though it was under his skin. It looked like they'd planted a silver dollar just below his right clavicle. Only as he got thinner, the catheter poked out more and more.

There was a divot in the middle where all his shots went. I made sure to be far away when that happened. A visiting nurse came on Tuesdays to administer the heavy meds and check vitals. Mom took care of keeping the catheter clean and giving Dad horse-pill-size immuno-boosters the rest of the time.

Except for today, of course. It was the first Friday in May and finally felt like spring, though, like Dad, I hadn't slept much the night before. Partly from pre-syringe jitters and also because we were rotating through the third of four lunar eclipses this year and I'd been researching the theory of all life ending after the blood moon sequence.

The bright side was, dawn came.

Mom abandoned us extra early today because she was in session hearing some controversial indictment about noise pollution at our local mall. She was one of the supreme court justices of Westchester County, New York. I had a hard time being impressed with that because they had never been able to curb fracking or stop the county from hosting an annual gun show. Also, whatever this noise pollution verdict was, I knew Mom would find something else to keep herself overscheduled soon enough.

She was constantly rushing around like the day was about

to disappear, leaving a trail of nutbags in her wake. She worked sixty-plus hours a week as arbiter of all things judicial. She also was on the board of five thousand different charities—we called them all "the sisterhood" because she only ever told us about the women at her meetings. One was for an animal shelter and we were currently sponsoring a guinea pig she named TinyGinsberg (after United States Supreme Court Justice Ruth Bader Ginsberg). In Mom's spare time, she was training for a triathlon with an obstacle course. She swore that at age forty-eight, she was in the best shape of her life and she owed it all to the power of *going raw*.

Going raw was Mom's newest theory about how to cure cancer and save the world. Before that it was eating cloves of garlic and trashing our microwave. Before that it was getting rid of all wheat, meat, corn, sugar, and laundry detergents in our house. At one point we boiled all our water and turned off all our electronics (that lasted exactly three hours). Mom had read so much about cancer research and hidden carcinogens that my brain got achy even looking at the latest article she'd clipped and posted under a refrigerator magnet.

I knew it was her wonky way of coping with Dad's insides turning into a battle zone, and I appreciated her efforts. I just hated feeling like finding the right legume was going to fix everything. It gave me too much hope and a false sense of control that ultimately came crashing down and/or gave me indigestion. My sister, Emma, was finishing her first year of state college four hours away and constantly texted me pictures of the stews and waffles in her cafeteria so I could see the world of cooked food. Emma used to be the one who could tell Sergeant Nutbags to chill out. Now we were rudderless. I was afraid of all things related to conflict, so I spent a lot of time silently seething, and Dad laughed a lot as if Mom were a well-meaning but misguided puppy. Which, in many ways, she was.

As Chelsea Diamond took the TV's stage blowing air kisses to her viewing audience, Dad set down his coffee and opened the top two buttons of his pajama shirt. I didn't mean to whimper, but his chest looked so bare and bony. He used to have sprigs of dark chest hair. When we went swimming at Wahonsett Bay he'd get seaweed caught in it and pretend to be the Loch Ness monster. There was not a single strand there anymore. Just this tender, splotchy skin.

"I know!" squawked Chelsea. "So simple, right? I'm living proof!"

I officially hated her and the peach pit she rode in on.

"It's okay," Dad said quietly. "Just read Mom's instructions and I can walk you through it."

Mom's scrawled notes on catheter sterilization were in the wonton section of the take-out menu. I had to thoroughly clean the skin around Dad's clavicle, wait thirty seconds, then stick the saline syringe into the magic divot to flush the valves underneath with a cleansing rinse. Hopefully without either of us fainting or screaming "Help!" at the sky.

"Got it," I whispered, pretending I wasn't shaking all over. I took out the four alcohol swabs I needed and lined them up on top of his book stack, tallying, "One, two, three, four. One, two, three, four."

"Hey," said Dad. "You're gonna do great." He tried to take my hand, but I was shoving it inside a latex glove, so we wound up swatting each other. I lined up the swabs again. And again.

"If it helps, Wendy just agreed to plant a peach tree in the third-world country of your choice," offered Dad. It wasn't fair that he was trying to cheer me up when he was the one broken.

"Let's do this," I said, putting on a second pair of gloves just to be extra sterile.

I ripped open a swab, wiped down Dad's silver-dollar-size lump and counted to thirty Mississippi. "Nice, nice," he murmured. Then I uncorked the saline syringe and lined it up with the little dip in the middle. Which really was a gaping hole leading into his fragile body, and I was about to dump some preloaded syringe that could've been filled with arsenic or glue or hairspray. I had no idea. I was just trusting blindly. Trusting my absent mom. Trusting the new developments in immunotherapy. Trusting whoever invented chest-catheter ports and decided saline was any kind of solution.

"Ready, set, go," I mumbled through clenched teeth. I pressed the needle into his chest; it made a horrible *pock* sound. We both gasped as I felt Dad's whole body tighten. He squeezed his eyes shut.

"Still good?" I asked in a tiny voice. He didn't answer. "Dad!" I yelled into his scrunched-up face.

"Yeesh," he said, trying to smile.

"Sorry," I whispered. "I just—are you okay? I'm sorry. I'm sorry. I'msorryI'msorryI'msorryI'm—"

"Pull it out. *Please.*" He was sweating along his pale top lip.

"Right."

We both panted while I took out the syringe and wiped another alcohol pad over his skin. Then I watched closely to make sure his chest was rising and falling. As opposed to oozing or collapsing. I wanted to run so far away and smash everything that made this moment. I wanted to hurl that syringe and suck the alcohol swabs until my insides burst into flames. Instead, I restacked Dad's untouched books. "One, two, three, four. One, two, three, four," I repeated. It was the only thing that felt certain. One plus one was two. Three would always be followed by four.

Dad's breath slowed down a bit. I offered him a sip of juice but he shook his head, eyes still closed.

"Amazing!" Wendy Wackerling cheered. The television sputtered with applause. "How can we get more of these extraordinary pits in people's hands?" she marveled. I threw two of my four latex gloves at the screen. They barely cleared the end of the bed and landed with a chalky outline around them on the navy carpet.

"Dad, I'm gonna turn off the TV, okay?" I didn't want to touch him again, so I did an awkward snap by his ear.

"Yeah," he said, clearing his throat. His eyes roamed around the room and then landed on me wearily.

"Are you okay?" I asked. "Do you want me to . . . ?" I didn't know what I had to offer. I didn't even know what I'd done. In the past year my dad had been through so many grueling treatments, operations, bouts of radiation, implants, and items of unsolicited wheat-free wisdom. And now I was sure I'd sealed his fate with one swift needle jab, just sloppy enough to puncture an artery or lung.

Dad closed his eyes again and whispered, "Go. School. Fine."

"Okay, but if it does something or you feel funny, please call me."

"Mmmmyup." He was drifting into what I hoped was a diamond-studded nap.

You're just napping. You're just napping. It's good to nap. You're just napping.

I mouthed those words twenty-five times while I watched him inhale and exhale. My dad detested naps. That was probably my hundredth clue that something was very wrong that first Friday morning in May when the world was erupting into either spring or everlasting darkness.

I scooped the syringe and wrappers off his night table and dumped them in the garbage. It took another five minutes to peel off the other two sweaty gloves I was still wearing. I went to the bathroom down the hall and turned on the faucet as hot as it would go. I shoved my powdery hands under the scalding water, watching them turn pink, holding on to the hurt as long as I could. No matter how hot it got, I couldn't scrub away all my ugly thoughts about coming home to Dad crumpled on the floor or shoved in a coffin and Wendy Wackerling shouting at him to wake up.

When I got downstairs I dialed Mom's number. As expected, it went straight to voice mail. *This is Naomi Rosenthal-Hermann. Your call is so important to me—*

Which was bullshit. Because what could be more important than her sixteen-year-old daughter possibly murdering her beloved husband of twenty-three years with a shot of saline to the heart?

Mom always said if she was busy to call her clerical assistant. Her name was Pippi and she was obnoxiously chipper. I couldn't handle her squeaky optimism right now. So I called Mom's voice mail again and left her a very passive-aggressive message about Chelsea Diamond's riveting story and hoping she was having a fun day and she should maybe check in on Dad since the saline shot had been fairly traumatic for both of us. Then I washed my hands one more time before grabbing my backpack and jacket and closing the front door behind me.

My best friend, Julian, was parked outside. His Volkswagen Jetta was leaking something all over our driveway.

"Sorry. How late are we?" I asked, climbing in. Julian was consistently five minutes early for everything. I was consistently five minutes behind. Today, I'd added an extra ten for possibly life-threatening needle procedures.

"Late enough to skip first period," he answered. We both had study hall first period, so it barely mattered. The Jetta started up with a ferocious cough; the front seat smelled like a forest fire. Julian had added about twenty-five new pinecone air fresheners to the rearview mirror but I could tell the cigarette in the ashtray had just been snuffed out.

"You know my dad's dying," I said, holding up a butt.

"Still?" Julian asked.

I punched him hard on his shoulder and he said, "Sorry! Sorry! C'mon. I'll treat you to free toast."

I didn't want to bawl before school, especially because I'd just started my liquid-eyeliner-makes-you-look-older campaign. So I cranked up Julian's newest Europop dance mix until my skin was throbbing. We didn't say another word all the way to the Unicorn Diner. Instead, I stared into the side-view mirror and tried to decide if the objects were larger in the mirror than in real life or larger in life than in the mirror.

Vacuum Decay

Also known as "catastrophic vacuum decay" or "cosmic death bubble." Space decays into a lower energy state, which makes a ginormous monster bubble, expanding at the speed of light. The bubble wipes out everyone and everything in its path—i.e., Earth, space, us.

Stephen Hawking says, "This could happen at any time and we wouldn't see it coming."

If we make it through the bubble collision, then we will most likely collide with other galaxies. Benjamin Shlaer (Tufts cosmology dude) calls it a "catastrophic sort of crunch."

Warning signs:
None, really. Which is the beautiful horror of it all. There's no way to prevent or prepare or even collect canned goods because it could happen in any space or time continuum.

Preventive measures:
Stay away from particle accelerators

Write to Stephen Hawking for access to the doomsday preface he wrote for *Starmus* book

Read more of Roxanne Palmer's article "Will the Higgs Boson Destroy the Universe in a Cosmic Death Bubble?"

Or better yet, don't

Chapter 2

DON JUAN CRUSTACEO

The Unicorn Diner was sort of like our secret clubhouse. Julian and I brought down the average age to midseventies because it was always crowded with blue-hairs from the retirement community behind the golf course. Our regular booth was on the side by the parking lot. It had optimal sightlines for people watching and checking in with the Unicorn ecosystem— i.e., the fish tank with three lobsters that never got eaten and a purple plastic seahorse sitting on a treasure chest with fake pearls dripping out the side.

Julian and I had a favorite lobster we named DJC, for Don Juan Crustaceo. He only had one claw. Julian said it was from a gang fight with a bunch of mermen. We loved to make up dialogue for DJC as he wooed the other diner customers. He had a thick Italian accent and no room for subtlety. As in, "Hello, ladies, would you enjoy to come inside my treasure chest and lick-a my pearls-a?"

DJC was quite the player. Plus, I was pretty sure he'd brokered a deal with the Unicorn cooks that he could never be slain. Not that there was a line out the door for surf and turf (that was the one dish on our laminated menus involving shellfish). Our sleepy suburb of Mountainside, New York, was landlocked and the nearest beach had been voted number two on a national list of the most-polluted waters for the past five years. Yum. Maybe that's what gave DJC his gleam.

"Is that a barnacle on your back or are you just horny to see-a me-a?" Julian said in an offensively slimy Sicilian accent as we stopped by the tank.

"Don Juan, you naughty bottom-dweller!" I answered in my high-pitched seahorse voice.

"Please-a. I want to give you pleasure-a with my pincers."

"Oooch, that sounds kinky," said someone behind us. Julian turned around and pulled our buddy Dara into a tight hug, even lifting her off the ground a half inch. I saw she'd dyed her short hair again. It looked like she had on a helmet of fire.

"False advertising," Dara explained. "Also, I misread the instructions and didn't dilute. But hey—" She pointed to a new pin she'd gotten for her apron that said, I'M STILL HOT, IT JUST COMES IN FLASHES NOW.

"How are my two favorite misfits?" she said, knocking me sideways with her wide hip.

"Eh," I answered.

"Amen, sister." She showed us the mugs of coffee waiting for us at our regular table. The porcelain looked way too clean and each mug had a leaping unicorn printed on its side.

"What the what?" said Julian.

"Stephan's orders. Don't shoot the messenger, but coffee's

no longer bottomless either." Dara rolled her big eyes. Stephan was the new manager of the Unicorn and was driving Dara insane. He had some vision about making this place into a fine-dining experience, which so far involved a lot more potted plants, a calorie count for each dish on the menu, and all of the staff having to memorize a list of "International Delight" dishes.

"Actually, do shoot the messenger," she whispered. "At least that way I get worker's comp." She put a few extra jams in my palm before rushing off to deal with a man complaining about runny eggs.

Dara was actually one of the few people who knew how crappy things had been for my family, because Julian and I came into the Unicorn so often to debrief. Dara hadn't had it exactly easy in the past year either. She was a single mom with a fourteen-year-old son who'd been caught lighting things on fire in his desk at school. So at age forty-nine she moved herself and her son into a one-bedroom apartment with her mom and took a third part-time job so she could afford some mandated behavioral therapy for her kid. Dara's mom sounded angry and agoraphobic. She drank whiskey all day and ordered a lot of kitchen utensils from cable channels. Dara was constantly trying to mail rubberized whisks to random P.O. boxes.

Whatever mayhem was going on at home, Dara showed up to every shift at the Unicorn with a new pin and a gritty smile. She swore she owed each sliver of her sanity to AA. Julian connected with her a lot on the power of twelve-step programs. They exchanged mantras and silent nods of recognition that I wished I understood on a deeper level. Julian was my best friend in the whole world, and yet there were so many pieces of his past missing to me.

Julian and I were four years old when we first met at the nursery school sand table. He wore a blue superhero cape and called himself Captain Booger. His magical powers included picking his nose and predicting the future by gazing into a big bouncy ball colored like the globe. Julian said that I could be his sidekick, Louise. My superpower was that I could swim through concrete. I was never allowed to touch his Ball of the Future, though.

One day while we were in Ms. Birdstall's first-grade class, Julian's mom decided she was in love with the cleaning lady and they moved out to an apartment a few towns away from us by Yonkers Raceway. Julian had not predicted that. No one had. Rumors rushed from carpool to carpool because *who knew there was a lesbian amongst us?*

My mom told me there were crazy custody battles and Julian was forced to testify against his mom in court. (Julian's dad accused his mom of reckless abandonment because she'd once left him in the car while she ran into the grocery store to get milk. Which everyone had done at some point, but Julian's dad was on a vendetta.) Meanwhile, Julian started losing patches of hair from all the stress and I clearly remembered him peeing his pants in the hallway when we were seven and trying to deny it even though there was a dark stain seeping down his leg.

It was like a modern-day witch hunt, Mom told me years

later. Julian's mom was only allowed to visit once a week, and even then it had to be supervised. After a few months, she just stopped coming. I was pretty sure she was living on the West Coast these days, but I tried not to pry.

Julian and I lost each other for almost a decade because his dad put him in some private day school where they learned math by contorting their bodies into numbers. Julian got really depressed and self-medicated by smoking and snorting anything that could make him feel lighter. He once told me about some acid trip he'd been on and I felt like a naïve idiot because I asked, "Does that come in pill form or as a spleef?"

Julian laughed a low, sad laugh and said, "Yeah, never mind. Why are we talking about this anyway?" essentially locking the access gate to that part of his life. I did know he went to Valhalla Treatment Center for rehab twice and to another private school that specialized in performing arts and was also sort of a correctional institution before I met him again as "freshpeople" at Mountainside High.

That was almost three years ago now. Julian had walked into World History, sat down behind me while I was writing my daily "All the Ways the World Can End" list, and said, "Really? Tsunami?"

I'd sucked in my breath quickly because a notebook was supposed to be private property and I didn't know any of my classmates well enough for one of them to be shoulder snooping. Certainly not anyone of the male persuasion. (On a scale of one to cool I was holding steady at a solid two.) But when I turned around with a clenched fist, Julian just smiled. He looked exactly as I'd remembered him, with maybe a longer chin and some new blond whiskers. The same turquoise eyes smirking behind his sandy, shaggy hair.

"Megatsunami," I answered. "It's not that far-fetched. Could wipe out Honolulu in minutes and keep traveling inland for sixteen miles."

Julian frowned. "But I just bought a bikini," he said.

That was the biggest reason why I loved and admired Julian so fiercely. He took the fog of all my obsessions and shrank them into the size of a two-piece. I never told Julian why I was studying all the ways the world could end because:

a) he never asked, and
b) I didn't have an answer. I just *had* to.

I'd been writing some form of this list every day since I was nine years old. I even knew the precise day I started: December 27, 2010. I was on winter break and my dad and I had taken the train into New York City to visit the big planetarium. There was a special exhibit about the future of intergalactic exploration. We got to climb inside some simulator where we floated upside down and my nose dripped backward because I had a cold.

When Dad and I got out of the cockpit, I sat down on a bench to wipe my snot and there was a movie playing on loop next to us called *Vacuum Decay: An Instantaneous End.* The subtitle said it all. There were clips of scientists in lab coats shaking their heads and pictures of meteors and quotes from people like Stephen Hawking coming out of the nebula. They couldn't be sure when it would happen or even if it already had happened once and was going to happen again. They just all kept saying vacuum decay was "a very real and cataclysmic possibility." Also, vacuum decay would bring "universal obliteration." And my favorite, "wiping out Earth and any memory of what it was."

I asked Dad for a pen and wrote those lines down on my forearm. Then I committed them to memory. Or really, my memory committed those lines to me.

Once I watched that stupid ten-minute horror-fest, I couldn't unwatch it. On the train ride home, I kept asking my dad how the Earth could be in that much peril and how come nobody was prepared. Dad answered, "How could we prepare?" which was the most terrifying answer possible. I didn't say another word the whole way home. I was so distracted that I ate the waxy paper that came with my hot pretzel and got a nasty scrape in the back of my throat.

I started my list of all the ways the world could end that night because I had to get it all out of my head. I added to it each day and made sure nobody else saw it. At least until Julian sauntered back into my life and shoved his nose into my apocalypse.

Of course, he was completely unfazed. He told me that the real threat was bioterrorism from homosexual robots and he was going to lead that charge. Also that before we all died, he was going to skip last period of school and go get Carvel flying saucers and I could come with him, but only if I committed to eating three.

I did.

Then we lay on the brown grass at Squirrel Park and talked about who was more influential—Thomas Edison, Buddha, or Whitney Houston. I showed Julian all my data on nuclear proliferation and he showed me the scars on his wrists, and that night I forced Julian to swear he'd never leave again and would be my best friend forever.

"Whatever that means." He shrugged. Which I took as a yes.

I was so thankful to have Julian back in my life. I knew I wouldn't have survived the recent past without him. Whenever my dad was getting carved up or chemo'd, Julian took me to the movies or through the aisles of Costco for cracker samples. Once I'd escorted Julian to an AA meeting in the basement of St. Mary's Presbyterian, but I didn't go inside. My favorite was when we dressed up and went to the fancy car dealerships on Central Avenue. We talked to a lot of well-groomed salespeople and even test-drove a Lexus. Then we took a long time to count all our pocket change as if that could make or break the deal. We found it hilarious, even if nobody else did. I always felt taller when I was near Julian. If the world were ending, at least we'd go down together.

Only we were pulling into the last two months of our junior year now, and Julian had applied to some exclusive dance conservatory in San Francisco. He was acting nervous and moody about it, but we both knew he'd be getting the thick acceptance letter soon. He was really passionate about modern dance and obscenely talented on stage. Plus, he'd already finished the high school credits he needed to graduate a year early by taking summer classes.

Logistically, Julian was being forced to move out. His dad had just gotten married for a third time—this one was a hedge-fund analyst named Katya who only had enough affection for her shihzoodle, Daphne, and told Julian he was "not her problem." She'd even written a prenup that stated her decision to be child-free. Katya had scheduled demolition of Julian's bedroom for the first week of summer break. (So she could build a bigger office with a treadmill desk and a heated dog bed for Daphne.)

Even if somehow Julian didn't make it into the conservatory, he was determined to escape this town.

I gulped lukewarm coffee to get rid of that thought. Julian was digging into the plastic squares of jelly with a spoon and offered me a taste of mixed berry but I shook my head no. Life would be so much easier if he could be not gay and I could be not so needy and we could run away and live off the fat of the land. Whatever the fat of the land meant. Probably fields of bacon swaying in the breeze.

"What's up?" Julian asked, waving his sticky spoon in my face.

I just shrugged, because him leaving and my dad dying and the smell of home fries creeping up my nose was just too much.

Julian reached across the table and took my hands in his. I could feel his caffeinated pulse bouncing between us.

"I don't know," I said, scanning the blue-haired horizon for something else to talk about besides the truth. "Did you read that new study about how all tap water is contaminated with Teflon now? But who can afford to drink bottled water every day, right? And speaking of water, do you think Don Juan's tank looks extra murky? I do. I think we should say something to Dara or maybe take it straight to management. What do you think? I can do the talking or you can really, because I use a lot of run-on sentences, which I'm pretty sure is hereditary. But whatever. Oh, and I was just thinking, not that you would, but could you please not go to San Francisco and never call and never write and forget that I ever existed?"

Julian's knuckles were turning white as he held on to my hands firmly. He blew the hair out of my eyes and made me meet his gaze.

"I'm not sure which question you want me to answer first, but I will say this: Yes, you use run-on sentences. And no, I will not abandon you."

Which gave me just enough courage to blurt out, "And can you tell me I didn't kill my father this morning?"

This time it was Julian's turn to take a gulp of coffee and cleanse his palate. While he did that, I described in detail what Dad's chest looked like and tried to imitate his wince. Julian watched carefully before answering.

"Listen up," he said sharply. "Your father might be dying. But you are not killing him."

I loved and hated Julian so much all at once. I couldn't trust my voice to be non-squeaky and warbly, so I just nodded.

"You know that, right?" he pressed.

More vigorous nodding.

"And you know it's not your job to save him?"

I pressed my napkin into my eyes until I saw floating blobs. I just wanted to hitch myself to one of them and drift away too. There was no other place to escape this feeling of everything falling apart.

"Too burnt?" I heard Dara ask. She often brought us plates of rejected bread that had gotten jammed in the diner's finicky toaster.

"Perfecto," said Julian. "And hey—if anyone can pull off that highly flammable-looking hairstyle, it's you." I knew he was giving me some time to compose myself. I opened my eyes and shoved some blackened toast into my mouth, mumbling agreement.

"Aw shucks," said Dara, fluttering her eyelashes quickly. "You say that to all the basket cases." Dara gave my cheek a pinch before taking off for another table.

"I feel like we should get going," I told Julian. "I want to try calling my mom again before second period starts."

"Wait," said Julian. "If you're going to call anyone for medical advice, it should be sweet Dr. G. Am I right? Answer is *yes* and *you're welcome*."

"You think?" I felt a smile peeking out from my haze of doom and pulled a business card from where I'd stashed it inside my jean jacket pocket. Actually, I had three copies of this card squirreled away in different pockets and a fourth locked in my top desk drawer at home. It read:

RADHAKRISHNAN GANESH, M.D., Ph.D.
Medical Oncology Resident
917-555-0198

"Now that's what I'm talking about," said Julian.

Dr. Ganesh was the newest addition to my dad's oncology team. He was also ridiculously handsome. Somewhere between thirty and timeless, with warm brown eyes and eyelashes that were long enough to be illegal. He was always so excited—to be doing rounds, to be studying immunotherapy, to be alive and part of the new alliance between Eastern and Western medicines. He loved to talk about how far we'd come in medical innovations just by looking back at our origins. (A quick search on the interwebs told me he was born in southern India and came here for college.) I especially loved how he used random American slang like "Can I get a what what?" and "That is what I am talking about!"

I could always hear him coming down the hall because his voice was so energetic and he gave a lot of fist bumps, especially when he liked my dad's vital signs.

Julian didn't believe me about Dr. Ganesh when I first told him. Or rather, Julian said that Dr. Ganesh was symbolic of my need for unrequited infatuation and addictive self-flagellation and that I was transferring loss into lust. (Julian read Piaget and Bettelheim in his spare time.) He was also pretty sure I suffered from "CTSD" (continuous traumatic stress disorder).

So about a month ago, when Dad had to do a hospital over-night (to replace his colostomy bag—party!), I begged Julian to visit for a look-see. Dr. Ganesh was doing his rounds and I could smell his sandalwood aftershave three rooms away.

"Ey-leah-nor!" he said when he saw me. "Can I get a what what?" (fist bump). Usually I hated going by Eleanor. My mom insisted on saddling me with this name because she thought Eleanor Roosevelt was one of the most underappreciated heroes of the world. I also had the clumsiest last name in the history of consonants, Rosenthal-Hermann, because Mom insisted on hyphenating. Everyone had called me Lenny since I was in kindergarten. Except Dr. Ganesh, of course. Somehow when he said my name, it sounded like it had five sultry syllables. Which was another reason his voice made me shiver.

"Damn," I heard Julian murmur. "One of us has to kiss that silly man."

Of course, I knew Dr. Ganesh could never really go for me. First of all, he was at least a dozen years older than me and had a regular habit of looking inside my dad's rectum. Also, I'd be wildly surprised if he was into awkward teen brunettes with overbearing unibrows and panic attacks who wore thrift-store jeans and still didn't really fit into a B-cup. But that didn't stop me from dreaming. Like, it wouldn't be totally impossible for Dr. Ganesh to be treating my dad on a night shift and then I'd be there looking out a hazily moonlit window and we'd share our deepest secrets and some Milk Duds from the vending machine as the sky melted into a sunrise.

"Maybe I should call him to describe what happened this morning?" I asked Julian now. "It's a saline solution. Not supposed to do anything besides . . . salinify?"

"Nice," Julian said.

"Or I could just text him?"

"Do it."

It took me approximately eleven minutes to compose these two lines of text:

Hi Dr. Ganesh, it's Eleanor Rosenthal-Hermann. Can I ask you a question?

Julian had already etched a map of the United States into his fifth piece of blackened toast and bitten off three more fingernails by the time I finished.

"Is that okay?" I showed him my phone.

"Sure, just let me see that." He snatched it and typed in **Do you like pina coladas or getting caught in the rain?** Then he pressed Send while I tried to pry the phone out of his hands, screaming, "Stopstopstopstopstop!"

Dara wasn't too pleased with our noise pollution and gave

us a scowl. Julian and I each put down a three-dollar tip on our one-dollar cups of coffee and picked out the pink chalky mints from the host stand before heading out to say goodbye to Don Juan.

I noticed there was a big plastic bucket on the floor under the tank and a hose pumping some bubbly fluid into it.

"There-a goes the neighborhood," said Julian.

"Who invited all the plankton to this party?" I chirped.

Julian tapped on the glass just as my pocket buzzed. I pulled out my phone and saw I had a text back from 917-555-0198.

Hahahaha.

How is my favorite Eleanor? You are very hilarious. Yes and yes!

~ Yours, Rad Ganesh.

Mass Extinction

A recent report from the World Wildlife Fund says that we've lost half of the world's wildlife population in the past 40 years.

Main causes:
    fishing nets
    poaching
    deforestation
    spilling crap into the water
    spraying crap into the air
    being crappy earthlings

Warning signs:
    tusks on your lawn
    summers without bees
    Don Juan Crustaceo losing all his lovers

It's no longer about survival of the fittest.
    We're all going down.

Chapter 3

VAGEORGIA

The Mountainside High School parking lot was the drooliest hub of mass extinction. There was so much horny potential for procreation, which mostly fizzled out into a lot of urgent face-mashing in gas-guzzling minivans or SUVs. What made me most annoyed was some unspoken and ozone-destructive rule that if you were getting some action in a vehicle you had to keep your taillights on. I knew at least two people in my school who had gotten felt up and worn out their parents' car battery in the same day.

Julian and I walked through the lip-lockers and joined the hall rush to second period without anyone asking where we'd been.

"Essays are in the basket. Once again, I wonder why I bother," said our English teacher, Mr. Dunleavy. I got a B, which was mildly insulting considering I'd drawn some poignant parallels between *The Grapes of Wrath* and the current water shortage in California, but all Dunleavy wrote on the bottom of my paper was, "Let's try to stay on topic next time."

Julian reminded me as we sat down that Dunleavy had been

at our high school for over a decade, teaching the same Steinbeck curriculum to snotty teens and pulling at the same four hairs on his head in frustration. Dunleavy had yet to get any of his own work published even in the school newsletter. He had a file folder full of unappreciated sonnets and a musical he'd written on his Casio about the life of Harper Lee—both of which he'd shared with Julian.

I tried not to get too jealous when other people fell in awe of Julian. He reeked of confidence and daring, and somehow made everyone feel like he was being extraordinary just for them. Even the crossing guard by our public pool once told me that Julian made her feel "heard" for the first time. Also, it was common knowledge that Julian was smarter than everyone in our school—including many of the teachers. A few months before, when we'd had to take statewide exams, we were supposed to write an essay based on a historical quote. Julian's essay began, "Give me liberty or give me meth." Then he launched into the biography of Terrence, the guy who used to sell Julian drugs outside Pocketful of Posies flower shop. It was a phenomenal treatise about how our judicial system was failing anyone nonwhite and how methadone clinics were like sweaty gyms full of gangs and false panaceas. Though ultimately Julian had to take the test over, I heard Dunleavy reading the essay out loud in the staff lounge, followed by applause.

After second period, I was pretty much alone until lunch. It wasn't that I had no other friends. I hung out with a handful of girls I'd known since third grade. But most of them were tripping after Becca Dinger, empress of off-the-shoulder sweaters. I'd been close with Becca back in grade school, but once she started wearing body glitter on a regular basis she lost interest in me. Also, she told me that my house smelled like mothballs and that I was insecure. Both of which I couldn't deny. Then she was the first girl in our grade to lose her virginity (to Kevin Kripps) and she reached instant celebrity status. Kevin and Becca already had a joint website where they posted pictures of their romantic getaways and musings on finding your soul mate.

Physics was a lesson in vectors that turned into chaos theory. Ms. Hubble (no relation to the telescope, but I'm sure it gave her a nerdy thrill) had us doing a lab that came to a crashing halt when the results for junior prom court were announced over the intercom.

The good news was that Becca was officially queen. The horrific news was that Derek Hooper was king. Becca started shrieking and lost her golf ball off an inclined plane, shattering a pipette in the process. While Becca's peons tried to clean up her mess, she announced to the class that she could never accept her position as queen without her boyfriend, Kevin, by her side. "The system is rigged!" she cried. "It must be stopped."

"Totally," chimed in a few girls.

"Rigged!" echoed some others.

There was actually nothing wrong or rigged about junior prom court elections, except for the fact that junior prom court was a ridiculous idea to begin with. The "elections" were held in the cafeteria and no one even campaigned. Plus, the prom itself was being held at a country club that had once been accused of spreading salmonella, and I wasn't exactly batting away offers from eligible young gentlemen.

The only dancing I was committed to doing was for Julian. He'd choreographed a solo for me in the Mountainside Spring Performing Arts Showcase, which was going up in less than two weeks. The piece made me giddy and petrified at the same time. I'd protested mightily when Julian said he wanted me to be alone onstage for three whole minutes. But the truth was those three minutes felt like the pinnacle of my small life so far.

The movements were simple but strong. All I had to do was stand in the middle of the stage with my head tilted to the side. There was a Pretty Petunia Princess doll that we'd found in my attic with one eye permanently shut and a head tilt exactly like mine. She'd been the inspiration for this piece. Then, when Julian cued me with some twinkly ballerina music, I had to waltz around the stage, my arms embracing emptiness. Julian told me I was evocative to watch as I did it. As soon as the music stopped, I collapsed on the floor wherever I was. That was the hardest part, since I had no practice in stunt work and never knew how to brace myself. Hence the trail of bruises up and down my left hip, thigh, and elbow. Each run-through turned my skin a deeper purple. I loved the marks of my persistence.

After my dramatic drop, Julian walked slowly onto the stage wearing an apron and carrying a turkey baster. He stood in front of me and the Pretty Petunia Princess doll and nudged us both with his toe. Then he took a long pause, surveying us both, picked up Petunia, and cradled her lovingly as he walked off stage.

Lights out.

Thunderous applause. Or maybe disturbed silence. Either reaction would thrill Julian for sure.

We ran through the movements a few times at lunch, but it was pretty treacherous since the stage was covered in dusty Fresnel lights, a roll of blank canvas, and a pile of twigs. The spring showcase was officially called *I Have But One Desire*, which was taken from a quote by the artist Georgia O'Keeffe. Julian and I called the show *VaGeorgia*, because it was an all-female cast (besides Julian) and the production had become intensely hormonal.

At the *VaGeorgia* helm was a tiny woman named Marty, who was at our school on some arts-in-education grant. She leapt around the room and talked with her whole body. It was clear she did not own a single bra. I loved Marty when I first met her at the beginning of the year. She'd traveled all over the world with a dance troupe and taken some ascetic vows where she shaved her hair to a salt-and-pepper fuzz. Her eyes were light gray and she smelled like potting soil. There was always a little piece of salad stuck in one of her front teeth, which I thought was accidental until she told our cast she placed it there to say "F you to all the societal expectations of female beauty."

VaGeorgia was supposed to be about claiming ownership over our femininity. I wasn't sure what that meant since I didn't think anyone wanted to own or even borrow mine. But when Marty said it, I felt like her words were the bongos and we were in some giant drumming circle. (She brought in a lot of drums to rehearsal—also a lute, a didgeridoo, and a Moroccan tambouriney thing.) Marty was focusing on Georgia O'Keeffe because she said O'Keeffe had been a crusader for women's anatomical power. She wanted the show to be "free from structural norms" and yet incorporate monologues, an a cappella medley of girl-power songs, and dancing.

Originally, Marty had told Julian he could do all of the choreography and she would do the producing and "lyrical composition." That didn't pan out, though. We never found out what exactly lyrical composition meant, and Marty insisted on starting every dance rehearsal with free-form movement that she called "exploring the female trajectory," followed by an invocation to our foremothers where we did a lot of primal yodeling. When and if Marty did hand the proverbial baton over to Julian, everyone was usually hoarse and tired. I could tell Julian wanted to choke her and all her foremothers, only he needed this last credit for his early graduation.

When afternoon classes were over, I tried to check in with my dad before heading to rehearsal, but he didn't pick up his phone. A good daughter would've gone home to make sure he wasn't lying in a pool of blood. A selfish, scared, graceless daughter would've shrugged, scarfed down a granola bar, and slouched her way into the auditorium. Marty was particularly on fire from the moment I said hello.

"We're on the stage. Let's go." She made the cast lie down with all the lights off as she led us through a guided meditation about traveling through our fallopian tubes to meet our hero-ines. "This is not just about one woman's desire, this is about *all* of our desires," she rumbled. "This is about every woman who has fought for our freedoms—Sojourner Truth, Betty Friedan, Malala, the Nineteenth Amendment. Open up your womb. Let the world see your sensuous light."

I wanted to be inspired, but lying there just made me think of the millions of microorganisms and adolescent bacteria bur-rowing into my skin. Not to mention the blanket of sawdust that had gathered on the stage since lunch. The one skill set I had mastered was being a germophobe.

"Now mindfully, carefully, make your way to your spots for the opening of the show," said Marty. A current of whispers whipped around the room. *Spots? Opening?* Nobody knew where to go or what to do.

"Yeah, that's what I was trying to tell you." Julian's voice boomed from the back of the theater. "We never set anything as the opening. Or the middle or closing for that matter. And we have no place to move even if we did know where to go."

There was a sticky silence as we watched Marty twist and lunge her way through the auditorium—working out some sort of answer with her wiry body.

"Okay, got it," she said. "Oscar, *lights*!"

Oscar was Marty's seventeen-year-old weirdo son who got dragged around to a lot of her rehearsals and rarely said anything. I honestly felt sad for Oscar because there were so many rumors about him in our cast. One was that he had a cleft palate and mostly used sign language. Another was that he came from a sperm donor with a criminal past and Marty still breastfed him. He was maybe dyslexic, or autistic, or fluent in nine languages. The only thing I knew for sure was that Marty homeschooled him while they traveled the world with her dance troupe. Also that he was about two feet taller than her and had a huge nest of dark curls that dangled over his eyes. Sometimes while we danced Marty had him improvise music on the upright piano that sat off stage left and was barely upright anymore. Everything Oscar played sounded like a variation on *Star Wars*.

The house lights went on and he loped toward the stage.

"Oscar, how close are we to hanging those canvases?" asked Marty. "I don't want to pin down any choreography until we know what this set is shaping up to be."

"I told you I can't hang anything up until you give me some time to make the frames," Oscar said.

"Right," said Marty. "And in order to make the frames . . ." She waited for Oscar to finish her sentence.

"In order to make the frames, we need to get more lumber. And in order to get more lumber, we need the truck to go more than two blocks without breaking down. And in order for the truck to go more than two blocks—"

"Okeydoke." Marty cut him off sharply and jumped onto the stage in the same breath. I saw Oscar chew on his bottom lip as he backed away and slammed the lighting booth door shut. I would never survive if my mom tried to homeschool me.

"Yes, this is right," Marty announced. "Let's all come back into a circle and check in, please." She had us all sit around the twig pile and pulled one out. The bark was thin and the color of snow. Marty looked at it like it was a precious gem, then gave that same look of misty-eyed appreciation to everyone on stage.

"I know this is a little disappointing, but I do think we need to close rehearsal for the day so we can respect our environment. It's a little like life, right? How often do we pause to thank a leaf or water a thirsty sprout?" No one answered her, even though she gave us an eon of thoughtful silence to come up with a response. "All right," she continued. "As we say goodbye for today, I'm going to pass around this exquisite piece of nature and when you receive it, I'd like each of you to say what this process means to you."

She passed the twig to her right. Lindsay McAden took it and tried to shrug off the assignment, but Marty just kept on smiling at her until Lindsay squeaked, "I think the process is . . . fun?"

There were lots of variations on the word *fun*—exciting, cool, interesting. Becca said she felt like it was intense. So the next five people said that too. I said it was challenging but helpful.

"Ooooh, what a fascinating choice of words," said Marty. "Can you elaborate for us?" I didn't actually know why I'd said "helpful," but what I meant was it got me out of the house and it gave my brain somewhere to focus, and sometimes when I was onstage moving or even following one of her meditations I didn't have to think about anything—not climate change or chemo or the alerts on my phone that told me how many critically endangered Javan rhinos were left in the world. But that was not something I wanted to share with this crowd.

Julian must've smelled my brain overheating from that question. He took the stick from me and said, "I am really enjoying this process and also feel like it's vital for us to move forward now and get that lumber. So I can take one or two people in my car. It's a beat-up Jetta, license plate starting EBW."

Then he stood up and got his backpack from the front row of seats. I followed his lead. So did most of the circle. Marty thanked us all again and said she would like to facilitate the lumber run, and probably Oscar too.

"Fine. Let's go," Julian said. His voice was chopped and impatient. "And I'm guessing you want me to drop you off at home?" he said to me.

I nodded, even though he was wrong. Still no message from my dad. My mom wouldn't be home for at least another three hours. So I didn't *want* to go home and act like everything was fine or manageable. I wanted to hide in the changing room or get caught up in the tornado of junior prom chatter or even lie pinned under a pile of lumber. Anything to not go home and just wait for something to get better. Or worse.

"Hey," said Julian. "Water your thirsty sprout, will ya?" He took Marty's twig, pretended to pick his nose with it, and then handed it to me for good luck.

Humpty Dumpty

One day, all the king's (or queen's) horses and all their wo/men won't be able to put this Earth together again.

A brief yet terrifying chart of the most devastating earthquakes since 1900

Name	Date	Location	Magnitude	Fatalities
Messina earthquake	December 28, 1908	Messina, Italy	7.1	123,000
Haiyuan earthquake	December 16, 1920	Ningxia-Gansu, China	7.8	200,000
Great Kanto earthquake	September 1, 1923	Kanto region of Japan	7.9	142,800
Ashgabat earthquake	October 6, 1948	Ashgabat, Turkmenistan	7.3	110,000
Tangshan earthquake	July 28, 1976	Hebei, China	7.8	655,000
Indian Ocean earthquake	December 26, 2004	Indian Ocean, Sumatra, Indonesia	9.1	230,210+
Kashmir earthquake	October 8, 2005	Muzaffarabad, Pakistan	7.6	87,351
Haiti earthquake	January 12, 2010	Haiti	7.0	316,000
Bernardsville, NJ, earthquake	August 14, 2015	New Jersey, USA	2.7	None reported, but Mom's assistant Pippi's sister's apartment building felt it really strongly.

According to my earthquake tracker, there are about 50 earthquakes recorded daily. There is probably one happening right now in the Aleutian Islands or somewhere in California.

Chapter 4

CHECKING IT OUT

I tried to open the front door quietly, in case Dad was still napping. He wasn't. He was standing in the middle of the living room like he'd just lost something and didn't know where to look for it. His pajama bottoms were so loose that he was clutching the waistband, and on top he had on a horrible tan fleece jacket with *Siegfried and Roy* stitched into the back. Mom had brought it back from some law convention in Vegas.

"What are you doing?" I asked. Not the nicest way to greet him, but I liked to face fear with misplaced anger.

"I'm not . . . sure," Dad answered with a lopsided smile. I could tell he really didn't want to be standing there, saying those words, feeling that shitty, smelling even shittier. He backed his way onto the couch. I hated our couch. It had too many colors chasing each other in a trippy paisley pattern and the pillows had no fluff left inside. When Dad sank down, the front of his jacket opened just enough for me to see a tide of red creeping across his chest. It had streaks that radiated out like fiery tentacles.

"That looks worse," I said, pointing. "Is it?"

Dad couldn't or wouldn't answer. I got him to stick a thermometer under his tongue. The first time it read 97. Then it read 102.

"Do we know what time Mom might be home?" I didn't even wait for him to try to answer that question. No one could answer that question, which was why this whole thing was so infuriating. Sometimes I felt like Mom was giving us all cancer of uncertainty.

"I saw she called," Dad said. "But I was in the bathroom." Which could mean two thousand different things involving his tubes and bowels and I wasn't going to make him elaborate. "I missed a call from Emma too."

"Emma my sister?" I asked.

"That's the only one I know," Dad answered.

"Whoa. Was it a drunk dial?"

"C'mon, Len. Play nice. She misses you."

"I'll call her back while I look for some Tylenol," I said. "Just stay here please." As if he had anywhere else to go or any energy to get there.

I knew calling Emma was not going to be helpful, but I didn't have a better idea. She usually only called home to tell me how messed up she got or how *consumed* she was with Walt Whitman and hashish and some guy in her chem lab named Manuel. I was enraged with her for leaving when our family was in crisis mode. To be honest, I was also incredibly envious. Emma had this amazing ability to jump into everything—puddles, people, languages—and leave her worries on a crumpled tissue for someone else to clean up. I didn't even think I'd finished dialing all her digits when she picked up, panting.

"Aha!" she yelled into the phone. "My little sister will be the tiebreaker. Lenny, don't think, just answer: Jonas Brothers or Justin Bieber?"

"Jonas Brothers," I said. "But what's the question?"

"Who's the first male singer you ever masturbated to. Duh!"

I couldn't decide if I was disgusted or excited by that question. I just knew I missed how we used to be small and have nothing to do but make up guessing games and pose on the living room floor with pretzel-rod cigarettes, pretending we were French cabaret singers. I spoke as quietly as I could, considering she was blasting some boy band that needed to be annihilated. I told her about flushing Dad's port and the red skin making a tarantula across his chest. She didn't say anything.

"Are you there?" I asked.

"Of course I'm here," she answered.

"Well? What do you think? Did I give him an infection?"

"No. I mean, I don't think so. But where the fuck is Mom?"

"Court," I said, enjoying Emma's outrage. Until it became all about her again.

"She was supposed to send me my black stirrup pants and her flowered shower cap for eighties night. Did I tell you I'm going as trickle-down economics and my new bestie Nicola's got an awesome Maggie Thatcher wig? Come in! You guys are cray-zeeeeee!"

Now it sounded like a small mob of Emma's friends had come into her dorm room to practice dolphin noises. I wanted to strangle Emma over the phone.

"I'll make sure to FedEx you from the ICU," I barked, about to hang up.

"Wait! What?" she asked.

"Emma, I need *help*!" I'd never spoken that clearly or desperately before. But I didn't know how else to get through the commotion. I needed somebody to be in charge besides me. It felt like there were pins and needles in my tongue while I waited for Emma to answer. I heard her tell several people to shut up and let her into the closet. Then she put on her Serious Big Sister voice.

"I'm sorry, Lennyboo. I really am. I love you so much and everything is going to be fine. What if I called Dr. Lowenfeld? He's the chief of everything cancer, right?"

"Lowen*stein*. He's doing a presentation in Toronto," I told her.

"Doesn't he have someone filling in? I'll just call and see who—"

I cut her off. "It's okay. I'll handle it." The thought of Emma contacting Dr. Ganesh sent a thunderbolt of terror through me. Not only was Emma loud and unafraid, she'd gotten all the pretty genes in the family—a nice rack, full lips, and honey-colored hair that was so wavy and soft I used to beg her to let me brush it before bed. Just for comparison, I used to ask Mom repeatedly if she'd had an affair with a poodle, because my frizz was so out of control. I could see Emma and Dr. Ganesh making out together in a medical supply closet without even closing my eyes.

"In fact, that's a great idea. I'm gonna call whoever's filling in right now," I declared.

"I am *totally* here if you need anything," Emma said.

"Me too. Gotta go love you bye!"

I stared at my phone for a solid minute, rehearsing my opening lines:

Hi, Dr. Ganesh, you might not remember me . . .

Hey Dr. G, 'member me?

DRG! It's ER-H! Wassup?

I decided I had to catch my breath first. And clean up this mess. While Emma was blathering, I'd taken out everything in the corner cabinet of our kitchen, looking for the Tylenol. Mom had a lazy Susan in there that was too lazy to spin anymore and on it were five different kinds of paprika, three half-moons of garlic, cinnamon, nutmeg, antihistamines, blood thinners, and calcium chews. There were medications in there dating back to when I was a baby and took some thick yellow syrup for an earache. Asthma, eczema, high blood pressure, anemia, insomnia. We could cure a nation of minor illnesses in that one cabinet. But of course, no Tylenol in sight.

I was so angry and scared and angry again. I wanted to throw everything against the kitchen window and make the glass or the earth or at least this day crack open and let us all out. It felt like nothing fit together and I had to make some sense or order of all these misplaced pieces.

First, I tossed everything that was outdated or smelled funky. I also dismantled the too-lazy Susan, sprayed down the empty cabinet, and chipped off the vitamins that had melted into the corner. Next I put the pills on one side and the spices on the other and crafted a little divider out of the back of an empty box of Girl Scout cookies. At least, I thought it was empty. Until three Thin Mints from the turn of the century with a green coat of mold fell on the floor and I thought it was a flying squirrel so I instinctually yelped and stomped on them. Then I poured Clorox into a bucket and wiped down every flat surface in the kitchen and dining room until I heard Dad calling from the living room.

"Just a sec!" I croaked. The bleach fumes clawed at my throat, which I actually liked. It felt like a protective shield covering my heart and lungs and all the words I wanted to say, especially when I came in to see Dad red-faced and panty on the couch.

"Just wondering if you found that Tylenol," he said. His teeth were chattering.

A simple request. I had found the bottle of Tylenol almost twenty minutes ago and had promptly filed it alphabetically on the "pill side" of the kitchen cabinet, forgetting to bring it to him first.

"So sorry," I said pitifully. "I'm . . . yes." I ran back to the kitchen and wasted more of my dad's precious minutes trying to get the water filter to work before filling up his cup from the faucet and handing him the pills. I could see them slip down his neck. He was so thin and empty.

"Emma said what about calling the attending resident," I said, pretending confusion. "Dr. Gernish?"

"Ganesh," corrected Dad. "That's a good idea."

Radhakrishnan Ganesh, 917-555-0198. Radhakrishnan Ganesh, 917-555-0198. Not that I hadn't memorized his number and repeated it under my breath every day since he gave me his card. I'd even devised one of my nerdy number games with his cell: *Nine plus one minus seven is three. Plus five-five-five is eighteen. Which is equal to zero plus one plus nine plus eight.*

Dr. Ganesh's message was short and formal. Mine was not.

"Hi, this is Eleanor Rosenthal-Hermann, Jeremy Rosenthal-Hermann's daughter. Also Naomi's, but I guess you know that or don't need to, but anyway. I was wondering. There's a lot of redness around my father's chest catheter. It didn't just happen. I mean, I was flushing it with saline and now it looks really red and I'm pretty sure he has a fever even though I'm not great with thermometers. This is a little hard to follow, sorry. Maybe we should just come in to the clinic? But I'm not sure if there are walk-in hours or if we should—"

It's always humbling to get cut off by a voice-mail robot.

"Left a message," I reported back to Dad. "We could also just go in if you want. I don't know if you really want to just show up at the clinic though, right?"

I meant that as a rhetorical question, but Dad nodded. I just stared at him, unmoving. He wasn't supposed to agree. He was the one who made this all bearable or steady in some small way. If Jeremy Rosenthal-Hermann needed help, then the whole world needed help. And by the whole world I meant the sun, the moon, the stars, and the planets (including poor Pluto). All the galaxies we hadn't even discovered yet. Maybe a side effect of Dad's new nocturnal awareness was hearing that silent warning of sudden vacuum decay or the seismic shifts bubbling up from Earth's core.

"Len, it's okay," Dad said softly. Whatever superpowers he'd acquired, he still had a radar for when I got yanked into my end-of-the-world fantasies. He sniffed my anxieties before I could even name them—he always had. Starting with that ride home from the planetarium seven years ago. I had felt his eyes on me, softly studying me like they did now.

"We're just checking it out," he said. "Get me some socks, will ya?"

"Yup. Yes. Just checking it out," I repeated numbly.

I'd never opened Dad's sock drawer before. I really hoped it wasn't full of old *Hustler* magazines, or worse, nudies of Mom in just her judge's robes. I reached in quickly, retrieving some brown argyles. The only things in there besides socks were a campaign pin for Walter Mondale and a flattened penny we made together at my school carnival when I graduated fifth grade. I felt so honored he'd kept that. I wanted to know what else he'd squirreled away.

But there would be plenty of time to go through all of Dad's stuff later. Maybe I'd carry that flattened penny in my pocket to his funeral. I saw myself walking slowly in a shapeless black dress, pressing the penny between my palm and thigh. Which couldn't come true.

"Stop! I don't even have a black dress with pockets," I told the Mondale pin. I slammed the drawer and shut myself in the bathroom. I washed my hands and said, "I love you, Daddy; I'm sorry, Daddy," twenty-five times to get rid of everything else in my head except here and now.

"Don't be an asshead," I spit at the wimpy kid with two new chin pimples staring back in the mirror. Then I washed my hands again until they stung and flicked the water into my face, running down the stairs to give Dad his socks. His feet were sticking out of his oversize sweatpants, the skin so translucent that I could see his veins snaking around the toes. And a small button of green pumping up and down. His pulse.

Mom had the hatchback, so we took the Jolly Roger—our fifteen-year-old station wagon that was due for retirement. Jolly had streaks of crimson along the backseat, which looked like a murder scene, but it was just from when Emma and I were playing beauty parlor with five shades of red nail polish. Jolly also had a pair of Groucho glasses that lived on the rearview mirror, a billowy canopy instead of an upholstered roof, and a radio that only got some AM sports station. It took a long time to get Dad in a semicomfortable position in the passenger seat, even though I'd brought his special doughnut-shaped pillow to sit on and a blanket from the couch since he couldn't stop shivering.

I put on the Groucho glasses for the ride too, because maybe they had a little magic left in their wobbly frames. I'd worn them to Dad's first chemo trip and he said it was the reason he didn't get queasy or have any bad side effects. The left eyebrow was missing and the plastic nose smelled like a gym locker room, but the mustache was still bushy enough for a laugh. I'd do anything to make this less harrowing for both of us. Plus, at least it wasn't me staring back in the rearview mirror.

I texted Julian before pulling out of the driveway.

Heading into the city with Dad. Wanna come?

He wrote back: **Sorry, knee-deep in lumberyard. Everything ok?**

Hope so. Fever.

Then I erased that because it looked like I was hoping for a fever. I tried:

Fever. Hope so.

Which made no sense grammatically and could be easily misinterpreted. So I settled on just:

Fever.

It didn't tell the whole story, but at this point I had no idea what the story was and I didn't know how to ask for help and, most of all, my dad was just waiting in the passenger seat while I rewrote texts.

"Okeydokey pokey," I said, gunning the engine a little.

"Woo-hoo," answered Dad.

Dr. Ganesh's office was about a forty-five-minute drive away—without traffic. It was nestled in "cancer row"—which is what Dad called all the research hospitals on the Upper East Side of Manhattan. I knew this area of New York City much better than I wanted to, thanks to Dad's dozen hospital stays in the past year.

"Can you believe we're still over there?" Dad asked, cutting into my daymare. He nodded at the radio. Apparently, a quarterback from the Buffalo Bills was dedicating his last win to the troops in Afghanistan.

"Unbelievable," I said, coughing out a piece of loose mustache and almost rear-ending the cab in front of us. Everyone in the tristate area had decided to go into Manhattan that Friday afternoon, so the crawl down the FDR Drive was taking more like an hour and a half. I kept trying to get off at earlier exits and wind my way through the city, but that just made the trip even slower and filled with angry pedestrians. Obviously nobody else had gotten the memo that we were possibly heading toward a galactic shutdown or that my dad was bleeding out from my morning syringe stabbing. Even the parking garage was backed up.

I'd forgotten about how we'd have to go through Dr. Ganesh's lovely but long-winded receptionist, Linda. Linda looked a little like the Pillsbury Doughboy and had sweaters that told stories in yarn. Today she had on a village with snowflakes and a dog howling at the moon. Linda moved slower than a slug on Xanax, and she liked to call everyone *darling*. As in:

"Oh hello, darling. I'm so sorry, Dr. Ganesh is done for the day."

"I know. But my dad isn't feeling well, so we thought maybe he could just take a look."

"He might have some openings—"

"We can't wait for openings!" I cut her off. Dad cleared his throat to let me know I needed to dial it back.

Linda looked at me as if I'd just slapped her. "If you're needing immediate assistance, the ER is just around the corner on First Ave."

"We don't know what we need." I tried to keep my voice at a lower octave. "We need to see Dr. Ganesh because he's familiar with the situation and he knows—"

"Ey-leah-nor!" Dr. Ganesh came through some secret door behind Linda, smelling like sandalwood aftershave and hope. "I just was hearing your message. This is so good you came."

He brought us into a putty-colored room in the back that had dim lights, an electric teakettle, and a desk with a framed

portrait of what must have been Mr. and Mrs. Ganesh—
gray-haired versions of his angular face. Three medical diplomas hung neatly above.

"Thank you so much for seeing us, Dr. Ganesh," said my
dad.

"I didn't mean to snap at Linda. And I know you're very
busy," I explained. "Can you just look at my dad's chest? Is it
okay? I mean, I know it's not, but how not okay is it?"

"Please, just relax. You too, Ey-leah-nor. It is so much nicer
if we can relax."

It was nicer. Blinding white teeth and his scruff of beard
helped too. Actually, everything felt calmer in here. Dr. Ganesh
would hold up the sky, or at least clear some stretch of the horizon so we could breathe again.

"Please sit," Dr. Ganesh said, taking Dad's hand and leading him to a cushioned chair. "Tell me what is happening."

"Well." Dad sighed. "I'm not exactly sure. I'm so sorry to bug
you like this."

"No sorry," Dr. Ganesh said. He took my hand and led me
to the chair next to Dad. His palm was so warm and sturdy. I
willed myself to let go even though I wanted to stay connected
to him until the world ended. Which it could at any moment.
Maybe I could ask him for his opinion on designer pathogens
or he could give me the access code for the medical journal ar-
chives I'd found online. I could buy him coffee or meet him
at one of those Irish pubs by the subway and talk about the

evolution or de-evolution of gene manipulation. Maybe cap the night off with bubble tea and karaoke . . . ?

Dr. Ganesh took Dad's temperature and checked his blood pressure. Then he had Dad lie down on the crinkly paper and massaged Dad's belly slowly. He was humming the whole time and nodding his head. He talked to Dad in a low, soothing voice. I didn't need to hear the words. The noise in my head—boy bands and spices and numbers colliding—started settling just watching these two men.

Then Dr. Ganesh asked me to step into the hall while he did the "other part of the examination." I could hear Linda packing up for the day. Muttering little reminders to herself, like "Gonna need to order printer paper soon," and "Could just throw a can of tuna in with those noodles. Make a nice casserole." She was totally unaffected by whatever catastrophe we'd just brought in—she saw this kind of suffering all the time. She left and went home and knew that day would follow night and she probably watched sitcoms with laugh tracks and ate processed cheese and *trusted* that life would go on. I listened to the swish of her pleated pants, hoping they could hypnotize me into trusting too.

Dr. Ganesh came back out. "Ey-leah-nor," he said with a gentle smile. "This is very good you came. I would like your father to stay overnight for some further testing."

"Why?"

"His white count is up too high. There's definitely infection."

"Why?" I said again. It was a word. Which was better than a wail.

Dr. Ganesh put his hands together in a sort of prayer pose. He met my watery eyes. "Is there anyone who can be here for you?" he asked.

I shrugged and shook my head and bit my tongue all at the same time. "You," I said. Trying to laugh.

"Okay," he said. "Then me."

Nanotechnology

Nanotechnology is the manipulation of matter on a teensy-tinesy, atomic, molecular, and supramolecular scale.

That's really small. For instance, this is a nanometer:

(It's too small to see without fancy microscopes.)
25,400,000 nanometers = 1 inch

This is how doctors have come up with the incredible treatments that pass through the blood-brain barrier.

This is also how some sickos could design a poisonous aerosol and act like they're just going to tag the big wall behind the high school football field with some cool avant-garde graffiti but then they're actually releasing nerve gas or something that makes everyone turn into zombies before the halftime show. Or on a much larger scale, like anthrax pen pals and government-building air ducts.

Probability:
The FBI is concerned, so we should be too.

Chapter 5

WHO CAN TELL?

"Why is he doing that?!" I yelled. "Make him stop!"

Dad was writhing and quaking in his hospital bed. Arching his head back so far I thought his neck would snap in half.

"Make him stop, *please*!" At least I had manners. Otherwise, it would be hard to tell the difference between a rabid bat and me. Flapping my arms and screeching around Dad's bed. Luckily, everyone in the room chose to ignore me. There were two male nurses surrounding him—one pressing on Dad's upper arms and the other doing some massagey thing to loosen Dad's jaw. A female nurse was unraveling tubes connected to a hissing oxygen mask and then in a whirl of foresty-smelling faith, in came Dr. Ganesh, with a bag of clear fluid that he swiftly attached to the IV pole.

"Hello, Jeremy. I'm going to give you a little oxygen now and we're just going to breeeeaaaathe." Dr. Ganesh's voice was low and firm.

"He just started shaking and I thought he was cold, but then his eyes rolled back and he was . . ." I didn't know whom I was explaining this to. I just had to make sure my dad wasn't dying.

He couldn't die without saying goodbye to my mom and sister and we had plans to do a road trip to the Jersey Shore in July and I think he even had library books out.

"That's it. Breeeaaaathe," Dr. Ganesh said again. He got the oxygen mask on Dad's face and directed one of the nurses with the IV needle. He put a heart-rate monitor on, too, and nodded at the electronic blips. "There we go," he said. "You're going to start feeling much better now. Muuuuuch better."

"He is?" I peeped.

Dr. Ganesh turned around to face me. "Ey-leah-nor!" He smiled. "Yes, of course. Here." He pulled off one of his latex gloves and held out a hand, ushering me forward. "Come see for yourself. He won't bite." He took my right hand and placed it on my dad's shoulder, which was slowly sinking into the bed, giving off little twitches as it relaxed. The combination of all of us touching made me feel like I was overheating and turning to ice at the same time. There was a small brown cloud of dried blood on Dad's pillow next to his ear. I shuddered.

"He's just breathing, right? I mean, sleeping?"

Dr. Ganesh nodded. Then he thanked each nurse personally for doing a fine job. The woman who'd been unraveling Dad's tubing looked at me with huge, kind eyes and said, "You did great, honey. I know this must be hard." Her lavender scrubs were so serene they made me weepy. She was a gorgeous woman with hundreds of tiny braids woven into a bun on top of her head. Her name tag read SAFFI.

Dad stayed asleep while everyone cleaned up around him. I hoped he would sleep for a while now. At least until I got some answers. Dr. Ganesh looked like he was heading out the door with the team of superhero nurses, so I rushed over to say, "Can I just ask . . . what was that?"

"Yes, this is a good question, Ey-leah-nor," Dr. Ganesh said. He gave me a fist bump, maybe as a prize for boldness. "Come with me, we will talk more in the hall."

We started walking toward the elevators. I thought maybe he was taking me to a lab or conference room to chat, but we kept roaming around the tenth floor without a word between us. We did three laps around the Island of Unanswerable Questions in the middle. That was the semicircle of desks that held all the secrets of life and death. Test results, urine samples, take-out menus, a misplaced vial of morphine—every answer would ultimately be pulled out of this mysterious island. As we walked by I heard nurses and doctors entering data on computers and comparing notes about leukocytes and parking tickets and medically induced comas and anyone doing something fun this weekend? all in the same breath.

I couldn't wait any longer. I turned to Dr. Ganesh so abruptly that a motion-activated hand sanitizer spurted out a dollop of foam. "Can I just ask you a couple of questions?" I said. "Or more like a thousand?"

"Ha! Yes. Let us just start with one," Dr. Ganesh replied.

"Did I just kill my dad?"

"I do not think so. Your father is very much alive in room 428, yes?"

"Okay, but then what was that? Did he just have a heart attack or . . . ?"

"Right. Okay, what I think happened is your father's temperature elevated so rapidly that he experienced what we call a febrile seizure. This is actually fairly common, but we see it mostly in young children. So now we have to get this fever down, have him rest, and then determine how it is related to the infection and where the infection is exactly."

"It's right here," I said, poking my chest. "Where I tried to clean out his port."

"Yes, well, this is one theory. But a fever of one hundred five degrees indicates something more systemic."

"I could've given him something systemic, though. I was the one who flushed his catheter port and then he was in so much discomfort and the fever. I mean, I washed my hands a bunch of times and I wore the gloves but we've been fostering this rodent named TinyGinsberg and I changed her water bowl last night, which must be a cesspool of all kinds of bacteriosis."

Dr. Ganesh smiled. "This is good. I did not know you were studying medicine," he said.

"That's a joke, right? Because I'm not."

"Yes, I joke. Ey-leah-nor, you are asking what? What gave him this infection? Your father is in a very immunosuppressed state, so many things can elicit a strong reaction. At this point, really, who can tell?"

"*You* can!"

That one came out a lot louder and angrier than I meant it to. Dr. Ganesh nodded slightly and kept walking. We were almost up to the tenth-floor lounge at the end of the hall.

"Sorry," I said in a calmer voice. "I just know there are a gazillion germs on the tip of a single fingernail and I wore the gloves but then I usually have antibacterial spray too but I read something yucky about propylene glycol, which I'd also like to ask you about, and mostly I'm just really worried that I caused all this."

Dr. Ganesh stopped walking and turned to face me. Which was lovely and terrifying. "Ey-leah-nor, we really don't know with any certainty what causes this infection. But we treat it and bring his fever down and then we see." He tapped his right pointer finger in the air, just a millimeter away from my left nostril. I pretended not to notice, even though he could probably feel every one of my nose hairs stand to attention.

"You are the hero of this story too, yes?" he continued. "You knew enough to bring your father in. This makes you a responsible young lady."

"I'm eighty-nine. It's all Botox," I said. He laughed loud enough for a couple in the lounge to look up. That felt great. Then we started walking again, and I just kept blabbing, because it was the first pocket of unterrified space I'd found in so long. "No, seriously. I'm not that young. Emotionally, at least. How old are you? If you want to tell me. Which you don't have to. Or . . . never mind."

"This is a fun question," Dr. Ganesh said. "I will have thirty-six years on May twentieth." He bought a bottle of water from one of the lounge vending machines while I did some fast calculations.

Yes, he was almost twenty years older than me, but his birthday was in May and mine was November 18, which meant we were really nineteen and a half years apart—almost to the day. Also, eighteen minus eleven (for November) was seven, and five plus two plus zero (the digits in his birthdate) equaled seven. And seven was prime, which meant we couldn't be divided.

"Now, I have a question for you," Dr. Ganesh said after taking a sip of water.

"Okay."

"I met your mother a few weeks ago and I assumed you all live together. Is this fair what I assumed?"

"Yes," I said. "She's just crazy." Dr. Ganesh scrunched his eyebrows. He didn't know how to respond to that. "Not *crazy*," I clarified. "I just mean she's always super busy at work and maybe in denial about this situation but fully functional. Overly functional, really. She's just at work now. She'll be here later. Or, I guess I need to tell her where we are, but then she'll be here. Wait, what did you ask me? Oh yeah, if we live together. Yes, we live together."

Dr. Ganesh looked concerned. "You must call and leave this message so she can come."

"Yes, I will," I told him. I didn't like that he used the word *must*. But he did have a good point.

He nodded slightly and whispered, "Thank you so much."

I sensed he was about to leave so I blurted, "Wait! Where are you going? I mean, can I just ask you one more question?"

"Shoot it," he said, fist bumping the air.

"Did you always know you wanted to do this? I mean, saving people's lives . . ."

Dr. Ganesh's smile dimmed. "Did I always know?" he repeated. "This is a yes and a no answer."

"What do you mean?" I pressed.

He took another swig of water, as if he needed to gear up for the rest of his explanation. Then he fixed a button on his lab coat that had come undone. "I do not say this to patients usually, but I tell you because I think you can hear it, right? Are we *keepin' it real*?" he asked.

"Definitely," I answered.

"When I was a little boy, I was growing up in an area of India called Pondicherry, and I wanted to be a singer. Just like this man, Bruce Springsteen. You know him?"

"Not personally, but yes." I tried not to giggle, but the thought of him singing "Born in the USA" made me really happy.

He continued. "I had a sister, born at the same time."

"Twin."

"Yes, twin. And she contracted leukemia." He paused. I could feel the *dot, dot, dot* drooping off the end of his words. That was cancer-speak for "she didn't make it."

"I'm sorry."

"Yes. I was not old enough to know her really, but I feel her loss in my body, you know? And I see the sadness in my parents. And I see this and I know I have to change this. I have to do this work."

"I'm so, so sorry." I hated that phrase but it really was the only thing I could think to say.

"Thank you. It is okay. I am very blessed to do this. I get to attend one of the top research universities. And there is much cross-pollination of these ideas between Eastern and Western treatment. So now there are many great possibilities with new forms of immunotherapy!" His voice was rising again.

"Wow, well I'm glad you're so hopeful."

"Oh yes! For this example, there is a drug we have in trial right now called Nivolumab. It is a full human monoclonal antibody that binds to a molecule called PD-1. We are looking at each individual molecule, which is quite astounding! There is so much more available to us through the use of this nanotechnology."

I wanted to tell him I knew a little about this stuff too, but he was too busy waving his arms excitedly and pressing his fingers together to show me how small a molecule could be. He went on, ". . . which augments the human immune response, instead of the traditional cytotoxic agents. Now, cytotoxins have proven enormously effective in stopping rapid replication, so we cannot ignore that method completely, but in combination we could resolve this on a physical and philosophical plane." He tried to catch his breath and started laughing. "Agh!

Ey-leah-nor! You have to tell me to stop before I am so majorly boring, right?"

"No, I love hearing you talk!" I said. "About this," I added, looking out the window and pretending to be fascinated by the traffic patterns on the East River Drive. I felt like this was the most informative, encouraging, slightly intimate talk I'd had in forever. I also felt guilty because I was forcing back a smile and meanwhile I didn't know if my dad was dying down the hall.

"So, in terms of my dad . . ." I said.

"Yes," Dr. Ganesh said. "All we can do now is wait for the fever to come down." The word *we* lit up in neon behind my eyes.

"The first forty-eight hours are very critical and I will not introduce any new treatments until the white blood count comes down. After that, however, I do think your father could be a fine candidate for this trial I mention involving Nivolumab, possibly in conjunction with Varlilumab. Of course, ultimately this will be Dr. Lowenstein's decision, because your father is *his* patient."

"Dr. Ganesh? Dr. Ganesh!" Saffi was rushing toward us, lithe and lovely, but her lavender scrubs looked a little wrinkled. "I know you're not officially on, but can you help out with room 453? The patient pulled out her monitor. She just had gamma ray done and we were told to keep her immobilized but she says she has to get up and walk."

"Walk! Yes!" Dr. Ganesh said. "Can I get a walk walk?" He turned to me sharply. "Ey-leah-nor, are you good so I can go in and speak with this patient? I think we have a plan. You are going to call your mother and then chillax and let your father's fever come down. We will check in again in a little while, yes?"

I put my hand up for one last fist bump, trying to savor that skin-to-skin jolt of courage before he and Saffi took off.

I stared out the lounge window for another ten minutes or so. If I closed my eyes halfway, the cars below looked like a glowing red worm. It would take Mom at least two hours to get in with this traffic on a Friday night. I knew I should call her, but I also felt like she didn't deserve to know anything after being out of touch all day.

When I did try her number, I got her voice mail again anyway. I omitted the part about pushing the needle into Dad's chest too hard and possibly causing a lethal infection. I actually left no details besides "fever" and Dad's hospital room number, ending with a smug, "Oh, this is your youngest daughter, Eleanor."

Then I turned off my phone and went back to Dad's room to watch him sleep some more. My new favorite thing about oxygen masks (besides saving people's lives) was that they made a wheezing sound when he took in air and filled up with a little white cloud to let me know he had breathed out again.

Then I could breathe out too.

Pandemics

Perhaps

After the

Next outbreak of

Deadly and/or debilitating

Ebola, influenza, or hoof-and-mouth disease, we can

Meet for

Iced tea and

Chat about the lessons we've learned since the

Spanish flu wiped out fifty million people?

Chapter 6

THE UTTERANCE OF COSMIC REALITY

I could feel the floor vibrating the second Mom got off the elevator (at 8:36 p.m.—almost three and a half hours after I'd gotten there with Dad). She was a parade of *Sorrys* and *Thank yous* and *I can't believe this*es. I snuck behind a few empty gurneys in the hall so I could spy on her. Mom rushed over to the nurses' island and told them how grateful she was for this incredible staff. She'd brought a big thing of dough-nuts and knew everybody's favorite flavor: "Nadia, you're chocolate frosted. Mariel—cinnamon spice. Saffi, I thought you might like this sconewich. Dr. Ganesh! The man of the hour!"

Even though I didn't want to give her credit, Mom had put in her time in these halls. She'd walked every inch of this scratched linoleum and knew every nurse's story. That was the thing with Mom—she drew everyone into her orbit. When she was there, she was really *there*. I watched her as she listened to Dr. Ganesh. She was crying and laughing and running through every human reaction in the space of a minute. Then I slipped back into Dad's room and waited. And here's something evil and ugly and true: I started stroking his head just so she could walk in and see me in that Florence Nightingale pose.

"Jesus, I'm so so sorry," Mom gushed. She dropped all of her bags and charged toward the bed, cupping Dad's face in her hands. Without sanitizing first.

"Jesus is fine. But can you please wash your hands?" I said. My voice was low and menacing. She nodded and went to the antibacterial squirter by the door. Then she came back and took his palm in hers, kissing it over and over again. She put her lips on his forehead.

"Feels cooler now," she said.

"Of course he is *now*," I snarled. It actually felt great to have the real estate in my head for anger. Mom clung to me in a drippy hug. She was rambling into my hair.

"You did so great, Lenny. I can't believe this. I'm so sorry. It's crazy, you know? I don't know what happened. My phone was off while we were in session and then when I went to turn it back on the battery was dead. I stopped at the phone store because I thought—I don't know what I was thinking. And then I went home because I didn't see there were any messages, and then . . ."

She went to a phone store. While Dad was convulsing. While he arched back in violent spasms.

"Do you want to tell me about it? I mean, I got the lowdown from Ganesh, but I'd love to hear your thoughts," Mom said, trying to connect with me eye to eye. I wasn't in the mood for reconciliation, though.

"Nah." I ducked under her gaze. "If you're going to be here for a little bit, I'm gonna get a snack," I said, bolting for the door.

"Plenty of doughnuts!" I heard her call after me.

I had to find Dr. Ganesh before he left. He wasn't at the Island of Unanswerable Questions. There were five phones ringing and lots of empty chairs.

I ran to the nearest bank of elevators, grateful to get an empty one. I didn't trust elevator ventilation and I'd read staggering reports by the Centers for Disease Control and Prevention on infections caused by hospital stays (also known as HAI— healthcare-associated infections). Whenever possible, I pressed the elevator buttons with my elbow and then held my breath until the doors opened again.

My fantasy was that Dr. Ganesh and I would catch each other's eye through the lobby's revolving door and do some fabulous dance montage. The hospital entrance was actually a pretty dreamy location. It had flower arrangements that were the size of toddlers and there were three walls of water emptying into a small wishing well. I never knew why people spent so much money on hospital décor instead of funding platelet research or coming up with a kinder alternative to the colostomy bag. But at this moment, I did appreciate the rainforest atmosphere. Especially the bamboo thatched hut that had an espresso machine coughing out steam. The noise compelled me to look over and see Dr. Ganesh, just as he was putting the lid on his coffee and reaching for a granola bar from the barrels of refreshments.

I didn't know what I was going to say, but I figured I could start by paying for his snack. I tried to thread myself up through the line at the cash register. "Excuse me, pardon me. I'm not cutting, I swear, I'm just—"

"Ow! Do you mind?!"

In my defense, I wasn't moving that fast. And I didn't mean to push. But I must've stepped on the edge of this old man's orthotic shoe. Age had taken away his elasticity, so instead of bending partway or bracing himself, he just toppled over into the yogurt case and put his elbow through the foil top of a Greek blueberry 2 percent fat. Horrible packaging concept.

"I'm so sorry," I said. "I didn't see you. I didn't know you were there. My dad's on the tenth floor." There was no reason to pull out the dad-dying-pity-me card. This man was obviously sludging through hell too. He had the yellowish face of somebody who'd been up days and nights without fresh air. Marking time just by the ticker tape on the bottom of a fuzzy bedside TV.

I stood there dumbly while the woman behind me rushed forward to help the old man back up because:

a) I'm a thoughtless asshead, and
b) I didn't have any sanitizer on me so the thought of touching this person's desiccated skin was petrifying.

"What were you doing?" he asked. Even his checkered fanny pack looked tired.

"I know," I said, which wasn't an answer. His elbow had a dollop of yogurt clinging to it. I handed him a fistful of napkins and said, "Blueberry's in high demand, huh?"

He didn't find that funny. I couldn't blame him. I put down a ten-dollar bill next to the cash register and said, "Please let me pay for him." Nobody in the line behind me was charmed by that gesture. Even the cellophane-wrapped apples looked disgusted with me.

Bolting out of the espresso hut, I scanned the tropical landscape for Dr. Ganesh. He was waiting for me by the milk and sugar-substitute counter. Or, not exactly waiting for me. More like stirring milk into his coffee. I reached into my bag and had to decide between a swipe of lip gloss and the Groucho glasses I'd taken from the Jolly Roger. Groucho won. The nose was hot and dented now, but I needed the glasses on for bravery.

"Hello, my name is Eleanor, I'm a Scorpio, and my hobbies include watercolor painting and destroying whatever hope is left for the infirm. And you are . . . ?"

Dr. Ganesh laughed and nodded his head. "I think this is a lot of eyebrows." He pointed at my face.

"Yeah, sometimes it's easier to say things when I'm somebody else. Can I get a what what?" I put out my fist and waited for him to bump it. He indulged me, then put the lid on his coffee cup and waited for me to either say something or let him go home.

"Right. I just wanted to say first of all thank you so much for being calming and brilliant. And thank you for getting my dad a bed and staying late and talking to me about nanotech-nology, which is funny—not *haha* funny but more like *what in the what?* funny—because I've been reading up on some of the incredible work that's being done with genetic sequencing, which is . . . well, incredible. And also, I wonder how it affects our treatment protocols for these global pandemics. Which—I don't know who gets to classify something as a pandemic, maybe that's the president or the surgeon general, but I would call can-cer a pandemic, wouldn't you?"

Dr. Ganesh wasn't smiling anymore. He looked confused and worn out.

"Actually, scratch that," I said. "Can I just give you a hug?"

"Um . . . I suppose so." He put down his coffee and opened his arms. His tracksuit smelled like cedary spices and a little like rubbing alcohol too. I'd never been this close to a man before, besides my dad and Julian. Unless I counted D.J. Trekorelli, who pushed me into a corner at the middle school winter carnival two years ago and told me he had feelings. I'd tried kissing him but it tasted like a salt lick so I told him I was bisexual and he ran.

As I sucked in a deep whiff of Dr. Ganesh's scent, I could feel all my neurons sending out a shimmery bat signal—*Alert! Man touch!*

He pulled away and I stared at the floor determinedly.

"I will catch you later, Ey-leah-nor," I heard him say before the revolving doors swept him away.

I wasn't ready to go upstairs and deal with Mom yet, so I stood in line at the café—calmly this time—and purchased a bagel, coffee, and a balloon that read IT'S A BOY! (Maybe it could make Dad laugh whenever he woke up from his opioid haze.) I sat by the wishing well and did some more research on my phone about Nivolumab and Varlilumab. Both of them were getting some really impressive results, but the test groups were pretty small. I wondered how to get Dad into the next trial before it closed. The whole application process was confusing. It was like buying concert tickets. They opened up the trial online and then the first fourteen patients to be sick or lucky enough to sign up at that exact moment got to have a dance party with a famous IV.

It also reminded me of that time when Dad and I got up at three a.m. to try to see this asteroid that was maybe going to light up the whole sky but also might hit the Earth. It was freezing down at the dog park and Dad stepped in some calcified dog poop and I knew he wanted to just go home and get back in bed but he waited with me and my binoculars until sunrise. We never saw anything extraordinary besides a cloud that we agreed looked like George Washington's profile. Which was a cold, sad relief.

It was important to get some perspective, so I picked up a handful of horrifying pamphlets in the lobby. According to the glossy foldouts, there were new pandemics and medical mysteries every day and I was standing at the forefront of human innovation. I knew it wasn't nice to waste trees, but I lifted a dozen of those brochures-to-worldwide-healing and decided to start a scrapbook of rare diseases for Dr. Ganesh. At first glance, my favorites were something called Jumping Frenchmen of Maine disease and maple syrup urine disease. Not that I was a connoisseur of scrapbooking, but this could keep me mildly distracted while I waited for Dad to wake up and actively snubbed Mom.

When I came back into the room, she was still glued to Dad's bedside, stroking his head and telling him about some roadwork being done on the New York Thruway. Dad's cheeks looked so limp and pale I stopped short. But the oxygen mask assured me he was alive.

"And here comes the greatest daughter on Earth, Lenny the Lioness," Mom announced. "Wasn't she amazing?" she cooed at Dad. "I really didn't mean to leave you both for so long, but damn this kid of ours knows how to rise to the challenge, huh? Is there anything she can't do?"

I sat on the vinyl recliner in the corner and started tearing out pictures for my scrapbook. "There are many things I cannot do," I said. "And please stop talking about me in the third person when I'm right here. It's annoying."

"Fair enough," Mom said in a small voice. She went back to her monologue for Dad, this time about the latest primary elections and the plumbing at the courthouse and really twenty different starts to a story that kept on veering into new tangents and tributaries.

At some point in the evening, Mariel brought us starchy cotton blankets and pillows that felt like they were stuffed with scraps of cardboard. Saffi checked Dad's vitals around eleven thirty and said his fever was now down to 102.5.

"Nice work," Saffi said to Dad, though his eyes were still glued shut. Even if he continued to look like a husk, at least we were moving in the right direction. Or a less dire one.

Soon after, I heard Mom's raucous snore. She was folded in half on her chair, her head nestled into the two inches of hospital bedding next to Dad's forearm. It looked like the most uncomfortable position possible, but I didn't dare wake her. It was actually the first time in the past twelve hours that I had felt something close to love or pity for her.

I pulled one of Mariel's blankets over my head on the recliner. Before trying to close my eyes, too, I had some more investigating to do on my phone. This time I was looking into who exactly was Radhakrishnan Ganesh, M.D., Ph.D. The man, the myth, the crusader for truth and possibility.

The name "Ganesh" came up in a thousand different profiles. Apparently, it was one of the most popular Indian names and it came from the Hindu deity Ganesha. All the images of Ganesha were of very feminine-looking elephants dancing—cuddly and fierce at the same time. I was surprised Ganesha was always referred to as a "he." Then again, the strongest men I knew—Dad and Julian—were definitely graceful too. The best definition I found was: *Ganesha is known as the Remover of All Obstacles and Deva of New Beginnings. Ganesha's head symbolizes the Atman or soul, and his body signifies Maya or earthly existence. His trunk represents OM, which is the utterance of cosmic reality. Ganesha is the muse for arts, sciences, intellect, and wisdom.*

Having grown up in a mostly atheistic home, I loved how vividly Ganesha's stories were written and illustrated. Also, I had always been infatuated with Dumbo, and one of my fantasies was to go to Mozambique and work at a national park that took care of endangered elephants. The more I read about Ganesha's cosmic trunk, the more I knew we were going to make it through this night.

I needed to find more info about *my* Ganesh, though. I finally narrowed down the results and found a few pictures of him on a soccer field. Another of him looking through a microscope. There was a paper he'd coauthored with five other doctors on advances in nanotechnology and the moral implications of accessibility. Some lab in Iowa listed him as a resident intern.

There were no records or pictures of Dr. Radhakrishnan Ganesh with a girlfriend. Which I knew shouldn't have meant anything to me, but I was glad no one could see my goofy grin under the blanket canopy.

I stayed up for another two hours, reading and studying. By the time the next nurse came in to check Dad's vitals at two a.m., I had:

a) Memorized all the major Hindu deities and their powers.

b) Fostered a small family of Asian elephants now being nurtured in an Oregon preserve. (I had three weeks to figure out how to explain the charge before it showed up on my "emergency only" credit card.)

c) Accepted the fact that I was smitten.

Totalitarian Dystopia

With a totalitarian dystopia, we wouldn't actually all die, but we'd want to. Spies used to wear sunglasses or hats or at least tiptoe. But now, everything is under surveillance.

Just a few of the scariest moments

1928: *Olmstead v. United States.* Supreme Court basically okays wiretapping of bootleggers.

1952: President Truman creates the National Security Agency (NSA) to protect/spy on the nation.

2001: Congress passes the Patriot Act.

2002: The Department of Homeland Security is established.

2008: Congress passes the FISA Amendments Act, which authorizes mass surveillance programs (and abuses).

2013: Japanese smart toilet gets hacked.

2015: Cousin Alan gets me a DIY drone for Hanukkah.

Chapter 7

BELIEVING

Like Wendy Wackerling had warned us just one day before, once I started believing, miracles happened. The next morning, I woke up to a completely different scene. A nursing attendant was opening the blinds and had turned on some classical music through the TV on the wall.

"Now, let's keep it that way, ya hear?" she said, swishing out of the room.

"What way?" I asked. "What happened?"

Dad was sitting up, eyes open. His skin had new colors and definition. He looked exhausted and had that damn oxygen mask on, but he scribbled on an unused napkin, *Something you want to tell me?* nodding his head at my gift-shop balloon. I told him that he had freaked the hell out of me, Nixon was president again, and there was a therapy donkey doing rounds in the afternoon.

Dad said, "Hee haw!" from under his mask and it sounded so weird that I started laughing and couldn't stop. Not even because it was hilarious, but because it was the first communication we'd had since he'd been shaking and writhing and I hadn't known if we'd ever talk again.

Mom took Dad's joke as a sign that she could finally go to the bathroom and pee. After my laughing fit, I told Dad I should head down to the lounge and call Julian to give him the full report because he'd called about twenty times but only left the same terse "Call me."

I had to admit it was rare and pretty thrilling to know something that Julian didn't already know. He usually had all the answers.

"It was so crazy," I started. "I mean, I don't want to really go into it, but remember when we saw that mouse snared on a glue trap next to the ficus in the diner? And we were like, 'Ew, we're never eating here again.' But then of course we ate there again. But that's not really the point. The point is, I kept thinking that my dad was that mouse. It was like he was caught in his own body, and I could see that he was trying to get out, but he also wasn't really conscious. It was horrible with a side of terrifying."

"Holy shiz. I'm so sorry," said Julian. I let him tell me how great and brave I was for a while. I didn't want to talk any more even though I knew he'd appreciate the rotating Island staff and Mom's grand entrance. I just wanted to be done with this unidentifiable infection and go home.

Julian read my silence, of course. "You guys getting discharged soon?" he asked.

"Good question," I said. "I sure hope so. But he's hooked up to oxygen and none of the doctors have come to check up on him today." Then I remembered I had some news Julian would love. "But there is a silverish lining . . ."

I told him how I'd initiated physical contact with the Remover of All Obstacles and that we'd chatted for a long time about personal stuff. "He's deeply passionate about his work. And has some dark family issues, of course. We really got into it," I said.

"Nice job, Len!" Julian did seem honestly excited. Though I noted that *Len* sounded childish to me. I preferred *Ey-leah-nor* now.

"He's really incredible," I told him. "And young and vibrant and humble. He has a great sense of humor. Did I mention he plays soccer? Or did. But now he's super busy curing cancer." I knew I was exaggerating, but it felt so good to be stretching my brain. The only other people in the lounge were a stooped man who looked a little like Elvis in his later years and a guy who must've been his son in a sweater vest, opening up take-out containers filled with pierogies. They didn't seem to care or notice that I was revealing a new breakthrough in cancer treatment. Elvis actually seemed to be deeply engrossed in the rerun of *Friends* playing on the mounted TV.

"So Ganesh is getting my dad into this drug trial that's been having phenomenal results. I'll send you some links. Basically, it's a monoclonal antibody that binds to individual molecules."

Julian was silent. I knew he wasn't following and it only emboldened me. "This is revolutionary stuff. So far, it's proven amazingly effective. It arms the immune system in this symbiotic way. It's huge. Do you want me to send you some articles about it? This is only being done at a few hospitals."

"Sure." Julian's voice was dull. Now I was getting annoyed that he wasn't as excited as I was. I knew Julian was a born cynic but I thought he could at least phone in some peppy responses. "Plus everyone in the drug trial gets a free elephant ride," I added to see if he was even listening.

"What?" he asked, confused.

"Never mind." It was a private joke with me and myself. I'd try it out on Dr. Ganesh the next time I saw him. Which I really hoped was soon. I couldn't take another twenty-four hours without his fist bumps of optimism.

After getting off the phone, I strode up to the nurses' island and said in my sweetest voice, "Excuse me, do you have a schedule for the doctors on this floor, please?" I didn't recognize any of the staff since the morning shift had started, so I just chose the warmest-looking woman with clean scrubs and a smiley-face button on her chest.

"A what?" She didn't look like her smiley-face button at all.

"A schedule, like who comes in when? My dad is in room 428."

"Okay, so are you asking who is his doctor?"

"Sort of. I mean, I know who his doctor is. It's Dr. Lowenstein. But he's in Toronto, so he has this attending resident, Dr. Ganesh, and I didn't know if he'd be in today or if we can contact him."

"I don't know a Dr. Ganesh." She spun around in her chair to get some consensus from the other nurses. "Is there a Ganesh?"

The back and forth was crazy-making.

"Ganesh?"

"Ga*nesh*."

"I think it's *Ga*nesh."

"He's the Indian guy, right?"

"Is he Indian?"

"Don't ask me."

Smiley-face-with-no-smile turned back to me and said, "I don't know exactly who he is, but it sounds like this Dr. Ganesh does work here."

"Thank you," I said through flared nostrils. "That's very . . . helpful."

By noon, I was ready to rip Dad's oxygen mask off for him. His temperature was hovering around one hundred and he was perfectly lucid but very soggy. He just wanted to be able to stand up untethered and maybe get a new gown. Mom and I had asked five different attendants when the doctors were making their rounds and got a series of shrugs. I knew they could see us wearing holes into the linoleum floor. There were little cameras perched in multiple corners of Dad's room. The Island of Unanswerable Questions was probably tracking our every gas bubble.

I was really tempted to call or text Dr. Ganesh directly, but I didn't want to bug him if it was his day off. I started texting,

When can I see you again? then chickened out. Instead I added five new pages to his rare-disease book:

- Abetalipoproteinemia, which was some inherited thing where people couldn't absorb fat and then couldn't walk or think. I just thought it had an incredible amount of vowels.
- Hartnup disease, which I really summarized as a glorified rash, and
- Blue rubber bleb nevus syndrome, which was a lot like horrible ulcers.

I wanted to make sure Dr. Ganesh didn't think I was making fun of these diseases, so I also included a page about the National Organization for Rare Disorders and a few of their success stories.

The hero of the day was a guy named Washington who couldn't have been much older than me. He walked with a swaggery kind of limp and was singing under his breath to the same beat. Washington was in charge of delivering meals. He came in at 2:30 with a turkey club and rice pudding, even though my dad couldn't eat anything with a mask covering his nose and mouth.

"Mmmm," Washington said, looking at Dad. "How're you going to eat this?"

"Thank you," I answered.

"We've been trying to get this thing off all day," chimed in Mom.

"Luke, I am your father," hissed Dad in his best Darth Vader impersonation through the mask. Washington thought that was awesome. He had a sweet, hiccupy laugh and he high-fived us all. An hour later, Washington stopped back in to say that he'd put in an order to get rid of the mask. Two hours later, another nurse tried to tell us that Lowenstein was still in Toronto and he was the only one who could okay that kind of order. But then I marched out to the hall and saw Washington talking with Smiley-No-Smiles and the mask came off at 4:25 p.m.

The first thing Dad did was rasp, "Long live Washington!" Then he drank five cups of lukewarm apple juice and told Mom, "Lenny was amazing."

"I heard," she said, pulling me to her chest. It was sort of a sideways hug and my neck was jammed into her throat, but Dad looked very pleased with our forced affection. I stayed there as long as I could before saying, "Okay, that's enough. I'm not pointing fingers, but we all smell like ass."

Mom agreed. She also said if it was okay with Dad, she'd love to get some fresh air and stop at a drugstore for deodorant. I was on board for that. I hadn't been outside for over twenty-four hours. The sky was already sifting into a pinkish sunset, but it looked so much wider and loftier than ever before. Mom and I peeled off in different directions at the drugstore and I spent a ridiculous amount of time staring at lip plumpers and counting all the different ways to spell *barbecue* in the potato-chip section. I heard Mom yelp, "I'm heading back, Len!" at some point, then decided to stroll even more slowly through the aisles.

When I got to the cash register, the girl ringing me up looked like she was maybe fourteen. Her name tag read HI! LET ME HELP MAKE THIS AN AWESOME DAY! SHEENA.

She had matching stripes of acne on each cheek and eyelashes shellacked into shutters. When she reached over to bag my items, I saw she was pregnant and had the name Luis tattooed onto the side of her neck. Her big belly and even bigger scowl made me feel guilty. I'd never had a job besides babysitting and I was buying three different kinds of gum, some frog stickers, and four bottles of hand sanitizer with my parents' earnings.

"Congratulationskeepthechange," I whispered while putting my leftover dimes on the counter, grabbing my stuff, and hustling out.

Mom was already back by Dad's side with smoothies in every color of the rainbow. Dad was able to take three sips of Spirulina Splendor before claiming he was full. I polished off something that tasted like sandpaper and toothpaste, just because I was starving and the turkey club was gone. I never actually saw Mom ingest of any of it, but she did reach into her drugstore bag, pull out a flowered shower cap, and start strutting around the room as if she were on a runway.

"I don't know if you really want to take a shower here," I said.

"No, it's for Emma," Mom answered. "I forgot to send her

costume. Did you hear what she's going as?" I just shook my head because I couldn't believe Mom was focusing on Emma's costume party when a few hours ago I thought we were planning for Dad's funeral. "It's trickle-down economics. So her friend has a Maggie Thatcher wig and I'm sending her—"

"Stop it!" I snapped. "Just stop! How horrible does this have to get before you take it seriously? We don't even know what's going on and you're busy at phone stores and buying shower caps like it's happy hour." Wrong metaphor, but Mom got the gist.

"You could've called Pippi," she mumbled. "I told you she always has her phone on in case of emergency."

"You're right, Mom. I could've." I snorted for effect. "Next time Dad is writhing for air and the nurses are calling code whatever I'll be sure to pick up the phone and chat with my BFF, Pippi. That'd be a lot more comforting than trying to depend on you!"

Mom looked like I'd just smacked her across the face. Which I wish I had the nerve to do but I never would. Dad took one of my hands and one of Mom's and gave us both a tight squeeze.

"We're okay," he said. "We really are."

I couldn't look at him or Mom. They both felt too unreliable to me.

"Please," Dad said to both of us. Or maybe he was talking to the nurses' spy cameras so they would stop looking at us imploding.

"I'm sorry," Mom said softly. "I know this was really hard on you both and I . . . yeah, I'm sorry."

"S'okay. Me too," I mumbled, then excused myself for an evening constitutional around the tenth floor. Unintentionally, I started retracing the steps I'd taken with Dr. Ganesh the night before. In the rest of the world, this stretch of time was called "Saturday night." I wondered what that meant to Radhakrishnan Ganesh, M.D. Was he at a dimly lit café with a long-legged blonde, laughing over tapas? Or holing up in the public library, his hand scratching the back of his neck as he tried to analyze new data in T-cell infiltration? The scenario I liked best was him in a one-bedroom Brooklyn apartment with lots of windows overlooking Prospect Park. The Ramones playing in the background as he sipped a beer, stirred a pot of homemade spaghetti sauce, and practiced handstands.

That's what my dad used to do.

It almost looked like Dad was stirring spaghetti when I got back to his room. His eyes were shut again, but his arms were floating a little bit up and down and in circles.

"He keeps trying to get that mask off, even though it's not there," Mom explained quietly. I'd hoped she would be sleeping, too, but she had her reading glasses on and was going over legal briefs by the light of her phone in her chair. "I ordered you a cot," she added, nodding at the rollaway mattress shoved between the foot of Dad's bed and the window.

"Thanks," I said. Then I gargled some of Dad's mouthwash

to trick my body into thinking it was time for sleep, even though I knew I'd be staring at the walls and counting heart-monitor beeps for another few hours at least.

Of course, because of the Law of Unfair Physics, as soon as I went to get coffee Sunday morning, the doctors did their rounds. Dr. Ganesh came by to check in on my dad and Mom reported that the first thing he said was, "Where is Ey-leah-nor?"

I didn't know if I believed her, but it didn't stop me from involuntarily bouncing a little. Then I rushed out of Dad's room and sniffed the halls for Dr. Ganesh's sandalwood scent. I heard his laughter coming from the west lounge, so I waited until the swinging doors opened and then tried not to pounce.

"Can I get a what what?" I hollered.

Stunned silence from Dr. Ganesh. He was surrounded by a circle of what looked to be graduate students, and I had interrupted him midthought. One young woman pulled off her paper mask and cap, shook out her raven tresses, and said, "Sorry, can you please repeat that, Dr. Ganesh?" while she frowned in my direction. Her lips stayed in that shimmery pout as she turned back to the good doctor. She was the kind of girl who could do whatever she wanted with a Saturday night.

Dr. Ganesh answered her and then asked the group about the patients they'd just seen. When the comments were done, he turned to me and said, "As it happens, this is the lovely young daughter of Patient C, whom we visited before."

Lovely. Young. Daughter.

I didn't know whether "lovely" was thrilling enough to cancel out "young" and I appreciated Dad's privacy being protected, but Patient C sounded so coldly clinical.

"No autographs please," I said. There were a few snickers behind him. "But seriously, I'm the treasurer and CEO of the Dr. Ganesh fan club. You guys are super lucky to be studying with him. I'm thinking of med school now just so I can do that too. He's like Salk and Sabin and he has the best tracksuits of anyone I know."

Dr. Ganesh shook his head. A few of the students whispered behind him. I wanted to clarify that it was a joke, or maybe a joke disguised as the truth, or the other way around. I also really wanted to give him the rare-disease book that I'd stayed up coloring. But this meeting already felt like it was adjourned. So I dug a crumpled bag of M&M's from my sweatshirt pocket and shoved it toward him. I'd gotten it that morning at the gift shop.

"What's this?" he asked, as if he'd just gotten the Nobel Prize in Medicine. "For me?!"

"Yeah, whatever," I said as coolly as possible. "I'm sort of allergic to chocolate and you can share it with the group. Or not."

"Thank you so very much," Dr. Ganesh said, looking deep into my soul. Before he turned away, I detected a wink. It could have been a hallucination, but I inscribed it into my memory for safekeeping anyway. "Let us continue with radiology, shall we?" he said, pressing the hall doors open with his thin hip. "I see you again soon, what what!" he called over his shoulder as he led his team of disciples away.

Which was vague enough to leave me agape. I didn't know if *soon* meant in the next few minutes or hours or days. I just knew it meant a future was possible. For me and my dad. Of course, I still hadn't found out when we would get to spring him free from this joint, so I retreated to room 428 to see what I could see.

Only Dad was gone.

"It's all good," Mom said, rushing over to intercept my freak-out. Apparently, while I was making a fool of myself in the hallway, Dr. Lowenstein had called from a two-second break in his Very Important Conference. He told Dad that he'd been monitoring the situation from up north (*via drone?*) and that Dad's high fever and infection were serious but "not unheard of." I hated when adults threw out phrases like that because it was so grammatically obnoxious and the words meant exactly nothing except that somewhere, sometime, somehow this had happened before.

Lowenstein also had phoned in an order for a bunch of invasive and time-consuming tests for Dad—MRI, CT scan, colonoscopy. Basically an all-day pass for the hospital camera crew to take action shots of Dad's mangled interior.

"Wait. Why so many new tests?" I asked. "What exactly is going on?"

Mom unleashed a whole stream of thoughts in no particular or cohesive order: "Modern medicine is this incredible amazing thing where we can replace organs and literally transplant an entire face onto another person's face, but there's also the day-to-day discomforts and uncertainties and it's not permanent, but what is really permanent, right? So we deal with this now and try to see what will help the most in the long run. Listen, nobody said this would be a cakewalk. First of all, nobody uses the term *cakewalk* anymore, and it's a good thing because I think it comes from the minstrel shows of the eighteen hundreds and people threw cakes at the best act. Point being, we're doing everything we can, this is a highly treatable form, and we're aggressively treating it. You and I both need a hot shower, so let's go home and then once these scans are done and reviewed, Dad will come home too."

I couldn't argue with her. Mostly because she was pulling out etymology, face transplants, and Buddhism in the same breath. Also because the thought of a hot shower sent shivers of joy to my armpits and it looked like Dad and Dr. Ganesh were going to be busy for a while. So I followed my mom down the hall to the bank of elevators and let one carry me down, down, down. Trusting in the unseen forces of gravity, modern medicine, and elephants marching toward new beginnings.

Water Pollution

From the Natural Resources Defense Council: "Dirty water is the world's biggest health risk."

The United Nations said 95 percent of the world's cities dump sewage into their water. America is one of the few places that supposedly has clean drinking water. But thanks to things like fracking, factory farms, and sewage overflows, there are more than 300 pollutants in U.S. tap water—including *arsenic*.

Bottoms up!

A Few Reasons Why We're Drinking Arsenic

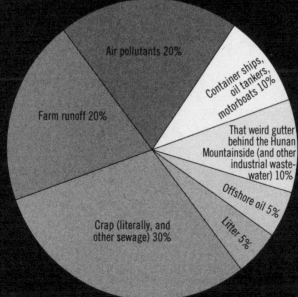

- Air pollutants 20%
- Container ships, oil tankers, motorboats 10%
- Farm runoff 20%
- That weird gutter behind the Hunan Mountainside (and other industrial waste-water) 10%
- Offshore oil 5%
- Crap (literally, and other sewage) 30%
- Litter 5%

Chapter 8

WOLFBALL

I was so slimy from two days of slathering my hands in antibacterial goo that when I got home I charged straight into the shower without even taking off my clothes. I knew I had to throw that outfit out anyway. I loved those green corduroys and it was one of my favorite hoodies, but I couldn't imagine how many times I'd have to wash them to feel like they were actually clean.

When I got downstairs, Mom was dressed in jeans and a new proud-mom-of-a-state-college-freshperson T-shirt, lining up plastic sandwich baggies on the kitchen counter and filling them with walnuts.

"Isn't a hot shower revolutionary sometimes?" she said without looking up. For each walnut she dropped into a bag, another went into her mouth. "I looked up *cakewalk* by the way," she went on. "Check this out." She showed me a video on her phone of someone in blackface doing a dance with lots of frantic-looking footwork. "Whoever won got the cake," she said.

"Thanks, I guess."

"Oh, and what do you think about Julian coming over here

for a sleepover while I head back to the hospital? You guys can see an early movie, get some pizza. By the time you come home from school tomorrow, Dad will be here too."

"Wait, what?" I loved the idea of not going back to the hospital, but I hated the thought of sitting in pre-calculus, daydreaming about all the cameras fishing through my dad's insides. "Are you sure?"

"Abso-tootin-lutely," said Mom. "Already called in a personal day for tomorrow, took my omega-3s, and I'm ready to rock." Mom did some crazy roundhouse-kick combo at me. Then she held up her phone. "I'll have it on my person at all times. Fully charged. If I remember to put the app on, you can watch me." (Mom refused to learn how video calls worked.)

The phone started vibrating, on cue. Emma's name and face lit up the screen.

"Ooh! Em's calling! I should take this so I can update her," Mom said, looking to me for approval. She bit her lip as if I'd caught her being naughty.

"Finish talking to me first, please," I said, seizing the phone and rejecting Emma's call. Then I put on my sternest voice to grill her.

"Are you going to stay with Dad until all his tests are done?" Mom nodded.

"You're going to call me as soon as the test results come back." She made a check mark in the air.

"And you have a couple of things to get in writing:

a) instructions on how we should treat Dad's port site at home and b) a schedule of the doctors on call."

"Got it," Mom said. The she paused and scrunched her eyebrows together. "Wait, a schedule?" she asked.

"Forget it," I said quickly. Mom took her phone back and pulled me into an unexpected hug.

"Oh, my sweet Eleanor," she said, her voice rumbling in between our skins. "You've been beyond amazeballs. That's what the kids say now, right? Amazeballerrific. I mean it." I melted just a little. I loved the way my mom smelled after a shower. It was a sharp combination of eucalyptus shampoo and the baking soda she used instead of toothpaste. The ends of her bobbed hair hung on to the last drips of water in dark coils. I wanted to stay in this scoop of calm between her shoulder and ear for as long as it lasted.

Of course, as soon as my breath slowed, Mom jolted back into her usual warp speed. "Okeydoke!" she declared. She pulled away and shoved two baggies of nuts at me. "One for you and one for Julian. Now take a few dollars out of my wallet and put on your shoes. He's picking you up in two minutes."

"You already called him?" That made me livid and grateful all at once. I hated her butting in almost as much as I hated asking Julian for favors.

"Sorry," Mom said. "I was just trying to expedite the process." Her phone was buzzing loudly again. Damn Emma. Mom gathered the rest of her nutbags while talking, blowing her nose, and combing her hair. "Love you so much, Len. Talk to you ASAP!"

By the time she slammed the front door behind her, my ears were making that *wah-wah* sound from life being too loud.

"Sorry you got a weird call from Naomi Rosenthal-Hermann," I told Julian when he pulled up a few minutes later. It felt really good to see him, like my world was recalibrating to its somewhat natural state.

"Don't be sorry," answered Julian. "I like your mom a lot more than you do."

I didn't know if I felt offended or vindicated by that statement, so I didn't argue.

"Do you want to talk more about the hospital?" he asked.

"Not right now. I told you the highlights."

"Well, if you do . . . ya know." He pinched my thigh. Which is what we'd decided lobsters did to show affection. I made antennae with my fingers and then pinched him back—hard.

The Mountainside movie theater was not exactly a Cineplex megatron. Our choices were something called *Wolfball* or a three-hour epic with a poster of Mel Gibson holding up a severed arm.

"*Wolfball!*" we said in unison.

Julian was feeling extra generous. He paid for our tickets, a box of Sour Smackers, and an ultra-ginormous jumbo popcorn that could fit a small child inside it. Then he let me pick where we were going to sit. I picked third row center, because I knew that was Julian's favorite spot anyway. While we watched previews, I sucked on Sour Smackers until my tongue ached. Then I chased them down with a fistful of salty popcorn. Everything in my mouth stung and I loved it.

"You don't have to sleep over," I whispered to Julian while they played some PSA about litter destroying the ozone.

"I know I don't *have* to. But it's either me or Adolf." Julian starting humming the music to *Schindler's List* and nodded at the guy who was the manager of the movie theater. His real name was Alan, and he wasn't responsible for a world-shattering genocide. But he did take his job way too seriously and he usually stood by the door, scanning the crowd with soldier-straight posture and squinty eyes. I was pretty sure he was part drone. One time when we'd tried to switch theaters, Alan literally threatened to call the cops on us. I wasn't sure what we could be arrested for, but we didn't wait to see.

"I'll take bachelor number you," I told Julian.

"Smart choice," he muttered while the lights dimmed for showtime.

The movie was blissfully stupid. It started with a kid from the projects who was so poor that his family slept in a bus shelter, but at least they had dry pasta, church, and each other. Someone saw the kid shooting hoops and promised to change his life. There was a montage of him dribbling for all of these important coaches, flying all over the world in designer sneakers, and getting to kiss a girl in a Jacuzzi. But he let his success ruin him. He stopped calling home. Then he did some drug that caused him to think he was part wolf and there were all these agents following him so he bit someone's face. His new life came tumbling down. He lost everything, including his sneakers.

That's when Julian leaned over and whispered, "I can't devote any more precious hours to this. Plus, I need something to eat besides sugar and salt."

"Me too. Don Juan's?" I asked.

Julian took hold of the popcorn bucket with a few kernels left on the bottom and gave it to Alan on the way out. "Thank you for this cinematic experience," he said, bowing.

Alan took off after us. "Um, what do you think you're doing? The movie's not over for another twenty-three minutes," he said in his robotic voice. We didn't answer him. The guy working concessions was drinking Sprite from under the spigot, so the last thing we heard was Alan saying, "Please tell me I'm not seeing what I think I'm seeing!"

"Are you seeing this?" asked Julian. He started humping the life-size cardboard figurine of Mel Gibson and then did this incredible flip over the ticket turnstile, followed by some gorgeous somersault-split-undulating-leap combo that took all the air out of the lobby. I ran after him as he burst out the doors and ran down the block, yelling, "Wooooolfballlllll!"

I caught up to him by Anthony's Cut & Trim, where we'd both been ruined by horrible haircuts in the past. The pictures of feathered hairstyles in the window were at least thirty years out of date. Anthony's angry cat was exchanging snarls with Julian through the glass.

"Are you afraid of anything?" I asked.

"Sure," said Julian. He stepped onto the peak of a hydrant and jumped off.

"Like what?"

"Like little kids' birthday parties. Yacht clubs. Terrorists. Terrorist yacht clubs."

"Come on," I said. "For real."

"Lenny, I've told you before. I doubt I'm gonna last past forty."

"Stop saying that!" I pummeled him on the chest, pushing him into a parking meter. I hated when Julian talked like this. I'd even drawn up a friendship contract where he had to swear not to discuss his theories about mortality or eat mayonnaise in front of me, but Julian refused to sign.

He wasn't actually ill in any way, except for a ridiculous amount of confidence, a morbid sense of humor, and a sprinkling of allergies. But for all of his skepticism, Julian got his palm read every year on his birthday and the last two times his lifeline wrinkle was pronounced "stunted." I told him he needed to use more hand cream. He told me he was ready to be reincarnated as a turtle.

"Hey!" he said, squirming under my palms. "It's not a bad thing. It just means I want to live for today. Ow!" He shoved me off of him and ran down the dusky street again. The worst part was he never looked back either. Julian knew I'd follow him wherever he went.

By the time I limped through the front doors of the Unicorn, he was already crouched down behind the tank, in the middle of a classic Don Juan Crustaceo monologue.

". . . so I told him every time I take a new lover-a, a flounder gets its wings."

I marched by as if I didn't hear or see him, though I couldn't help noticing the water in the tank looked really low and murky. One of the non–Don Juan lobsters was on its side, its tentacles way too inert.

"She's like a Botticelli with none of the curves-a," Julian whispered, letting me sulk. He joined me a few minutes later, sliding into our booth like nothing had happened.

"I'm getting a full meal and you're treating," I told him.

"Is that so?" Julian replied.

When Dara came over, she was wearing one of her real-hair-but-not-hers ponytails, with cotton-candy-pink lipstick and thick fake eyelashes.

"I love this look," I said, even though the ponytail was a shade lighter than the rest of her rusty strands and one of her eyelashes kept flopping.

"Definitely hot," Julian added.

"Fake it 'til ya make it," Dara said, snapping her gum. She looked happy at the compliments, though. "No burnt toast left, sorry."

"That's okay," said Julian. "I'm treating my girl to a real meal tonight. We'll take two of your finest grilled cheese sandwiches on wheat bread. A dollop of mashed potatoes just for the lady folk," said Julian.

I was grateful that he remembered my favorite order, but I didn't want him to get off too easy. When Dara started gathering up the menus, I stopped her and said, "Actually, I'm gonna do one of the International Delight dishes. Which do you recommend?"

"Woo-hoo! Look who's finding her sass. I always have a scoop of tuna. But you know Aniket is from Delhi and he makes something awesome with tomatoes and curry."

"Perfect!" I slapped the menu down, feeling pretty triumphant. "You know, I have a new friend who's Indian and maybe I'll bring him here."

"Really?" Dara asked. Julian was biting his lip, giddily waiting for me to go on.

"I mean, he's more than just a friend. He's a man." Julian started cracking up, and even though I whined, "What? Stop!" I was laughing too because it was a ridiculous statement.

Dara put her hand up for a high five. "You go, girl," she said. "All I have is sobriety and a pair of crappy false eyelashes." She reached up to work on the spidery lashes, then peeled both of them off and fixed them under her nose like a tiny mustache.

"Okay, I was wrong," said Julian. "*That* is hot."

"I'm gonna try it out on Stephan, see if he has any sense of humor. Did I tell you he's putting up some mirrored tiling in the entrance so he can look at his face more? Not sure what that means for your beloved lobsters."

"Wait—what?!" My yelp almost blew Dara's lash-stache off and it definitely turned some heads. "Sorry," I said, a little quieter. "Let me get this straight, though. Is he planning on throwing them back in the Atlantic? Because I get the newsletters from the Natural Resources Defense Council, and there is an all-time high right now in acidic runoff. He can't just dump them at the nearest beach and hope for the best."

Julian and Dara both looked at me with their mouths drooping open. Then Julian took my hands in his and kissed me on the knuckles. "Oh man," he said. "Sometimes you are so awesome. In the saddest, sweetest way." His eyes were sagging like he might cry, but he was also pressing his lips together as if he was holding back a huge guffaw.

Dara scratched the top of my head and said, "I don't know what his exact plan is, but I'm 99 percent sure it wouldn't involve Stephan taking the time to bring your lobsters to the beach. I just love you for even thinking of that possibility."

I didn't have time for all the pity. I stood up abruptly, splashing out half of my nonrefillable coffee.

"Well, we have to stop him," I announced. "Tell Stephan that I want to take the tank home. I can buy it from him if he wants. How much is he asking—a hundred dollars? Two hundred?"

"I . . . I don't think he's asking anything," Dara stammered.

"Is he in the office right now? Or should I write him a note so we have some official documents? I can probably go as high as four hundred dollars, just have to take out my babysitting money and a loan from my aunt."

Julian stood up and sort of pressed on my shoulders until I sank back into the banquette. "It's okay, we'll figure this out."

"Yeah, I'm not even sure they're getting rid of the tank completely. It was a guess," Dara said, backing away.

"Just ask for Stephan, please!" I called after her.

"Okay, why don't you tell me a little more about the Ganesh?" Julian asked. I knew he was trying to distract me, which was fine. It was actually fun to recount the hug and the maybe-wink. Julian looked up Dr. Ganesh's hometown of Pondicherry on his phone and the pictures all had enchanted-looking temples and towering mountains. Then he updated me on the *VaGeorgia* mayhem I'd missed. Marty had spent two hours having everyone in blindfolds drawing their inner erotic creatures. Then Julian hung some lights with Oscar.

"He's a weirdo, yes. But he's also talented as hell," Julian reported. "You should see these murals he's working on backstage."

I was too preoccupied with the idea of just taking off with Don Juan's tank to really pay attention. Dara dropped off our meals a few minutes later and tried to scurry away, but I caught the edge of her apron and tugged.

"Working on it!" she assured, then rushed away.

"Hey, freak," said Julian. "Just relax, will ya?" The International Delight was internationally inedible. I bit into what I thought was a piece of tomato but it was so spicy I spit it out, whimpering. Julian switched plates with me and let me devour his grilled cheese instead.

After a few minutes of munching, he broke the silence with, "Did I tell you Chris and her new wife offered me a room in their house?"

If he was looking for a way to yank me out of my crustacean schemes, this did the trick. I was stunned. Chris was Julian's mom and he never brought her up in conversation.

"How did she . . . ? When did she . . . ?" I stuttered.

"I told you the counselor at Valhalla was big on role-playing with your demons and made me write her an email a few years ago." I nodded vigorously even though I didn't remember him ever telling me that. "So she's written me back a few times, but I didn't know what to say, and then I was looking at real estate in the Bay Area, which is ridonkulously expensive . . . so I wrote her to just ask what kind of rent she pays."

"That's great!" I said. Julian didn't respond. "Is that great?"

"I don't know what it is. Maybe it's great. Maybe it's just setting me up to be disappointed all over again," he said. "I've never met her new wife. You know, Tatianna left."

"Sure," I added, again doing my best to sound like this was old news, though I had no idea about any of it. Tatianna was the scandalous cleaning lady who had whisked Chris away a decade ago.

"I haven't seen her in years," Julian mumbled angrily. "It's probably one of the stupidest things I've done."

"I think it's great," I offered.

"And in other news, my dad just rewrote his will so Katya gets basically everything. As if she needs it. She recently informed me that she has a special Fitbit that she wears only in the bedroom. Is that fair that I have to know that?"

"Ew."

"Yeah, big ew," said Julian. "So, can we get out of here now? You can write a note to Stephan if you want. I'm gonna go pay at the front."

The irony was that Stephan had also replaced the paper placemats with these vinyl tablecloths, so I had nothing to write on. I used the back of Julian's receipt to scrawl,

> Dara—Sorry if I was pushy and thank you for
> being the bestest. Please let me know how to
> arrange tank pickup and payment. Xoxox, L

I left my phone number and email address on it too, even though I'd promised in Health & Home Ec never to reveal personal details like that.

"I'm gonna bring you home soon!" I told Don Juan on the way out.

"That's what she said," Julian answered for him.

When we got back to my house, I changed into some pj's and offered Julian a pair of my sweatpants, which were baggy on him. We spent a while feeding TinyGinsberg pieces of cracker and telling her how lucky she was to be a rodent with no social responsibilities or noticeable hang-ups. I was so exhausted from two nights of almost no sleep that I was having trouble forming complete sentences.

"How about we camp out on the couch?" Julian suggested, which sounded delicious to me. He took the long part of the L and I curled up on the shorter leg.

Julian was catching up on emails on his phone with one hand. With the other he started scratching my scalp and kneading my neck. I felt my whole body loosening under his touch. I had about five chapters of social studies reading left to do, but I skimmed through exactly two paragraphs of my Cold War ethics textbook before nodding into a drooly sleep. It was so blissful to have my limbs stretched out all the way and hear no beeping or gurneys going by.

The next time my eyes opened it was 1:29 in the morning and I was so thirsty I thought my tongue would crack. For a good minute I had no idea where I was, or why there was a small blue light next to my pillow.

It was Julian. He was up, scrolling through pictures on his phone. I leaned in to get a better look. Most of them were of two older women—smiling, hiking, holding up plates of spaghetti.

"Is that . . . your mom?"

Julian shut his phone off quickly. "No. Or maybe. Just trying to figure out the distance between her place and the school. I'd rather rent a one-bedroom anyway."

"Sounds smart," I said, sorry I'd interrupted him. "Just make sure you get a month-to-month lease, in case you hate it. And flood insurance, 'cuz you'll be crying your eyes out missing me."

"Ha!" Julian answered. "That's my Lenny. Always preparing for the worst."

ELEANOR ROSENTHAL-HERMANN

28 Mosswood Rd., Mountainside, NY 10538

May 7, 2017
Mr. Al Gore
Chairman, Climate Reality Project

Dear Mr. Gore,

Long time, no write.

I know you're busy so I'll keep it brief. I just re-watched your last talk about our global responsibility and the oceans rising more than anyone has ever predicted. I also read your poem about Neptune dissolving at a science fair last year. I have admired you and believed in your vision since I recycled my first juice bottle and I just want to say:

a) Thank you.
b) I'm sorry.
c) Are solar panels really going to do anything?

Sincerely,
Eleanor

Chapter 9

EXQUISITELY VULNERABLE

On Monday morning, I called Mom once from the
Unicorn parking lot, once from the gym locker room, and
three times during lunch. I kept on getting no answer. So much
for being all charged up and ready to rock.

"What if I took your car for a joyride into the city so I can
find out what's going on?" I asked Julian before fifth period.

"What if you give it a few more hours and I'll drive you in
after rehearsal?" he answered. "You do know that if you skip out
on this shitshow, I will cut you out of my will."

"You wrote a will?" I honestly thought it was possible.

"Don't get excited," he said. "The only stuff I'm leaving
behind is my Ken doll collection."

There really was nothing I could do except wait. And look
at my physics quiz cluelessly. And then write a letter to my physics teacher, Mr. Monroe—(no relation to Marilyn)—that I'd
tried to look at our velocity-time graphs but I'd had a family
emergency and I did take his class and our approach to kine-
matics very seriously because I thought there was a lot at stake
and way too much social inertia. Plus, had he noticed that we

were on average two degrees warmer this spring and there was so much fog we lost the moon for a week straight?

Mr. Monroe took the note and my mostly blank test without saying a word.

After that, I called Mom two more times from the bathroom and chewed twenty-four pieces of gum, trying to chomp out my anger and sense of foreboding. Then, just as the final bell rang for the day, Mom texted: **How was school sweetie? Still waiting for results. Brb, C U l8er.**

She was big on using text abbreviations, even if they didn't make sense.

I was big on blaming her for everything wrong with this moment.

"I'll take that ride," I told Julian as we stepped into the auditorium for more *VaGeorgia* lunacy.

"Five o'clock," he said. "Don't be late."

The invocation of the day was for another victim of honor killings in Pakistan. This was why it was so hard to be truly upset at Marty for all her touchy-feely warm-ups. They were actually meaningful and I could hear her hiccupping back emotion as she spoke. Of course, to the left of me I could hear this profound conversation in whispered response:

"Are you wearing my lip balm?"

"No, am I?"

"You totally are."

"Ew, sorry. I'll get you a new one."

"It's okay, I have like a gazillion. How's that thing on your toe?"

"You wanna see it?"

"No! Well, actually, yes."

Marty was oblivious to the chatter. She had us improvise movement while she chanted a Pakistani folk song, followed by a game of duck-duck-goose using the words *trapped* and *free*. It was already past four when the loading-dock door swung open backstage and rattled so loudly there was a collective jolt.

"Sorry," said Oscar as he came in with a huge framed canvas that he laid next to the back curtain. He went back out and the same thing happened when he returned with a second canvas. "Freakin' vortex," he muttered. I had to give him credit for putting at least a Pause button on Marty's circle games. And he probably didn't know it, but the crazy winds we were dealing with were caused by a leaking arctic vortex and a melting southern hemisphere. So that was a nice vortexional shout-out.

Oscar brought out three more canvases. They were each at least seven feet long and covered with gorgeous O'Keeffe-esque collages. It looked like a mix of paint, photographs, tissue paper, and a few large unidentifiable objects.

"Are those bones?" asked Sylvie Ditmas.

"Please say they're not tusks," squeaked Lindsay McAden.

"That's . . . incredible," said Becca Dinger. The Prophet had spoken. The rest of the girls oohed and aahed. Oscar shrugged off the compliments and said something to Marty in what sounded like Dutch. Then he disappeared back into the light booth to collect more bones or study the art of being odd some more.

Marty clapped her hands, invigorated. She turned back to the stage and said, "Okay, I think we should spend today working on the overall shape of this showcase. At the end we can hang these spectacular pieces Oscar has rendered. Now, who has something they'd like to present?"

The a cappella group was missing its soprano.

The two monologists were feeling shy.

"Becca has an awesome song that she wants to sing," offered Sylvie.

"Stop it!" Becca said, standing up, obviously pleased. "Only if you guys do backup," she demanded. Sylvie, Lara, and Madison were immediately in line behind her. There was a good five minutes of giggling and nail biting while they huddled to iron out the specifics. Then Becca turned toward the rest of us with a fluttery flourish and sang in a raspy voice,

> *I . . .*
> *have . . .*
> *but one . . .*
> *desire . . .*
> *and that is you.*

Her backup dancers echoed, *That is you*, while wagging their hips slowly.

Sylvie jumped up and down shouting, "Yes! We nailed it!"

Becca rolled her eyes and then bent forward in a deep curtsey.

"Oh . . . kay," Marty said. It was hilarious to watch her face try to wriggle its way out of dismay. "Okay," she said again, more definitively this time. "Thank you for using the title so prominently and for exploring what it means to desire. Is there more in development, perhaps?"

Becca shrugged. "I guess. But I dunno. I have like no time to do anything between now and the show. My boyfriend, Kevin, is working a double shift and I swore I'd keep him company." Marty opened her mouth to say something, then stopped. "Plus," Becca said, "this is really emotional work, you know?"

I couldn't tell if she was full of it or truly attached to these two lines of drivel, but that was the answer Marty was looking for. She nodded solemnly and mouthed, *I know*, to Becca before turning back to the rest of us.

"Who else?" she asked pleadingly.

Julian pulled me by the wrist up to the center of the stage.

"Wait," I whimpered.

"For what?" he answered. His cheeks were fiery and his hair was matted into sweaty spikes. There were few things that made Julian more wrathful than bad art.

I tried to speak to him without moving my lips so we could have a little privacy. "I just didn't know we were performing in front of everybody today."

"Now you know," he said. Then he turned to the rest of the class and instructed them where to sit in the audience.

"Oscar," he hollered toward the lighting booth, "can you bring up L5, M3, and O2, please?" He pointed to the lights above as he named them. When they actually came on, Marty hooted.

Julian ran down to the locker room and got the Pretty Petunia Princess doll, apron, and turkey baster while I stood dumbly onstage, waiting. We had to play the ballerina music from his phone, which made it sound more tinny than haunting. I felt my skin quivering while I did my waltz of solitude and I stared at the exit sign in the back of the house so I could forget where I was. The music was taking forever to end. I bailed early and dropped to the floor. The only redeeming moment was hearing a few hushed voices:

"Is she okay?"

"I dunno."

"She meant to do that, idiot."

"Whatever. I *do* want a new lip balm."

Julian walked on slowly, glaring the audience into silence. Then he added a stunning leap-lunge combo, picked up Petunia, and walked off.

Disturbed silence. Very disturbed.

"Thanks, you can cut the lights there, Oscar," Julian called. I just stayed lying on the stage floor. I was considering lying there for the rest of human existence.

"Mmmmm," Marty said. "Mmmm-hmmmmm." She sounded like she was impersonating a moped or channeling a ghost. "This is the end of the piece, yes?"

Julian nodded. He offered me a hand so we were standing up facing the class together.

"I see," Marty said in a very measured tone. "I am really intrigued but I don't want to project my thoughts on it before I hear yours. Do you want to tell us how this relates to Georgia O'Keeffe or the theme of desire?"

"Do I *want* to?" Julian repeated. "Not really."

"Right," said Marty. "There is so much here. What I like about the first part is that, Lenny, you are not particularly graceful or even coordinated but you lift your neck in this exquisitely vulnerable way." She smiled at me.

"Thank you?" I said, even though it sounded like the opposite of praise.

"Damn," I heard from the crowd.

Marty spent another ten minutes analyzing Julian's physical choices and the use of a turkey baster as a symbol of reproductive and creative prowess. She asked more questions about the possible links between Georgia and the doll or the purpose of my "distressing stumble." She mentioned again how I lacked poise, which added to the impact of the piece. Julian didn't say a word. He'd been through so many auditions and critiques in the past few years that I was sure this bored him more than anything else. For me, though, it felt like I was being publicly spanked. Repeatedly.

At some point that wasn't soon enough, Julian interrupted to say, "Thanks so much. Maybe we should see what else is show-ready?"

Marty agreed. Of course, nobody had anything else to present, so then she said everyone could pick an instrument from her duffel bag and we would improvise a group composition.

"No," cut in Julian again. He was done with the shenanigans. "You can't make us bang on drums and toot recorders for an hour and a half next weekend. We have posters up, tickets sold, and Rice Krispies treats for intermission. We have so much potential here. I can teach a group number right now. Just think about it." He narrowed his eyes for effect before speaking again. "Is this really how you want to honor Georgia?"

For the next hour, Marty handed the reins over to Julian and he worked us hard. He improvised a tricky but energizing dance combination for us all to try. He even figured out a way for us to make these human sculptures that looked like O'Keeffe's hollyhocks and rams' heads. I was really awestruck. Especially because whenever someone got lost or complained it was too complicated, Julian stayed calm and focused, repeating each move and counting the beats. When Marty tried to butt in, he literally leapt over her and kept going.

But when five o'clock came and went and Julian didn't stop rehearsal, I got peeved. I tried to bulge my eyes out at him and point to the ancient clock over the stacked folding chairs in the back corner. He either ignored me or was too impassioned to notice.

It wasn't until Oscar appeared again and asked Marty loudly, "Are we hanging the collages tonight?" that anyone dared to stop Julian's flow. Marty was diving into Julian's choreography too, and somersaulted over toward her son.

"My dearest," she said, "I did tell you we'd do that, didn't I?"

Oscar didn't care either way. "It's fine. But I'm gonna get going because I have a six o'clock call to Prague."

"Six o'clock?!" Marty laughed. "How could it be almost six?"

"Oh my goodness that is so not okay," Becca gushed. "Kevin's gonna be *so concerned*. I have to go." She ran down to the locker room, with Sylvie, Lara, and Madison in tow. I wondered what it felt like to never have to be alone.

"Sorry to keep you late," Julian said to the rest of us. His eyes found mine. "*Really* sorry."

"Yes, but I think this was so fruitful and expansive, right?" Marty said.

"Please go home and memorize this. Do it ten times in front of a mirror and have it clean and ready to go for tomorrow," Julian instructed.

Everyone collected their stuff and started heading to the locker room. I couldn't handle the idea of listening to the girls compare boob size down there even though I did want to change my tank top and pee. So I said to Julian, "I'll be outside. *Waiting*."

"Gotcha. Two minutes," he answered. I pushed open the side door, slid my back down the brick wall by the bike racks, and closed my eyes. I guess I appreciated the arctic vortex at moments like these, when I needed a blizzard to clear out my brain.

"I don't want to project my thoughts before I hear yours, but do you really want your neck to be that exquisitely vulnerable?" someone asked in a grumbly voice. I thought it was Julian trying to make me laugh.

"Nice one," I said. "Can we just leave? That woman needs a lesson in social graces and maybe a new vibrator."

"Wow. I'll mention that to her." That was definitely not Julian's voice. I blinked my eyes open and found Oscar standing over me. He was holding a copy of some thick book in another language.

"Oops," I said. "I mean . . ."

"Yeah," he said, smirking. I'd never seen him up close like this before. He had Marty's light gray eyes, like deep-set marbles. A thin nose with a smudge of moss-colored paint on it.

"Sorry, I was just . . ."

"Huh," he said. He opened his book and sat down next to me, uninvited.

"What is that?" I asked.

"*Moby-Dick*. In Portuguese."

"Shut up," I said, because it sounded like a joke. Oscar just smiled. His smugness made my skin crawl. "Okay," I said. "Then how do you translate 'dick'?"

I immediately regretted that one. Oscar started cackling softly under his awning of curls.

"Fine. You know what? Didn't you say you have some phone date with someone in Prague? Maybe she'll appreciate your language skills. You think you're so smart and worldly and you can just float all over the globe and nothing will ever affect you. Go ahead. And you can breastfeed until you're eighty-nine for all I care. But one day . . . one day we're *all* going to die."

I stood up to go, even though I had no idea where and I really wanted him to leave because I got this spot first.

Oscar kept staring at me. He wasn't amused or sneering anymore. Just studying me as if I'd come from another planet. Maybe I had. Maybe I was the only one who knew how dark and doomed we all were.

"What are you looking at?!" I screamed.

"Nothin'," he answered. Then he closed his book slowly and stood up. He walked over to the bike rack, unlocked a dented blue mountain bike, and peeled off.

Oversanitizing

According to a recent World Health Organization report, our fanaticism with germ killing has resulted in antibiotic-resistant bacteria all over the globe. Especially because of supersize sanitizing agents like triclosan and triclocarban.

Someday soon the surgeon general is going to announce that hand sanitizers are the leading cause of cancer.

That will be hilarious. Cancer always has the last laugh.

Chapter 10

IF YOU'RE GOING TO SAN FRANCISCO

Julian and I didn't get on the road until six thirty, which pissed me off royally. Julian said, "I understand that you're mad and that I effed up. But hopefully we just beat all the rush-hour traffic?" Then he gunned his Jetta's motor and did get us down to the hospital in record time.

Still, it was dark when we got there. We had to walk through a steady stream of people in scrubs coming out of the lobby—hailing cabs, eating potato chips, returning to life. The only person I recognized on the tenth floor was Smile McNoSmiles. I could tell from the stacks of half-eaten cafeteria trays that even Washington had already come through and left for the day.

When I walked into Dad's room, there was a pigtailed pixie in front of his bed doing starlight jumps in a hot-pink sweat suit. For a split second, I thought someone had sent my dad a stripper.

"Excuse me, what's going on?" I asked sharply.

The sprite whipped her head around with an ear-to-ear smile glazed onto her face. It was my mom.

"Helloooo!" she sang, as if Julian and I had come over for a cocktail party. She drew us both into a lung-crushing hug. When I wriggled free I saw her outfit also had hearts bedazzled onto her chest and BAD in rhinestones on her right thigh.

"What happened to *you*?" I asked.

Mom laughed loudly. "Dad and I were freezing in here last night, so I went out to pick us up something warmer to wear. All I found open was a Victoria's Secret two blocks away."

Dad held up a sweatshirt that was black with a pink sequined cat in the right bottom corner and ears on the hood.

"I'd rather freeze," Dad said.

"I think both of you look fantabulous," said Julian. "May I?" he asked, pointing to Dad's feet.

"Why hello, Julian," Dad said. "And of course you may." Julian sat on the end of the bed and started massaging Dad's feet through the covers. Dad smiled and closed his eyes. This was their routine. Julian had taught himself acupressure online to help with an old Achilles injury and he'd used me as his guinea pig for a while so I knew how comforting it could be.

"Inhale one, two, three, four," Julian said softly. Dad breathed serenely, following his lead. I had to forgive Julian in that moment. I was so grateful that he could bring this kind of tranquility to my dad. I knew I couldn't. I was too scared to rub Dad's feet that way, or to trust his deep breaths. Within seconds of coming in, I'd started pacing and rearranging the little mouthwashes that the staff seemed to bring in every few hours for Dad. I also refolded the spare blanket and gown in the corner and dusted the windowsill with a few alcohol pads.

Meanwhile, Mom was doing slow-motion jumping jacks, followed by something that looked like dry-land breaststroke.

"Mom is teaching me some new ways to keep my body limber in bed," Dad explained. He quickly poked his arms out in a T and started mirroring the swim lesson.

"We've learned a lot about vowels in the past twenty-four hours," Mom said. "A—adrenaline. E—endorphins. I—intimacy."

"Catchy," Julian commented.

"These are all tips we picked up from Chelsea Diamond. Did you watch that too, Julian? And did I tell you both that she got back to me?"

"No," we said in unison. I didn't even know that Mom had been trying to get in touch in the first place.

"She's very sought after—as she should be," Mom said. "So sadly, the answer was 'Not at this time,' but I thought she worded it so sweetly. Even her font is lovely. I'll show you."

While Mom started scrolling through her phone for the lovely-fonted note, I tried to get some sense of what was going on with Dad. He kept thanking Julian and letting his eyelids droop.

"Hey, Dad," I said. "Before you float away, can I get an update on test results and stuff?"

"Right," he said. He pulled himself upright and looked at me squarely. "I actually had Ganesh write some notes this morning so I didn't mix up any of the names. Sarge, can you hand me that pad of paper?"

"Pad of paper—check," said Mom. I watched her hand him the notepad and kiss his bald head. He fit perfectly into her armpit. I felt bad that I kept rolling my eyes when Mom talked and doubting her sanity. She was dealing with this with an extra dose of nuttiness, but I wasn't exactly stable either. She curled over Dad like a protective wing, then whispered something into his neck and let go.

"Okay, well there's Varlilumab and Nivolumab, which is also called BMS-9365-something," said Dad.

"BMS-936558," I said. "I've been reading up on both of them."

"Wow, look at you," Dad said. I studied Dr. Ganesh's scribbles. His handwriting was much messier than I'd thought. Everything slanted to the left a lot.

"Okay, so you know both of those drugs are sounding very promising in terms of the liver and the lymph nodes," Dad said. "The clincher is here." He flipped to the next page on the notepad and showed me a diagram with lots of circles and arrows. Dad squinted at the drawing and hummed a little. As if he were analyzing some cubist retrospective at the Met. "I think those dark spots are the lesions. Let me get this right. And that's the myelin wall. And I think this set of arrows down here is the blood-brain barrier. Is that right, Sarge?" He turned the paper on its side and narrowed his eyes for serious studying.

"Wait, did you just say blood-*brain* barrier?" I asked. My

teeth felt thick and hairy. The back of my throat filled up with saliva.

"It's okay," Dad said.

"No it's *not*!" I squawked. Dad and Julian both instinctively reached out to hold one of my arms.

Mom chimed in. "The good news is they're small and easily zappable."

"Wait—*they*? How many lesions are there? How big? How long?" I asked.

"Size doesn't matter," Julian said. Mom chuckled. Dad and Julian high-fived.

"Are you serious?" I kicked Julian in the shin. He whimpered.

Dad took my hands in his and said, "Look, this is not entirely unexpected. And to answer your question, there are between four and seven lesions that they will easily zap with gamma knife therapy. Which is very precise and doesn't involve any surgery. Once we've done that, then we'll start on the Varlyloola stuff."

"Varlilumab," I corrected. "Why didn't you tell me all this?"

I was getting louder and whinier, but I couldn't help it. I needed to prove this was all wrong and someone was at fault. Even though Dad was the last person I wanted to be accusing.

"Sorry," Dad said. "Dr. Ganesh just left about an hour ago."

"So sweet, that man," said Mom. "And again, he asked for you, *Ey-leah-nor*."

That did unclench my stomach, at least a fraction of a knot.

Dad peeled off the pieces of paper with Dr. Ganesh's drawings and words and handed them to me, as if they were a peace offering. I buried my nose in the big muddled notes he'd written on the side. *Lymph nodes, liver, brain, Lowenstein.* They needed Lowenstein's final approval, Dad went on. But Lowenstein was held up in Toronto for another thirty-six hours.

"What does that mean, 'held up'?" I growled.

"Another person in high demand," Mom said. "Speaking of, I just found the email from Chelsea Diamond. Just a little backstory: I told her how much of an inspiration she was to me and Dad and asked if she would come visit or speak at the hospital. Does anyone want to read it?"

I groaned instead of answering and unwrapped more alcohol pads to clean off Dad's night table. Mom decided to read the email aloud. It was only three lines to the effect of *Sorry about your troubles. I don't make house calls. Good luck.*

"That's a form letter, Mom," I scoffed.

"No it's not," Mom shot back. Then she lost her bravado and said in a small voice, "Is it?"

I didn't care if I was the resident asshole. Nobody else was taking this seriously. I refused to make eye contact with anyone. Instead, I folded the papers from Dr. Ganesh together tighter and tighter until the wad was almost as small as a bottle cap.

"What are we doing about this? Right now?" I demanded.

"It's okay," Dad repeated softly. "Right now, we're waiting for

Lowenstein to schedule the gamma ray. Then they assess whether I qualify for the trial, and meanwhile we can start on radiation. I think two weeks after the brain mets are out." I just huffed in response. "It's okay," he said for the hundredth time, proving that it meant nothing.

I mashed my lips together so I wouldn't say, *No it's not and you know it.*

"Now c'mon, this is boring," Dad said to the room. "Tell me what's going on in the real world. Julian, any letters for you from San Fran?"

Julian kept looking at Dad's feet as he mumbled, "Actually, yeah."

I wanted to roar, but I couldn't find enough air in my lungs to start. It was National Punch-Lenny-in-the-Gut Day.

"You got in!" Mom cheered. "I knew it!" She launched into singing some hippie song, *If you're going to San Francisco . . . ,* bouncing and gliding around like she was on an acid trip. Dad was singing now too. I was the only one just standing there, trying to obliterate the party with my storm-cloud face.

Julian looked up at me and shrugged.

"When did you find out?" I knew he couldn't lie if I asked him directly. It was part of his AA pact of being accountable to the higher power of truth.

"Just . . . last week I guess," he said.

"I have to pee," I muttered, stomping out.

I could've peed in Dad's bathroom, but instead I walked all

the way down to the one by the elevator. It smelled like hot ammonia and there was no lid on the toilet seat, but it would do fine for my purposes. I locked the door, balled my hands into tight fists, and pounded them into my head twenty-five times really fast while I counted out loud.

I stopped for five breaths and took inventory. My knuckles burned. My head was full of static. But I knew I could get up to one hundred punches before things started looking really blurry.

Pounding was my favorite obsession, or maybe it was a compulsion. All I knew for sure was that each blow to my head was sharp and clear and rocked me completely out of my circuit of anxiety. When I pummeled myself in the head, all I could think about was the darkness and pain. *My* pain that I gave to *me*.

I'd started this lovely self-destructive activity two years before, when there was an outbreak of meningitis one town over from where I lived. Maybe "outbreak" was an exaggeration. There was a 14-year-old girl who died, though. She played intramural lacrosse and some of the girls in my grade had seen her a week before at the lacrosse meet. When she died, they made a dance video for her that our principal played during morning announcements. No one could figure out where she'd contracted the disease, and all my research pointed to contaminated tap water. I knew it was a rare incident, but it just shook everything inside me. I tried boiling all my water for a week, then switched to almond milk. Which, ironically, led to crushing headaches.

Instead of taking two aspirin and calling someone in the morning, I kept trying to measure my agony. I couldn't tell whether it was bad or bubonic. Two weeks after the outbreak-of-one, kind of on a whim, I went home, locked myself in my closet, and pulled my hands into two tight fists. I clobbered myself in the head. Hard.

That first round of self-boxing was actually magical. It felt surprisingly cleansing, like I'd just knocked out all the cluttered voices and broken through to a pocket of fresh air. I pounded my head twenty-five times that first day. Thirty the next. Then thirty-five. By the end of that week I'd raised the bar to one hundred, pulsing on my toes and grunting a little like Rocky in between sets of twenty-five. The sound effects were probably what tipped Dad off. It was a fall Saturday afternoon and I thought he was outside raking, but he must've come in and heard me. He knocked on my door and demanded to know what I was doing.

"Hammering . . . stuff?" was not a genius answer by me. Dad had a lot of follow-up questions and I was feeling very tired and unsteady, and then he was inside my room and I couldn't look him in the eye and come up with a new story.

He sat me down and made me explain exactly what I liked about harming myself and how it gave me relief. Then he opened one of my notebooks and a pen and we wrote a list together of other things that could make me feel breathless, but in a good way.

1. Swimming at Wahonsett Bay
2. Bicycling up the hill at Pinebrook Boulevard
3. Fajitas

Dad threw a sweatshirt at me and told me to get my shoes on and meet him outside. He got our bikes out of the garage and spritzed them with lube, then took off for Pinebrook at record speed. I had no choice but to try to catch up to him. Both of us panting and gasping at the red leaves clogging the sewers.

Before coasting back down, Dad pulled off to a patch of grass and got off his seat. He walked over to me and put his hands around my head.

"Promise me you'll do this instead. I love this beautiful, giant noggin."

I didn't say anything because I was still gulping air spastically from the tough climb.

"Promise," he said again, holding out a pinky. Waiting until I hooked mine with his.

I did take that oath seriously and I did stop the hitting. Until this moment, that is. I didn't feel like Dad was holding up his end of the bargain either, though. He could have called me when Dr. Ganesh was there or said something to me besides "It's okay."

Fifty-three, fifty-four, fifty-five. I was definitely out of practice. My hands felt more damaged than my head, no matter how hard I rapped. I wondered how forcefully I'd have to strike to crush one of my fingers or shatter a knuckle. I didn't know why humans were created with these ridiculous digits and appendages that really served no purpose. I didn't know why any of us were here if we were just going to perish.

"Hello? Hello!" Someone was rattling the doorknob. "Are you okay?" It sounded like an older woman, who then started some diatribe about whether this was really a public restroom and who was in charge of maintenance.

"Be right out!" I mustered. I was now up to seventy-two and had just hit my stride. I really didn't want to stop before getting to a multiple of twenty-five, but I could tell Miss Maintenance wasn't budging. I turned on the faucet and waved my hands in front of the automatic paper towel dispenser. It emitted a loud clucking sound but nothing came out.

"Sorryforthewait," I slurred as I opened the bathroom door. The hall light seemed blindingly bright now and the woman waiting had sprouts of gray mustache. As if I was in a place to judge.

Walking back into Dad's room, I did feel at least a shade victorious. Everything was just foggy enough to be less real. Mom was slapping down piles of playing cards on the tray table attached to Dad's bed.

"Want us to deal you in?" Dad asked. "Hearts."

I stood there for a good thirty seconds, watching the three people closest to me drift in and out of focus. I thought it would feel crumbier to betray my dad. I also wished he'd look at me deeply and know what I'd just done. But we were obviously on different planes. I took some cards from Mom and propped myself up on the window ledge. The numbers were skiing off my cards and everything in my head was ringing. I looked around again and broke into a stupid grin. No one else could hear it. No one knew what it felt like to be achy and tipsy and me.

We played two rounds of hearts before Dad started squirming a lot and trying to reposition himself in bed.

"Did you press the button?" Mom asked. Dad nodded, looking up at his morphine drip with glassy eyes. I hadn't noticed he was still hooked up until that moment.

"What's happening?" I asked.

Mom cut in before he could answer. "Do you guys mind clearing out? Lenny, I'll be home just a little after you."

Dad told Julian again how great the acupressure felt and thanked him for coming in. Mom was about to change his pillow arrangement when Dad said, "Actually, let me talk to Lenny privately for a minute first."

She left without a word. Then Dad took both of my hands in between his, closed like a shut book. He used to tell me bedtime stories this way. Opening up our palms and tracing the lines in my skin with his once-upon-a-times.

"Hey, do you know how much I love you?" he asked. I nodded, avoiding his eyes. "And do you know what a champ you are for getting me to the hospital when you did?" I shrugged.

"Okay, how about this—why don't you look up plane tickets to San Francisco and we'll get you out there for a visit?"

"With you?" I asked. It was like a knee-jerk reaction. It took Dad and me both off guard.

"We'll try," he said, pulling me in for a hug. His skin smelled so sour I winced. "You're my girl," he whispered as I rushed out.

Julian was waiting by the elevators. So was the mustachioed woman who'd ushered me out of the bathroom just a half hour ago.

I smiled at her and said, "Hi again!" so gleefully that she got confused and looked behind her. Then I gave that same fake smile to Julian and asked loudly, "Were you going to tell me? Or just send a postcard from the Golden Gate Bridge?"

"I just thought you had a lot going on," he said.

"Shut up," I shot back. That scared the woman enough that she motioned for us to take the next open elevator by ourselves. I pressed the L button two times with each elbow and sucked in my breath defiantly.

When the doors opened again, Julian said, "I thought you stopped doing that."

I blew all my stored-up air and rage in his face. "What do you know about me?! You don't know anything! And I don't need you to know anything! I don't need you at all!"

Storming through the tropical paradise of Lobby, I stopped at every hand sanitizer I could find and rubbed in the foamy elixir until my skin was screaming as loud as my anger. Then

I hurled myself through the nonromantic revolving doors into the chilly night.

"Listen," said Julian. "I'm not leaving for another few months. Can we just have fun and not act like this is the end of the world?"

"Ha!" I threw my head back to add exquisitely vulnerable drama. I almost hoped people were watching. "You're so full of yourself. As if you could end the world. Goodbye, Julian."

I slung on my backpack indignantly and started strutting away. I hadn't planned on breaking up with my best friend. I just wanted him and everything he had been to me to be gone.

"Oh . . . kay," Julian said. It was probably the first time I'd actually shocked him. Or maybe he was just confused about logistics. "But do you want a ride home first?" he asked.

Damnit.

Carbon Monoxide

Yosef Schlockitsky[1] got on his motorcycle to go into town but never arrived. He was found on the side of the road, sleeping. He slept for six days without waking. When he did get up, he had an erection that lasted a month.

The culprit?

A Soviet-era uranium mine that is leaking high levels of carbon monoxide, poisoning the villagers of Kalachi in Kazakhstan.

Sounds like a joke, but not when you're Yosef with the boner.

Or any of the other 160 people in Kalachi who've fallen asleep for days at a time, or suffered headaches, hallucinations, and bladder problems.

Carbon monoxide is odorless, colorless, and all around us. We have sensors for carbon monoxide levels in our house, but I don't trust them anymore.

[1] Name changed to protect the sleepy.

Chapter 11

PEOPLE WHO NEED PEOPLE

It was always cool in Dad's toolshed, and smelled a little like cow dung, which is why no one went in there except for me. It was just about ten feet by ten feet of space, cut into the stone foundation on the side of our house. It had a dirt floor, one toaster-size window, and a door with a metal latch that only locked from the inside.

Dad hadn't actually used his tools or tried to fix anything besides the occasional leaky pipe in years. But he had the shed well stocked. Five huge bags of mulch, a few pairs of gardening shears, a circular saw, a power drill, and my favorite: the manual pencil sharpener that he'd drilled into the one wooden beam.

This is where I was making my secret end-of-the-world bunker.

I was pretty proud of how minimalist but efficient I'd set it up to be. It took a lot of research not only for the best quality but also I could only buy stuff once a month because of limited funding. Mom had given me an emergency credit card the first day of high school and I'd figured out how to keep the balance pretty steady by making deposits from my bat mitzvah/

babysitting money. (That is, if I kept sponsoring Asian elephants to a minimum.) She never checked the statements she got as long as the bottom line continued to add up.

I had just a few pieces of card tables from random garage sales and a small cooler of nonperishable foods. A bag of walnuts because if we were caught down here I didn't want to spend the end of our lives hearing Mom talk about how those things could've saved us. The first-aid kit was the hardest piece to put together. I'd read so many different versions of what was essential and I didn't want to make any mistakes but I also couldn't afford a lot of the top surgical equipment. So far I'd collected painkillers, anti-inflammatory meds, bandages, antiseptic cream, a sterilized needle and strong thread, cough medicine, cotton wool, iodine, and a roll of string (for emergency amputations—those were my least favorite instructional videos to watch).

On top of the mulch I had a dozen space blankets I'd gotten online. Four for our family and some extras because they folded up very compactly and I really did like most of our neighbors. I had to look into new insulation to help with extreme cold and protection against airborne gasses or poisoned runoff being absorbed by the soil. And I wanted to replace all the canned foods because I'd just finished this article about the difference between BPA-free and non-BPA. Whoever said that knowledge equaled power didn't have the Internet as a source for info. Or my brain scrambling all the pieces of knowledge and power into a kaleidoscope of despondency. Looking around now, I felt dizzy from all the stuff I knew and could never unknow.

I'd started this project way before Dad's diagnosis. When I was in sixth grade we did a unit on Chernobyl and Three Mile Island. I asked Dad if I could use a corner of his shed for a "science project." I set it up as a little diorama and took a picture for the class, but nobody was as enthralled with the bunker as I was. As I kept adding to it, I just made sure everything could be folded up or stuffed into corners and under tarps. Dad didn't seem to mind. And when I showed it to Julian, all he said was something pretentious about needing to get an interior designer in to add some color. Neither of them really understood how important this bunker had become to me. I came in here at least once a week to bring in a can of beans or a pack of batteries. Sometimes just to lie on the floor and feel the earth under me. It was no longer about where to go in case of nuclear annihilation or bioterrorism. It was where to go to escape *today*.

Today was fanged and fiery and wrong in five million different ways. I needed to thrash out my mom, dad, Julian, Lowenstein, and perhaps the entire San Francisco Bay.

I checked the shed's lock again—five taps with the right pointer finger, five taps with the left. I turned off the naked lightbulb and let my eyes adjust to the gray world of streetlights coming through the miniature window. Then I stood in the middle of the room, scrunched my hands into two fists, and started pounding for real.

Nobody could interrupt me this time. I socked myself in the head fifty times without stopping. Grunting and grimacing, I sounded like a wild boar and the sides of my head felt like they were caving in. I paused for exactly five breaths and then started in for fifty more. I was going for five hundred this time. At my next breath break, my right pinky was bleeding and too stubborn to bend. Everything from the wrist down was on fire and everything from the neck up was made of lead. But I had to keep going. I gnarled my cooperating fingers into lumps and went back in. Fifty blows just above my ears. Breath. Fifty on the top of my skull. Breath. Fifty on the back by that ridge. Breath. Fifty on my forehead and face and anywhere my hands could make contact. Pounding, pounding.

Until I was lying on the shed floor, letting everything rattle inside me. I felt exhausted but semi-triumphant. My jaw was drooping. My face felt hollow. My fingers were crumpled and limp.

After a few minutes of panting, I heard Mom's car pull into the driveway. I let myself in through the back door and got up to the bathroom to rinse my face and hands before she called, "Lenny? You eat yet, hon?"

It was almost 10:30, and I was woozy but famished. "Coming!" I answered. My voice sounded froggy. Echoing in my bruised skull.

When I lurched through the kitchen door, Mom was humming and making piles on the dining room table—stuffed manila folders, thick textbooks, her laptop, two plastic bags of take-out.

"I stopped at Kaling Me Softly," she said. "Ordered way too

much but I didn't know what you'd want." Kaling Me Softly was a vegan fusion café near the hospital that had posters in the window promising a new world of health and vigor by way of seaweed.

"Thanks," I said limply. Everything she opened smelled like farts.

Mom tried to remember her order: "Cashew tempeh ball. Seaweed slaw. I think one of these comes with rice." I just shoveled stuff into my mouth without tasting. My hands were shaking too much and the whole world was pulsating.

Mom was telling me about how healthy everyone was in Asia because of their connection to the rice paddies, but I noticed she didn't eat a single grain of rice. She was slowly unwrapping chopsticks and sipping some organically sustainable fermented-tea drink priced at $7.95.

"This is very odd tasting. You want to try?" she offered.

I shook my head no. Or maybe I meant to, but instead I just stared and thought I was shaking my head because it was so hard to feel solid.

Mom put down her drink and tugged at my hand. My hand happened to be scooping mung beans into my mouth. So we both watched the beans rain down on the table and then laughed awkwardly.

"You okay?" Mom asked. "I mean, I know that's a stupid question. Of course you're not okay. But, are you . . . how are you?"

I wondered what she saw. Whether I smelled like burnt

rubber from smashing my insides together or if the whites of my eyes looked too white. Secretly, I was glad she noticed something was going on. But there was no way I could explain what.

"I'm okay. Just a lot. Show goes up next weekend."

"Ooooh yes!" Mom said. "You got Dad and me tickets, right?"

"I . . . will." I didn't know if she was saying it just to be nice or if she really thought Dad could sit in a wooden auditorium chair while I had a dancegasm on stage.

"Really looking forward to it," Mom said. She took one of the take-out containers, sniffed it, and then put it to the side. "Well, I guess I should get crackin', huh? Have this report due for the governor's commission tomorrow at ten and I have to analyze forty-five immigrant testimonials. Also have to call Em and just see how she's doing. Do you mind if I play a little Streisand to keep me motivated?"

"Go for it," I said. Then I pushed the rest of my seaweed into a little mountain and announced I had a ton of homework to do. Which was true even if I had no intention of doing it. I just couldn't pretend that trigonometry mattered or that anything was calculable. I needed to look at the reports I'd downloaded about gamma knife therapy, drug trial waivers, sun swelling, and this horrifying disease called Kazakhstan sleeping sickness. Also, I had Dr. Ganesh's note and diagram folded into a small disk in my pocket, and I had to kiss it and tuck it away in my emergency suitcase upstairs.

I went up and locked my bedroom door. Then I lay on my belly and shimmied under the lip of my bed to retrieve my suitcase. I'd waterproofed the outside with spray and put a combination lock on it three years ago.

Eighteen to the right.

Twenty-three to the left.

Zero.

Which took me a while to configure, but eighteen divided by two was the same as three to the second power. And zero was the period on the end of that sentence. Also the empty hole we were all falling into.

Inside the middle section of the suitcase, there were journals and salt pills arranged in rows. The pockets were the most vital, though. That's where I stowed all the things that meant too much to me. I unzipped carefully, took everything out, and lined it up on my floor. I'd done an inventory just a week ago, so I knew the tally by heart. Still, it felt soothing to count again.

1. Thirty-nine empty jam packets from my breakfasts with Julian at the Unicorn Diner. Because Julian was born on December 27, I'd purposely collected twelve strawberries and twenty-seven mixed berries.
2. Two ticket stubs from *Avenging Everything*—the last movie I'd gone to see with Dad. It really had no plot except for an angry bike messenger delivering the wrong

packages, but Dad and I would see anything for the sake of a tub of popcorn.

3. Twenty-five pill bottles that were supposed to hold his magical cure but were collecting dust unmagically on the lazy Susan downstairs. There were some pills rattling around in a few of them, proving their uselessness.

4. A prescription for Xanax that Mom got my doctor to write two years ago because she thought I was washing my hands too much. I'd told her I filled it. As if that would solve anything.

5. Eleven pages of notes I'd taken on blood moons, surveillance techniques, and West Nile virus.

6. Three form letters I'd gotten back from Stephen Hawking, Al Gore, and the Centers for Disease Control and Prevention. My letter-writing campaign had really bombed. I'd written to Hawking about the Higgs boson/quantum-fluctuation theory. I'd asked Al Gore for his opinion on seafront real estate. The CDC was maybe a little overambitious. I calculated how much water and space they'd save if they removed all public water fountains (open drains for disease) in the tristate area and then drafted a petition for them to endorse. Everybody wrote back something to the effect of *Your concern is my concern, but I'm not that concerned about it at the moment.*

7. Forty-one photographs of Ambrosia Steinhart in a padded envelope.

I rarely looked at these photos, and nobody in my family knew I had them. They'd lived in our hall cabinet for the first fifteen years of my life, along with two defunct humidifiers, three bundles of *National Geographic*s, and four shelves stuffed with moisturizers, cotton balls, and appliance manuals. Emma had found the pictures a few years ago, one rainy afternoon when we were making tampon tiaras.

"Agh!" she screeched. "Lenny, do you know who this is?"

"No."

"This is Dad's infamous *ex-lover*." She said that last word so slowly I could feel it ripple through me.

"Stop it," I said, even though I knew Emma was right. It was actually common knowledge in the Rosenthal-Hermann household that Ambrosia was Dad's girlfriend before he met Mom. They all went to college together. Apparently, Ambrosia was a punk performance artist and she and my dad smoked lots of weed and drove a van cross-country with two pennies, a guitar, and a dream. She was ravishing—wide, mischievous eyes, dark hair down to her butt, and heart-shaped lips. She claimed to be related to Dee Dee Ramone. The story goes that my dad proposed to her in a tent by the Michigan dunes.

She said yes, and also that she was pregnant—with their poetry professor's baby.

Mom swooped in while Dad was nursing his wounded heart. They graduated. Took things slowly. She went to law school in Chicago. He did the Peace Corps and taught in a one-room schoolhouse in Nepal. They met up again in New York five years later and leased an apartment month by month. It was very careful, their love. Their first pet was a goldfish named Airplane. They each bought their own groceries for the first year of living together.

And then, without telling anyone, my mom bought a red chiffon dress at Saks, my dad rented a top hat and tails, and they got married at city hall on a snowy Wednesday in December. Both of them said it was "the smartest thing I ever did."

The mystery and passion of Ambrosia Steinhart haunted me, though. She was a reminder of what could've been. Her sexuality was so loud and unafraid and I wanted to hate her, but really I envied her. Most of the pictures were taken either on the beach or with some D.C. monument in the background. Ambrosia was always laughing—in a pair of ragged overalls, kicking up sand; splashing in the crest of a wave; flipping the bird at the Lincoln Memorial. There were also a few nudies. Her body sprawled on a rumpled bedsheet; another in the grass. Her sparkly eyes and pubic Bermuda triangle were like three smudges in the white expanse of her milky skin.

I checked my bedroom door. Locked and relocked it ten times. Not that Mom could hear me sifting through these sexy pictures silently. But I felt so guilty looking at them. I wanted to empty my body and fill it up with Ambrosia's—her curves, her wild hair, her fiery self-righteousness. She made me feel hot and daring.

I pulled my faded T-shirt down just enough to poke out my left shoulder and pouted my lips. Then I got my phone off my bed and snapped a selfie. It looked nothing like Ambrosia, of course. More like a close-up of my scrawny bicep and freckle patch. But I liked the way my nose faded into the background and I did have a halfway decent mole on my chin.

I studied Ambrosia's body again. She looked like a strutting peacock, expanding in every direction. I tried posing again—this time arching my back and spreading my arms like wings. *Snap.* Then I got my camera to balance on my bookshelf and took some more. *Snap, snap.* With just my reading lamp on, the shadows made it pretty eerie.

Next I dove into Ambrosia's eyes—so gleeful and flirty. She knew she was making everyone near her excited, riling up the world. For this, a little cosmetic enhancement was needed. I tiptoed across the hall and raided Emma's closet for her Vincent Davicci Luminescence kit. (Emma spent two summers as a department store "skin consultant.") After sneaking back into my room, I swiped on a layer of Shimmering Stardust eye shadow and outlined my lids with brightener.

Snap.

For my lips I drew on Bruised Berry followed by Lickalicious GlossyGirl. Then I sucked in my cheeks so hard, I let out an unintended whistle.

Snap, snap, snap.

Puckered, petulant, slightly ajar with a hint of tongue.

Snap, snap.

If I was imitating Ambrosia, I reasoned, maybe it was just a game.

Except I knew exactly what I was doing.

And I couldn't blame it on the kale or my crushing headache or any other external influence. I was as close to sound as I'd ever be and I knew this was wrong. I should've stopped before I even started. But I had no time for morals or tact. Everyone was either in love or dying or both. The earth was cracking open in fault lines too big to measure on any seismic scale, and people were dropping into deep inexplicable slumberfests because they knew it had to be safer in the unconscious.

I snapped. I snapped more of my neck, my earlobe, my eyelids. I snapped a shot of my left kidney with just the edge of my Hello Kitty underwear. I snapped one of my hands clutching my not-quite size 34B boobs, trying on Ambrosia's *What? Who, me?* look.

I couldn't blame it on the ozone. Or on Stephen Hawking's aloofness. It was all me. It was me, snapping and snapping. It was me who knew all along what I was going to do with those semi-sultry lips. It was me who looked through all those selfies, picked out the sexiest ones, and sent them to Dr. Radha-krishnan Ganesh. One by one.

Shaking, not thinking. Thinking, trying not to think. Typing again, just, **Are you there?**

No response. I kept looking at my dark phone screen, as if it would give me some answer. I hadn't even thought through what I wanted him to do.

Sorry. That was a mistake, I wrote.

No response again.

Are you on tomorrow?

Still nothing.

I tossed my phone on the bed. I had to get out of here and throw away everything. The photos, the jam packets, the tickets, the letters, the pill bottles that didn't or shouldn't or couldn't save anybody. I stuffed it all back into the suitcase, put on the padlock, and shoved it under my bed. I wanted to light it all on fire and do a high dive into the flames. I opened my door to see if I could at least get it out to my bunker and bury it under the mulch.

Mom had turned her music up way too high. I heard Barbra crooning, *People who need peeeeeople.* She sounded more woeful than I remembered. Kind of like an abandoned puppy. Then the band underneath her faded out, but a muted yowling kept going.

That's when I realized it wasn't Barbra Streisand making that mournful noise; it was my mom. Naomi Rosenthal-Hermann, age forty-eight, an untrained singer sitting at her dining room table in front of an insurmountable pile of work, wondering how she got here, how she could survive as a widow, how this all would end, how her heart could possibly break more.

At least, that's what it sounded like to me.

Designer Pathogens and Bioterrorism

Fun facts!

- "You can download the gene sequence for small-pox or the 1918 flu virus from the Internet." (Nick Bostrom, *The Atlantic*, 2012)
- Half of Hollywood is walking around with bio-weapons in their lips. Botox—which is actually a neurotoxic protein produced by the bacterium *Clostridium botulinum*—is one wrinkle away from *botulism*. Which is fatal.
- It's just some DNA tweaking and we'll be deal-ing with bubonic plague possibilities—which, I recently heard was not imported to the US by rats, even though they eat, sleep, and make love in garbage. (Not sure rats can "make love," but sounds better than "rat sex.")
- At the same time, genetically engineered bacteria—aka *adjuvants*—boost the human immune response and help prevent fun icks like pertussis, cholera, and HPV. So if we want to have any hope of stopping AIDS, heart disease, MS, and cancer, don't we *have* to design new pathogens?

Chapter 12

YOUCA WEAVE MOW

Text number fourteen, sent at 7:03 a.m.:

Hi Dr. G this is Eleanor Rosenthal-Hermann. I dropped my phone in a puddle and had to replace it. So nothing that you may have gotten from my number in the past twenty-four hours was really from me. Is this still you?

It had been over nine hours since I sent the last seminaked picture of myself to Dr. Ganesh. Still no word back. I'd spent the first part of the night listening to Mom sob downstairs, being too chickenshit to do anything to comfort her. Then I spent an hour or so trying to figure out if my phone could tell me whether a sent text had been viewed. I fell asleep around three in the morning, while reading my notes for the social studies midterm I'd forgotten about until then and listening to a podcast about space colonization.

Text number fifteen, sent at 7:08 a.m.:

Hello, this sounds crazy but I know another Dr. Ganesh. If you got a strange set of texts late last night, they were for him.

Text number sixteen, sent at 7:09 a.m.:

The other Dr. Ganesh I know teaches photography so that's why I had to send him pictures. They were an assignment.

By the time I dumped myself in a shower, got dressed, and went downstairs, Mom was at the kitchen table, already back from a brisk jog in her BAD sweat suit. Only, when I looked down I saw she wasn't wearing any pants. Her legs looked way too bony.

"Is this . . . intentional?" I asked.

"Ha!" Mom boomed. "I started to get in the shower and then I realized I really needed some coffee." She raised her BEST MOM EVER mug at me. "Cheers!"

Whatever I'd heard leaking out of her the night before was gone. She'd swept it up, ironed it out, mopped the tears, and pulled her bob back into two perky pigtails.

"Cheers," I mustered, raising an imaginary cup.

"So, what's the plan, Stan?" she asked.

"Um . . ." I wasn't sure what she was asking.

"Well, I'm heading to the courthouse and you have a very important job today. Do you remember what it is?" I shook my head no. "Three tickets for *I Have So Many Desires* please. Front row center."

"*I Have But One*," I corrected.

"Can you get three?" asked Mom.

"No, I meant—wait, why three?"

"Me, Dad, and Emma's coming home next weekend!" Mom said with cheerleader glee.

"Emma—why?" I felt weak in the knees.

"Homesick, I guess," Mom said quickly. I highly doubted

that, but I also had too many other questions that I needed to get out first.

"Wait, do we know that Dad will be out by then? What about the gamma knife thing, and we still haven't gotten Lowenstein's approval, and what about—"

Mom had no time for doubt. She shushed me and said, "Listen, Chicken. I feel really hopeful about this new direction. Just between you and me, I think Lowenstein's a little grumpy that Ganesh thought of this trial without him. Yes, there's some politics to the whole thing because Dad's got these lesions, which they don't usually allow with the Varilililum." She paused to put on a kooky voice and salute me like a soldier. "We. Will. Prevail!"

She winked and flexed her biceps while I tried to process everything she'd just said. I didn't know which part made me squirmiest—the fact that Dad wasn't supposed to be on these meds with lesions or all of Mom's theatrics. I didn't get to ask for clarification on anything, though, because Julian beeped at that moment.

"Yowsa!" Mom said, springing from her seat. "Time for some pants, huh?" She shoved my backpack at me and gave my forehead a peck. "I'm hoping to be home from work regular time. Dad says he doesn't think anything's happening until Lowenstein is back tomorrow. Meet you at oh-twenty hundred? I'll pick up burritos or something."

I watched her gallop upstairs before slowly letting myself out the back door and cutting across our neighbors' yard to the street parallel. I heard Julian honking again in my driveway, but I kept walking in the opposite direction. If I took this back route and ran for the last four blocks, I could potentially get to school in time for the late bell. I knew it was childish to be literally running away from my best friend, but I felt bruised all over and like I couldn't trust Julian at all. I'd actually thought about texting him the night before and hashing it out. That was before I started sending lewd selfies to one of the pioneers in immunotherapy. Now I had no stamina for reconciliation.

My phone started vibrating just as I was getting to the Mountainside parking lot and I did some awkward cross between a leap and a lurch.

It wasn't Dr. Ganesh. It was a text from Julian that read, **Really?**

I wrote back: **You said you wouldn't abandon me.**

His response: **I've worked so hard for this. Why can't you be happy for me?**

I sent him a smiley face, which I hoped he knew was text irony, then walked into school.

I bombed the midterm. I was usually good at memorizing dates but I could never put anything in context. I couldn't see how there was a Battle of the Bulge the same year Henry Winkler was born and also Mount Vesuvius erupted somewhere nearby, so the world almost ended and began at the same time. I also mixed up Khrushchev with Churchill in the quote section and I ran out of things to say in my essay about the Lend-Lease Act.

I checked my phone in between classes approximately forty-seven times. At 11:18 a.m., I sent Dr. Ganesh a text saying, **After the puddle incident I left my phone at my friend's who looks like me and I'm really scared she did something weird and inappropriate with the camera.**

I followed that up with, **Could you just write a Y for Yes or an N for No if you got something strange and tasteless from this number?**

No answer.

My final stab was, **To whom this may concern: This number has been hacked!**

For lunch I decided to avoid the world all together. I went to the library and looked at pictures of people in West Africa affected by Ebola, followed by washing my hands for ten minutes in the girls' gym locker room. That was mildly helpful—the skin between my right thumb and pointer finger was rubbed raw. For a few minutes all I could feel was the sting of hot water touching new skin. Which in some sick sense was my definition of success.

The rest of the day moved glacially slowly. My science lab was literally about waiting for water to boil. I didn't get a message from Mom until two thirty, and then all it said was, **Holding patrn w/Lowenstein. Staying @ court. Brblol.** I wrote back,

Gr8, and tried to think of a new excuse for skipping *VaGeorgia* rehearsal. But Marty had the auditorium door open and she was standing outside ushering everyone in.

"This is it," she urged. "The final push!"

The room was complete chaos. It looked like a dust storm and it stunk like BO. The first two rows of seats were filled with light fixtures and power drills. Oscar was on a ladder stringing up another floating collage of blossoming femininity. Julian was going over a dance combination with Marty, weaving their bodies in and out of the pools of light on stage in a ridiculously graceful swirling motion I knew I'd never be able to replicate. My great fear of him being destroyed by my ditching him this morning was tossed out. My even greater fear that he'd barely notice my absence and feel free without the albatross known as me around his neck was now louder than ever.

In the locker room, Becca was showing her minions a hickey that was just under her left armpit. I didn't know what could be sexy about getting your skin sucked, especially there. It also inflamed me when the tiniest Becca wannabe—Leigh—squealed, "Ooooh, I can count your ribs, you skinny bean!" I never saw Leigh eat anything besides sugar-free gum. I hated how many girls in my grade were starving themselves or posting pictures of their bathroom scales. Julian had told me stories of some anorexics in his rehab program and said if I ever did that he'd poison me in my sleep. Which I guess was an effective threat because I ate mostly what I felt like eating. I also had the perspective that my dad had given up his butthole and part of his intestinal tract and I had no right to abuse mine.

"Can I just tell you, Kevin is so into my body," Becca said. The girls panted and giggled. Somebody even clapped. "I'll show you after rehearsal. I mean, whoever feels like coming to Troops."

"Me! Me! Me!" came the chorus.

Troops was the army-navy surplus store in our town where Kevin worked part-time. I'd actually been in there a few times to scout out radiation meters and protective hoods for biohazard attacks. The owner, Mr. Steig, was two hundred years old and had a shriveled arm from Korea. He listened to a tinny radio and did word jumbles behind the register while coughing loudly. It was always ten degrees too hot in there.

"Ladies?!" Marty hollered. "Lots to do today!" No more warming up or touching our inner muse. Marty was going over someone's new monologue and Julian was leading everyone else through an intricate dance routine.

"Lenny, you're there." He pointed to a tape mark on the stage without a shred of emotion. "Just watch out. Still a lot of nails on the floor."

I knew he was busy and this was not exactly the time to get into it, but I felt stunned that he gave me no eye contact, no recognition, no nothing. I'd never had a major fight with Julian before, probably because I worshipped him too much. Also I'd witnessed how easily he cut off his mom, his stepmom, even a guidance counselor who once told him he should go into computer programming instead of dance. Julian seemed totally unaffected by our split now. In fact, he was literally leaping with a new joy.

It took approximately thirty-eight seconds from the moment Julian said the word "nails" to the moment when I felt one under my left heel and skidded into a stepladder, making a huge clattery one-klutz band and falling on my ass. The most unbearable part was chomping down on my tongue. My mouth filled with warm, salty blood.

Everyone stopped. Marty was the only one who thought to ask, "Are you injured?"

I was seriously tempted to yell, "Yes! My vagina and my heart and my trust in the past, present, and future are all damaged irreparably!" But I didn't say anything. I just pulled myself up slowly and kept sucking on my tongue.

"Do you need to take a break?" Julian asked with a sigh. I couldn't tell if he was annoyed or concerned. My jaw was shooting arrows of pain up into my head. If I'd fractured my face or had to get some sort of tongue grafting done, Mom would have to choose which hospital bed to sit by and I knew she'd choose Dad, or maybe we could be at the same hospital but I wouldn't want Dr. Ganesh to know what I did because biting your tongue off had to be the stupidest injury in the history of boo-boos.

Marty came up behind me and started working my shoulders with her small, muscly hands. "I want you to respect your body," she said in a low voice. "Why don't you go up into the lighting booth and sit down for a few minutes. There's some coconut water in my thermos." She steered me off the stage while I tried to envision tongue reattachment surgery. If there even were such a thing. I knew nothing about the human body, really. We were all just hanging on by these tiny tendons.

I got into the lighting booth and locked the door behind me. It was stuffy and dim in here. There was a low ceiling that was seeping some sort of insulation I'd bet was a descendant of asbestos. I knew around the corner it led directly into the catwalk above the stage, and normally I would have been curious to spy on everyone down below, but I had no interest in investigating or staying there one second longer than I had to. I reached over the light board with all the switches and levers and shut the window leading into the auditorium so I couldn't hear what was going on onstage. More importantly, they couldn't hear me while I battered my head.

I tried one of those mantras that I'd seen on the Breathe network: *Hi Fear. You can leave now. You can leave now. You can leave NOW.* Only with my puffy tongue it sounded more like, *Youca weave mow. Youca weave mow. Youca weave MOW.* Then I slammed my fists into my head with everything I had left. *Youca weave mow!*

"Whoa, that can't be helping," came a voice in the dark. Even though I had no idea who was there and whether I was about to get murdered in a lighting booth, I wasn't as alarmed as I was aggravated. I was only up to seventy-two hits and I had to get to at least one hundred. I started up again. But the voice came through once more, angrier this time. "Stop!"

An overhead fluorescent light went on, and Oscar Birnbaum sat up from a lumpy futon mattress that was shoved into the farthest corner of the room. His long legs were twisted in a pretzel, and when he stood up it looked like a clown car of limbs. He had to bend his neck down to keep from bonking his head into the rafters. "Can you please stop doing that?" he said.

"Can you please stop spying on people?" I said through flaring nostrils. He was blinking as if he'd just woken up. I hated him for looking so tall and uncomplicated. "You have no idea what I'm doing," I added. I shrugged as if that could shake off his judgment.

"You're right. But it doesn't seem to be helping," he said.

"How do you know?"

"Educated guess."

"Ha!" I said. "Educated? Are you in school right now? How does that work exactly? You put on your school slippers and walk into the kitchen before Mommy rings the bell? Does she grade you at the dinner table or take you on class trips?"

Oscar just stood there, waiting for me to run out of insults disguised as questions. Then he said, "I can explain homeschooling to you if you want. We have standardized tests just like you. It's not that mysterious." He pointed to a landslide of textbooks and a closed laptop on his little futon nest. I noticed we actually were using the same elementary physics book in my class.

"How do you make any friends?" I asked.

"I don't need to make friends," he answered. "I don't want to be attached to places or people." I couldn't decide if that was the cockiest or wisest thing anyone had ever said to me. I just knew he was looking at me with those marble eyes and it was making me feel itchy. "Until the cord be broken the bird cannot fly," he mumbled.

"Excuse me?"

"It's a famous quote from Saint John of the Cross," Oscar said.

I shrugged. "I'm Jewish. Anyway, your mom told me to come up here because I tripped on one of your nails."

"First aid's there, if you want it." He pointed to a red metal lunch box above the lighting board with the words YOU ARE BRAVE, YOU ARE BEAUTIFUL written in wide letters with permanent marker on the side. Hanging from the lock was a small ambery crystal. I opened the box and took out a sleeve of alcohol pads. Not because I needed one, but I also didn't want to go back into the auditorium and pretend I was all better.

I wasn't. I doubted I ever would be.

Oscar folded himself back on top of his lumpy mattress and cracked open his physics book while I spent a ridiculously long time wiping the bottom of my feet and inhaling alcohol fumes. The bleeding in my mouth had stopped and I now had to find a secret place to beat my head one hundred times uninterrupted. I was thinking maybe the locker room, since everyone else was occupied on stage.

"Hey," Oscar called as I was letting myself out of the booth, "it's none of my business, but don't do that thing where you hit yourself again."

"Yeah. It is none of your business. Thanks."

It took Oscar three long steps to be right in front of me, blocking the door. "Seriously," he said.

I hated how close and insistent he was. I felt like I was going to break out in a rash from being this exposed. "Why do you care?" I mumbled.

He shook his head. "I don't. I'm just being a good Samaritan. Which I mean in a purely secular context."

I didn't know that Samaritans were from the Bible and I didn't want to hear him expound upon that. I tried to ignore him and reach for the doorknob, but he intercepted my right arm and snagged me in the most awkward arm shake in history. We both looked down and then backed away.

"Sorry," he said. "Just promise not to do that. Please."

"Fine," I said. "If you promise to stop . . . just stop." I pushed past him and lunged out the door, thoroughly confused. I crouched in the back of the auditorium by the piles of untouched lumber for the rest of rehearsal, watching the waves of menstrual ferocity onstage. It wasn't as if anyone missed me or even noticed my absence. When it was over, I merged myself into the crowd heading down to the locker room and decided I'd even follow them into town to check out what they had at Troops. I couldn't stand the idea of watching night creep in all alone in my house. Mom wouldn't be home for another two hours at least and I had no focus for homework. If I holed up in the bunker I would just be tempted to text Dr. Ganesh some more lies or crack my skull open with my fists and I'd somehow just made a pact with Oscar the homeschooled freak that I wouldn't do that. I wondered if it meant anything to him. Probably not.

As I fell in line with the girls leaving, I heard Julian call out from the stage, "Lenny, do you want to go over the choreography you missed?"

"No thanks!" I yelled back. It felt a little electrifying to refuse his company.

For the whole fifteen-minute walk into town, Becca told some story about swimming with dolphins in Florida with her super-rich uncle who had a new wife and motorboat, both named Tina. Tina was going to take Becca to her plastic surgeon when Becca turned twenty. Nobody dared interrupt, even to ask what I was doing there.

When we got to Troops, Kevin Kripps was not in the window. Becca started chewing on her lip and pacing.

"Let's go to the drugstore," she ordered. "Leigh, do you wanna do some laxatives with me?" Leigh looked stunned. Everyone else just waited, mouths open. "I'm *kidding*, you losers!" Becca said. I wanted to shoot her in the hickey. When we got inside the drugstore I made sure to stay close to Leigh just in case she got tempted to check out the diet section. I also bought a chocolate milk and chugged it right in front of her so she could see it felt good to actually nourish yourself.

When we came back out, Kevin was hanging up some new gas masks on a clothesline next to a flakey-faced mannequin. I recognized a couple of them from my airborne toxin research—they were the MSA Millennium masks that were used in the Persian Gulf War. They were supposed to be excellent at filtering out nasty particulates, and they had a drinking tube built in that connected directly to a canteen.

"We're going in, right?" I asked.

Nobody answered me. As I soon learned, the usual routine was for the girls to stand next to one of the parking meters pretending they were really engrossed in some conversation until Kevin climbed through the maze of steamer trunks and fatigues to tap on the glass window. Then—and only then—Becca walked up to him and blew a wisp of fog onto the glass so she could write him a secret message. He did the same back, then disappeared. Then more waiting by the parking meter.

I was not a fan of the waiting part. I really wanted to know if that new gas mask was for sale and how much Steig was asking. I already had to budget for Don Juan's lobster tank, and after hearing the girls discuss plastic surgery and endangered dolphins in the same breath, I knew I had to get better bunker equipment before we all were smothered by a cloud of botulism. So I said, "I'm heading in to look at something. Possibly purchase. Anyone coming?"

"Whoa!" said Becca, putting her hand in front of me.

"Kevin loves you so much," I said. (Julian always said, kill 'em with kindness.)

"Right?" she said, pushing the door open and marching in ahead of me.

Mr. Steig was at his usual perch, unjumbling words next to his radio. Kevin came out from behind a rack of pea coats looking concerned.

"You okay?" he asked.

"Yeah!" said Becca. "Just wanted to come in and see ya!"

"Oh . . . kay. But I don't think Steig wants a whole crowd unless you're buying something, babe."

"Lenny's buying something," offered Sylvie hopefully.

"Well, I might. How much is the MSA Millennium you were just hanging up?"

Kevin looked amazed. "Hey, you know about the Millennium? Steig! I'm showing her some stuff."

The mold and mustiness got more intense the farther in we walked. I could feel sweat collecting under my bra. But it was worth it—the gas mask collection in the back was even more extensive than in the front. Steig had the Millennium, the Advantage, a bunch of Russian PBFs, and a huge section of Israel Defense Forces equipment. I felt like I should go with something made over there because it was cheaper and it made me feel at least a little like a good Jew.

Kevin agreed that the Israeli civilian gas-mask kit was the most bang for the buck. It could be used for nuclear or chemical attacks. The canteen was included and it had adjustable straps. I was grateful that I could fit into the small adult size, because the kids' kits were much more expensive. Kevin told me he'd talk to Steig about giving me a friends-and-family discount. He also showed me his favorite tag that he'd shellacked to one of the shelves.

THIS EQUIPMENT WILL NOT PREVENT YOUR DEATH, BUT IT CAN POSTPONE IT.

He thought that was hilarious. I found it mildly funny.

Kevin looked really pleased as he led me and the mask kit up to the register. Steig grunted, "No returns," and rang me up for $129.99. That was exactly five dollars off, and about forty-five more than I had in my babysitting savings. I handed over the emergency credit card and started calculating how much I'd have to babysit in the next month to get the account balance back up. Steig gave me a complimentary Troops magnet and went back to his puzzles.

When I got outside, the girls were huddled around Becca. Sylvie was elected to come forward.

"Um, Lenny, that was very not cool."

"What was very not cool?" I asked.

"I don't know how you know that much about gas masks or

if any of that was even true, but I think you should know that Becca and Kevin are super serious and you're not going to steal him away from her."

"What?" It was hard to know whether I wanted to laugh, spit, or scream. Sylvie looked back at the girls for support. Leigh was shielding Becca's face from me. I guess even my presence was now deemed a threat. Madison cleared her throat dramatically and gave the hitchhiker thumb, as in *Get lost*. The verdict was clear.

"Yeah, it doesn't matter," Sylvie said. "When you betray Becca, you betray all of us. Lenny, it's time for you to leave."

Artificial Intelligence

	Humans	Robots
Can do long division without using paper	Yes	Yes
Can perform brain surgery successfully	Yes	Yes
Can reproduce itself without any intimacy issues	No	Yes
Needs constant snacks, sleep, and positive reinforcement	Yes	No
Has any sense of morality about wiping out the human race	We hope	NO!!

Chapter 13

DR. THATCHER'S STICK

Even the best gas masks on the market couldn't filter out lies or loneliness. Tuesday night, after the Troops fiasco, I made one last attempt at texting Dr. Ganesh. I wrote,

ERROR ERROR ERROR

All messages from this number to be disregard.

The typo was insulting, but I wanted it to look like a robot generated it. I didn't even hope for Dr. Ganesh to respond to that. I just needed to feel like I had thrown out some sort of lifeline before sinking completely.

The next day was Wednesday, which was miserable with a side of yuck.

I was mad that Julian didn't even stop by to offer a ride, even though I would have refused. I was mad that my morning news email included an exposé on E. coli in most of the water supplies of North America and I hadn't gotten even an automated response to my calls to our assemblyman. I was particularly mad that Mom mentioned in passing that she was taking off a few more days from work, which was surely a sign of the apocalypse, but when I quizzed her about it, she acted like it was no big deal.

"I just thought, with Emma coming in tomorrow, and Dad has a few more scans . . ."

"Enough with the scans. What is the plan of attack?" I asked.

Mom didn't know. She said that the first set of scans had to come back first, and Lowenstein was in New York for just a small window of time before heading out to another conference, but hopefully there would be an hour for a face-to-face chat before he left and they could go over everything.

"Not *hopefully*," I barked. "That man is not leaving until we get some answers. Why does everyone who looks into microscopes forget how to talk to humans? That guy is a complete asshole. Are you going there now? Because if so, I'm coming."

Mom just stared at me. I'd never really sworn like that in front of her before. She took off her reading glasses as if she had to study me through a new lens.

"I wasn't planning on going in today until later," she said calmly. "I believe Lowenstein does his rounds in the afternoon and I will make sure to see him."

"Do you need me to—"

"No," she cut me off firmly. "I'm sorry this is hard for you, Lenny. But what I really need is for you to go to school now."

I sludged through most of the school day without saying anything besides, "Sine, cosine, sine," and "The invention of the pendulum clock." Both because I was called on, not because I raised my hand.

VaGeorgia rehearsal was uneventful and isolating. Julian worked onstage with a small gaggle of girls on some pyramid-looking human sculpture. Marty took the rest of us outside to the bike racks and gave us a bunch of poems she'd written describing O'Keeffe's life. I thought they were halfway decently written, though she used the word *moist* way too often. We had to recite them out loud while walking in slow motion.

On our one pee break, I restarted my phone three times just in case technology or mercury in retrograde or a synchronized uprising of human-designed robotics was to blame for my lack of Ganesh texts. Still nothing. So I hatched my most futile plan yet. I walked down the hall and called the front desk of the hospital, asking to be transferred to "my good friend and esteemed colleague, Dr. Radhakrishnan Ganesh." I used a vaguely British accent, because I couldn't do Indian without sounding really rude.

Then one of the tenth-floor nurses—I think Mariel—grilled me.

"Who is this?"

"An old colleague of the esteemed Dr. Radhakrishnan Ganesh."

"Your name?"

"Doctor . . . Thatcher."

"Can you spell that please?"

"T-h-a-t-c-e-r." I heard her sigh. "Oh dear me, I left out the *h*." She giggled. Then I heard a ripple of giggles and realized

I was on speakerphone. "Is your refrigerator running or do you like Prince Albert in a can?" I blurted and hung up.

Slipping back into the auditorium, I thought I heard my name being whispered by Sylvie and Madison. Sylvie saw me and started flapping her elbows to cue everyone to shut up. I wanted to tell her that she could keep going—I had too much else to worry about besides being kicked out of their cult. There was no time for another confrontation, though. Julian called us all back onto the stage and had us start going through the full ensemble piece again. And again. Until we got it right.

We didn't finish up until seven that night, and I pretended walking home in the dusky light didn't freak me out. The house was empty and smelled like guinea-pig poop. I gave Tiny-Ginsberg some pretzels since we'd run out of her food days ago. She screeched at me angrily, and I had to admit she won the prize for most forsaken.

I called Dad to see how his day had gone. He sounded subdued and said that Mom had left just a few minutes ago. Also did I know that Emma was coming home for the weekend and there was a reality show about robots and humans dating? Pretty soon, he started snoring.

"Hey," I said. "Is that a lawn mower or are you just happy to see me?"

"Huh?"

"It's okay," I said. "Those new drugs must knock you out."

Dad sighed. "No, they couldn't even start me on the new stuff yet."

"What? Why?"

Dad said Lowenstein was back from Toronto but he had "some major concerns" about the drug trial and wasn't ready to give it the green light.

"It can't cause any *harm*, right?" I asked. "Why not just try it?"

"I hear ya, kiddo." Dad yawned. "We're appealing."

"We need to start it *now*!" I knew that I sounded alarmist, but I didn't care. Apparently, neither did Dad. I could tell from his long exhales that he was falling back to sleep again.

"Love you to the moon," I said, trying to be softer.

"And back," he mumbled.

I couldn't understand why Dad was being so passive about this. It was like they'd drugged him into submission.

Butts in at 4:20, texted Emma.

Then a few seconds later: **Hahahahaha! I love autocorrect! Bus not butts!**

I couldn't even answer her. There was nothing funny about her phone rescrambling her words or robots dating humans and I was beginning to think that Dr. Lowenstein was a cyborg himself with his lack of empathy. I stormed out to the bunker with my phone and wrote everything to Dr. Ganesh I should've said to begin with.

As in, **Okay, it was me, and I know that was wrong. Can we** please pretend that never happened unless you need to talk about it but I don't because I know it was a mistake and I'm really sorry I put you in an awkward position and it will never ever happen again? But I really need to talk to you because Dr. Lowenstein is refusing to start the trial and I'm getting nervous because time is of the essence and I don't really know anyone besides you who understands.

This time, there was a message back within minutes. It was a little cryptic, but at least it was something.

Eleanor, I am very sorry I cannot be at the meeting tomorrow. But you are in the best hands. Take care.

What meeting? I texted. Again, no response.

I pounced on Mom as soon as she pulled into the driveway. "Is there a meeting at the hospital tomorrow?"

"Hello to you too, my dear."

"Hi. Sorry. Hi. What is this meeting about?"

"I don't know." She shook her head. "There's always a meeting."

"Okay, but why would Ganesh text me about a meeting?"

"The question is, why would Ganesh text you at all?"

I rolled my eyes. "We can talk about that later. What's going on? Did you see Lowenstein today?"

"Yes." There was a horrible pause. "Can we please talk about this inside, Lenny? I'd really like to take off my shoes. I thought you'd be getting ready for bed."

I trailed after her, not letting up for a second. "I already spoke to Dad. He sounds like a zombie. Which is a whole other story, and I also want to speak to whoever is administering his meds. But he was coherent enough to tell me that they didn't start the PD-1 yet, and they *have* to. Dr. Ganesh said he could."

"Yes, but Dad is not really a patient of Dr. Ganesh, sweetie. Lowenstein is the one who is leading this trial and he's the head honcho, so we have to—"

"No! We don't *have* to do anything! We don't have to blindly accept what this guy says just because he has fancy diplomas on his wall and gets speaking gigs in Canada! I don't even think he's human anymore!"

"Okay." Mom breathed slowly. "Excuse me, please." She walked past me and poured herself a glass of white wine from the fridge. Then she took a jar of flax seeds from the counter, opened the top, and tipped it toward me. I pushed it away.

"I'm skipping school tomorrow and coming to whatever meeting is happening," I told her. I left her in the middle of the kitchen, munching.

That night, I stayed up until two in the morning doing more research on clinical drug trials, then dumped out my padlocked suitcase and made a list of all the meds that Dad had ever been on since diagnosis, in case that could be informative. I also jotted down a few alternative treatments I'd been looking up, like noni fruits, soursop leaves, cannabis oil, and some village in the Andes Mountains where people had mutated genes but were disease-free.

I refused to open the envelope of Ambrosia pictures again. In many ways, she'd gotten me into this mess. I wondered if she even knew how much she'd scarred my dad. If he died, I was going to track her down and send her a copy of his obituary.

I'd forgotten I'd stowed my rare-diseases book in here. That diverted my attention for a solid four minutes. I even added another page for something I'd read about called pink tooth of Mummery and made up a few more, like "laughing too much at knock-knock jokes disease" and "overproduction of sweat glands while eating kale disease." I knew Dr. Ganesh wouldn't be at the meeting. But I was determined to find him and make this right somehow.

Of course, what I really wanted to do was hit my head five hundred times without stopping. Just smash and slam myself until I demolished every knotted brainwave inside. But I thought again about Oscar Birnbaum making me commit to that stupid promise. Standing there in all his trilingual nonchalance, unnerving me. I was sure he'd forgotten about that moment entirely, which only made me feel worse. To me, that exchange was somehow the only thing vaguely keeping me tethered to Earth.

Thursday morning, I called the high school office to say Eleanor Rosenthal-Hermann would be out because of a family crisis. I was talking to a voice-mail box, but it felt good to name this ominous feeling out loud. Mom told me the meeting with Lowenstein was set for 11:50 a.m., which I thought was an obnoxious way of saying, "I'm too busy and important to waste a few minutes and just say noon." It also meant we needed to leave our house by ten just in case of tie-ups. At 9:52, Mom came back so flushed from her morning jog I thought she would explode.

"We'll be fine," she assured me. I told her I was waiting in the car and stomped outside.

An hour later, as we sat in traffic, she said, "Maybe the train would've been faster."

"Or leaving on time," I muttered.

"It'll give Lowenstein a few minutes to have a cup of coffee," Mom assured. "Or discover a new genetic sequence. Did I tell you there was an article in the *Times* about him being on the forefront of modern immunology?"

"Wow," I said blandly.

Then she prattled on about all the things Emma wanted to do when she got into town and how impressive the Binghamton bus schedule was.

Lowenstein had not discovered a new genetic sequence or had a cup of coffee in the forty-five minutes we gifted him with our lateness. He was in a secret chamber behind the nurses' Island of Unanswerable Questions, waiting for us with a can of diet ginger ale and a frown. His hair looked thinner and lintier than I remembered.

"So sorry for the delay. You remember my youngest daughter, Eleanor? My eldest is coming in later today on the bus. She's studying public policy and transgender normatives, which is as confusing as it sounds, but I'm sure you can appreciate the expansiveness of college curriculum these days. Lenny, I think I told you Dr. Lowenstein was honored by New York University for the work he did integrating premed students into the lab for more hands-on studies."

"Yes, yes," he said, waving her away but obviously a little flattered. "This is fine. Are we ready?"

"Yes, please," I said.

Lowenstein led the way into Dad's room. Dad was propped up in one of those vinyl lounge chairs with his WAHONSETT IS FOR ALGAE LOVERS T-shirt, which I appreciated, even if it looked five sizes too big on him now. There wasn't really enough room for us all to sit. Lowenstein leaned against a wall. I started rinsing out Dad's plastic pink water pitchers in his sink. Mom kissed Dad's forehead and then perched herself on his bedside commode.

Lowenstein opened a manila folder, looked at the notes inside for a few seconds, and closed it again. He cracked his neck and cleared his throat.

"I'm sorry I was away earlier this week. I'm sorry that I didn't order these scans sooner. And of course, I'm sorry we're having this talk now." He stopped and looked right at me. His brown eyes were tiny behind his glasses. His gray sprouts of eyebrows, on the other hand, needed their own zip code.

He cleared his throat again. Coughed a bit. I wanted to hand him a SARS mask.

"So, as I mentioned, it looks like we won't be able to put you in this trial after all," he began.

"What do you mean 'won't be able to'?" I asked.

"Well, these latest scans disqualified us."

"Who's the judge? That guy from *American Idol*?"

Dad winked at me after I said that. Which could've meant he thought I was hilarious or that I needed to shut up and let the doctor talk.

Lowenstein cleared his throat two more times before continuing. "Well, we knew there was risk of this, but there are significant new metastases—including these glioblastomas, which are tricky . . ."

His mouth was moving and the rumble of vowels and consonants was clearly coming from him, but I couldn't process anything he was saying. I poured out the lukewarm water in Dad's plastic bedside pitcher and started rinsing it over and over again. The soap wasn't doing anything except making my hands slippery, and every time I dropped the pitcher in the sink I knew it was collecting more bacteria from the bottom. This whole room was dripping with disease.

"But the progression has been so rapid . . . We originally thought that the targeted monoclonal antibody treatments would work because they've been so successful before. But then we had to move on to a more defensive approach, which, as we know, often runs the risk of depleting the body's resources. And now . . . well, it looks like we've run out of time. And options. Again, I'm so sorry."

I tried adding some antibacterial gel and scrubbing with that.

I turned on the hot water until it was steaming. The faucet was the loudest thing in the room.

"Lenny," Mom said over the roar, "do you have any questions for Dr. Lowenstein?"

I turned the water down and faced him straight on.

"Questions, questions. Oh yeah, here's one," I spit. "Are you giving up?"

Out of the corner of my eye I saw Mom suck in her breath. Dad held his hand out to me and said, "Honey, we're not giving up. We're doing everything we can. There's just not much else to do."

I hated that Dad was sticking up for this schmuck. I dumped the water pitcher again and pumped some more soap into it. "Dr. Ganesh said that there were a few trials available. There's also a ton of drugs being tested on brain lesions, like Durvalumab or that other one . . . Pembrolizumab? Which is on the list of immune modulators."

Lowenstein looked astonished by my medical knowledge for maybe a millisecond. Then he said, "I'm familiar with that drug as well, but it would be too much on his system."

"*His?*" I said, pointing to Dad. Lowenstein nodded. "You mean *my father*? Because he's still in the room and he's still very much alive and if you're just going to say, 'Oh well,' then maybe you should address him directly."

"Lenny—" started Mom.

I stood in front of her to block all interruptions and kept

talking directly into Lowenstein's face. "Here are a few more things you may want to know, because he's a person, not just one of your statistics. His name is Jeremy Reuben Rosenthal-Hermann. He's forty-nine and a half years old and he was the first Jew to make partner at his law firm and he's the proud father of two daughters and used to be in a band called the Mermen and plays racquetball and can do five-digit long division in his head."

Lowenstein looked a little queasy from nodding and fake smiling at me. Which only made me talk louder. I told him about when Dad and I went on a Girl Scout father-daughter trek through the Catskills and Dad filleted a fish with his bare hands. I told him about how he taught me to ride a bike and whistle and sing in French.

"Did you know that he played guitar professionally for a year? And he has a notebook by his bed at home where he collects good jokes. Here's a G-rated one for you. What's brown and sticky?"

Mom stood up and said, "Okay, Lenny, let's give Dad some time to—"

"A *stick*!" I shouted. Then I cackled pretty maniacally.

Lowenstein was being too important to laugh. He opened his manila folder again, which I was now convinced had porn inside because he was so excited by it.

"Forget it," I snorted at him. "No offense, but you're a little bit useless. This is why we're facing mass extinction today, you know. Because each life counts and each life is part of the global survival. So if *you* can't do anything helpful or even humane for my dad, then just tell me where Dr. Ganesh is. *Please.*"

Mom scowled at me. "I'm so sorry, Dr. Lowenstein," she said. "I think we just all need to process this."

"Of course," he said. "And please feel free to reach out if you have any questions."

"Yeah—my question is, where is Dr. Ganesh?" I repeated. I knew no one was going to answer me, so I marched out to the nurses' fortress. "Where is Dr. Ganesh? Excuse me, where is Dr. Ganesh?"

There was obviously an epidemic of deafness going around the floor. I charged behind the counter. It was actually ridiculously easy. But it got everyone's attention.

"Sorry, but you can't do that."

"Sorry, but I just did. Who is going to tell me where Dr. Radhakrishnan Ganesh is?"

"He's not on the floor today."

"Is he in his office on Seventy-First Street?"

"We're not allowed to give out that kind of information."

"Well then what kind of information do you give out?!" No one answered. "I'll be right here until someone answers me! Is Dr. Ganesh expected today or is he in his office?"

Saffi—the beautiful nurse with braids from the first night I'd brought Dad in—spun toward me on her chair slowly. Calmly. She didn't say anything. She just found my eyes and nodded.

Office? I mouthed. She nodded again. I ran to the elevator bank and used my elbows to press all the arrows pointing up (an escape trick I'd memorized from some heist movie, though no one seemed to be following me). Then I opened the door to the stairwell and slipped in extra quietly, running down the ten flights on my tiptoes. I got a sick thrill from hearing my mom at the top yelling, "Lenny? Lenny, *wait*!"

World War III

Approximate Number of Operational Nuclear Warheads

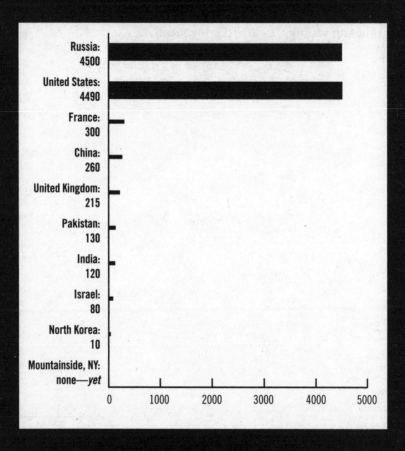

Chapter 14

SMALL TALK(ING)

Linda with the yarn-story sweaters looked up so lovingly from her desk that I almost broke down before the door closed behind me. I really just wanted to bury myself in the acrylic sunset that was spread across her pillowy chest.

"Darling!" she chirped. "How is that wonderful dad of yours? And is it nippy outside? I brought a windbreaker but I don't want to presume."

"Pretty warm out actually." I tried my hardest to sound cheery. "Is Dr. Ganesh here by any chance?"

"Yes, but he's booked solid until the end of the day. And I'm heading out at two, otherwise I'd try to slot you in. So sorry," Linda said. She pulled off her clip-on earrings and placed them by her phone. Then she started shutting down her computer, mumbling things like, "Exit application" . . . "Save changes" . . . "Yes, and quit."

"I know it's Friday afternoon and it's getting late. It's an emergency, though."

She stopped humming along to her easy-listening radio station and snapped to attention. "Is your father here?"

"No. He's in the hospital. Which is why I need Dr. Ganesh to . . ." I wasn't sure how to finish that sentence. I needed Dr. Ganesh to change Lowenstein's mind and convince him that the drug trial would be miraculously efficient. I also needed Dr. Ganesh to change the progression of time and reverse the racing reproduction of cells in my dad's body and tell me we could do this. We could find an opening somewhere. A bunker in the sky or at least in my brain where we'd be safe. Plus, I needed to apologize for sending him dirty pictures.

Linda was waiting for me to explain.

"I just need to talk to him. Please?"

"I'll tell him you're here," she said. "Rosenthal-Hermann, yes?"

"Yes. First name—Ey. Leah. Nor," I said weakly.

Linda waddled down the hall and knocked on Dr. Ganesh's door. I could picture him at that desk with the photo of him and his parents. His parents who'd lost a child and the wise son who had pledged to find a cure.

I heard his trademark "Helloooo!" and then Linda mumbling something with the door closed. When she came back, I pretended to be reading a pamphlet on endocrine health.

"Okay, darling, you're in luck," Linda sang. "I guess he has a few more patients coming in, so if you can be back a little after five, he'll be finishing up then. I won't be here, but you just press two-zero-two-eight at the security door, twist the lock to the left, and come on up. Same code for the office door."

"Thank you thank you thank you thank you!" I sounded like a cat's squeaky chew toy. Linda opened the door and ushered me out.

I had a little too much hope walking away from that moment. Enough hope to go to the drugstore and pull out Mom's emergency credit card again and charge up forty dollars' worth of eye shadow, hand sanitizers, tweezers, a thank-you card with a frog on it, and six bottles of some pink wine cooler.

It wasn't that I wanted to get drunk with Dr. Ganesh, but I needed something to unknot this night. I had very little prior experience drinking. I'd taken a few sips of my dad's beer over the years. And last summer at our cousin's wedding, Emma made me try vodka, which was horrible and amazing all at once. My mouth was on fire and I was doing a rubbery chicken dance that made me feel taller than the clouds. The next day was rough, though. I vowed that this time I would sip slowly.

Pregnant Sheena at the cash register clearly did not remember me. Or was willfully trying to forget.

"Hey! How's it going?" I practically screamed at her.

"Fine thank you and how are you," she said in her dreary monotone while scanning my items. She stopped at the wine coolers and shot me a look. "ID?" she asked.

I did a very dramatic impersonation of someone looking through her pocketbook for a piece of identification. Then I shook my head and said, "This is ridiculous, but I seem to have left all my ID at home. But I swear—"

She cut me off. "Do you want to save a life and donate a dollar for AIDS?"

"Whoa, who's *for* AIDS?" I asked, trying to crack her. I didn't know why I needed this girl to like me so much, but I did. I kept thinking how I couldn't trust any of my so-called friends and she was about my age and there wasn't that much separating us except maybe social stratification and income inequality and I could help her bring up her baby if she was all alone because I needed to do something more meaningful than nose-dive into this vat of self-pity.

"I think it's awesome what you're doing," I told her.

"What am I doing?" she asked. I nodded at her belly. "Oh yeah," she said, looking more angry than excited. "You want this stuff in one bag or two?"

I still had over three hours until I could buzz Dr. Ganesh's office again. I signed a few petitions on the street—mostly to save dogs and get rid of oil rigs. Then I walked down to the old Park Avenue Armory building and wandered through the room with all the knights in chain mail.

"You guys look ridiculous," I told the mannequins. There was something so pitiful and enraging about their dusty steel collars and gauntlets. They looked like oversize toys. At least we didn't waste all that time forging iron for shields and swords anymore. Everything was electronic or invisible to the naked eye. The next world war was going to start from somebody's robot's second drone once removed.

"Can't have that in here," said a small woman in a blue smock. She had glasses taking up most of her face and flashed a badge that said ARMORY DOCENT at me. Then she pointed at my cell phone, which kept buzzing in my hand from Mom calling repeatedly.

"Sorry," I said, trying to turn it off at the same moment that she called again. "I'll just . . . yeah." Back out on the street, I answered just in time to hear Mom midsoliloquy.

". . . do a loop with the car but we can't file a missing persons report until it's been at least three hours I think."

"Mom!" I shouted. "I'm right here."

"Aaaah! Aha!" she yipped. Then I couldn't tell whether she was laughing or crying. Dad took the phone from her.

"Okay, okay. Hey, Lenny, hon. I'm sorry this is so hard."

"It's not your fault. Please stop saying sorry."

"Fair enough. Where are you?"

"I'm—I'm fine."

"But where are you?"

"I can't tell you."

Dad conferred with Mom, then came back to the phone.

"Listen, honey, we won't ask any questions, but we really need you to come back. Mom's going out to the bus stop in a little while to pick up Emma. She says she can swing by wherever you are. Just give us a corner or a coffee shop and she'll meet you there."

"Sorry, Daddy," I said. I could feel a sob caught under my

ribs and I really didn't want it to get out. Once I started, I didn't know if I'd ever stop. "I'm safe. I'll check in again soon." I hung up before he could offer another solution and went into the nearest bake shop so I could at least sit down. I chewed on some ice and ordered a croissant that sort of devolved in my hands into a fistful of French dust. Then I sat in my pile of crumbs and wrote a list of all the things I needed to say to Dr. Ganesh, including:

1. Pembrolizumab is listed in both colorectal and brain tumor trials. Coinkidink or brilliant sign of possibilities?
2. Cancer should be put on the list of catastrophic pandemics so we can get federal and even international support/funding for research.
3. FYI my dad's band once played to a sold-out crowd at Jones Beach.
4. Those pictures I sent were a huge joke with a side of mistake wrapped in a burrito of ugly.

I rewrote it twice to look neat but not overly formal, in case Dr. Ganesh asked to see my work. I also used my phone to look up where the phrase "good Samaritan" appeared in the Bible, because it had been bugging me since Oscar had said it the other day. It wound up being in a parable Jesus told about someone getting beat up on the road to Jericho and all the people who walked right by him before the Samaritan stopped.

I walked by people who were suffering every day. Most of the time I backed away if someone looked particularly troubled or contagious in any way. I wondered how many people I'd passed just today who might not make it until tomorrow.

I had a half hour to go until five o'clock when I put in the secret code at Dr. Ganesh's security door. I used the empty lobby as a dressing room, pulling out some of my new makeup compacts to pluck a few stray eyebrows with my tweezers and smear on some lavender sparkle shadow. Then I took the stairs to the eighth floor instead of dealing with elevator germs. Adrenaline always helped rescramble my neurons at least a little.

When I got into his waiting room, I heard Dr. Ganesh walking down the hall explaining how his new running sneakers made him feel like a grasshopper and also how caffeine could be therapeutic but he didn't understand why Americans paid so much for drinks made with cold coffee.

His extra last patient of the day was very old. It wasn't fair how old and alive he was. His tan pants were belted just below his chest and he wore a sailor's cap that looked like it was attached to the rusty hair underneath. He was leaning on Dr. Ganesh while they walked. Then he thanked the good doctor and announced he was going to go home and have eggs and tomatoes. Dr. Ganesh wished him well and said they'd talk soon. He locked the door after the sailor left. When he turned around there was a smile on his face. Then he saw me on his waiting room couch, and shut his lips into a tight line.

I stood up, but he motioned for me to sit down again, which I ignored. He sat in the chair farthest away from me. I couldn't be deterred, though.

"Thank you for seeing me. Not *seeing* me, but just using your eyes. Or whatever you're using. Just—thank you for letting me come here."

"You are welcome," he said stiffly. "Linda said it was an emergency."

"Yes! I mean, not the nine-one-one kind but—yes!" I'd wanted to save the wine coolers for later, but it looked like now was already desperate. I pulled out two bottles and tried to hand one to Dr. Ganesh, but he waved me away.

"It's sour apple passion," I read. "I guess if you like sour apples, you must be passionate about it, huh?" I twisted off the cap and took a long swig. It tasted like carbonated caramel. "Yum," I said, trying not to wince. I took another big gulp and felt everything start to melt. I hadn't noticed until that moment that the labels had pictures of a couple running on the beach. I thought I should tell him it obviously wasn't us—I'd never look like that in a bikini.

"Is this alcohol, Ey-leah-nor?" Dr. Ganesh asked.

"Well, sort of. I mean, it's mostly sugar, which is unfermented alcohol, right? Or maybe it's alcohol that's already metabolized?"

Dr. Ganesh either didn't understand the question, didn't have an answer, or, most likely, didn't care. "Please," he said, "you cannot have that in here."

"Of course not! Just a sec!" I gulped about eight more ounces of apple elixir because this was already going so poorly and Dr. Ganesh looked disgusted even though he was supposed to be the one person in the world who could accept me and offer hope.

"Okeydoke," I said, draining the first bottle. I needed to look at my list. Or at least recite some data. "So the emergency is— well, do you know what Dr. Lowenstein told us today?"

"Yes, Dr. Lowenstein is my mentor. We have spoken a lot about this case."

"This case" really stung. I wondered if they added the number of my dad's metastases and did long division with his life expectancy. I was part of "this case" too—the trouble-some daughter with misplaced outrage, chronic halitosis, and obsessive-compulsive, continuously annoying idiosyncrasies with a dollop of Electra complex on top.

"I need you to tell Lowenstein that we have to do the trial," I said.

Dr. Ganesh folded his arms.

"Or I shouldn't tell you what to do. Did you read that thing online about Europe approving Pembrolizumab for first-line treatment? Something like 74 percent for one-year survival, which is way better than Ipilimumab."

"These are PD-1 targeters," Dr. Ganesh said glumly. "Your father wasn't able to tolerate the BRAF inhibitor we tried." He didn't even acknowledge that I'd memorized some pretty hard words and statistics. Especially when the room was tipping to one side. I grabbed another cooler and opened it, taking a slug.

"Ey-leah-nor, *please*," he said. I'd never heard his voice that close to anger before. His ears pulled back a little and his whole face looked tight. I wanted to tell him that anger didn't scare me and that I was grateful he could be this open with his feelings and that this was good for us as a couple because emotional honesty was the only real source of human potential. "*Away*," he ordered, breaking into my reverie. I tucked the bottle behind me and blinked hard to refocus.

"Right," I said. "Okay, if you're on the anti-pembro team, there's another monoclonal antibody I saw mentioned a lot. Durva-something?"

"Durvalumab," Dr. Ganesh said. I put my fist out for a bump because we were having a conversation now! But he didn't move.

I stopped, stumped. Honestly, I had this list of things to tell him and lots of numbers swimming in my head but I'd envisioned Dr. Ganesh softening by now. He would say something to the effect of we were in this together and he had an enchanted loophole or had misread the charts. Plus, he had taken so long to respond to my texts because he was doing some really meditative work with his inner conscience. And now he was ready to say that he respected my mind and my heart and let's forget about protocol and age differences and he wanted to take my whole family to India where the cure would spring up out of a saffron-scented fountain.

I had no idea how to get him to say anything close to that, though. So I sat down and tried to start over. "Sorry. I meant to ask, how are you?"

Dr. Ganesh did laugh a little at that. "Thank you, Ey-leah-nor. This is small talking, I see. I am fine. Now, how can I help you?"

"Okay, you're right. Except it's small *talk*. Not small *talking*." He nodded. I took my rare-diseases book out of my knapsack and handed it to him. "It's a work in progress," I said.

"For me?" he asked. When I nodded, he gave it a quick glance, thanked me, and rolled it up so it fit in his lab coat pocket. I wanted to tell him that it took a lot of hours to make and maybe he could read it now as an icebreaker, but he was looking more and more impatient. So I took a few more gulps from the second bottle before trying to form words again. This time Dr. Ganesh closed his eyes and shook his head.

"That's the last sip. I'm just very thirsty and confused. Are you saying you agree with Lowenstein?" I asked. Then, because my tongue was getting so slippery and impatient, I added, "Lowenstein rhymes with jellybean. And spleen machine. And rowing team. Or teen. Or . . ."

Dr. Ganesh waited for me to be done. Then he said, "Yes. I agree with Dr. Lowenstein. Unfortunately, the trials you have spoken about have either been filled or your father would not be eligible at this advanced stage. I thought it would work—"

"You said it would work!" I jumped in.

"But because of the aggressive metastases this is no longer viable."

"Then we'll find another trial. There's a gazillion of them."

"Drug trials are not always the answer."

I stood up. And fell down on the chair. And stood up again. "You were the one who brought up the trials in the first place. *You* said we were going to cure my dad!"

"Yes." Dr. Ganesh was eyeing the door now. "And this is where I owe you an apology, Ey-leah-nor. I said . . . I said too much. I should not have told you all those personal things. I should not have made this promises."

"*These* promises."

He looked so claustrophobic and sad. "I don't like to say this, but there is nothing else we can do."

I stamped my feet to show him I meant business. "Define *nothing*," I said.

"No treatment that we think could prolong your father's life without excruciating side effects."

"No treatment at all?" He didn't answer. "None?!" I screamed. I wanted to cry. I wanted to wail and beat my hands on his chest. But I could barely breathe and my mouth felt so sticky with apple syrup. "So that's it?" I asked feebly.

"I am sorry."

The silence afterward choked me.

"Tell me how long we have," I heard myself croak. "I know you know."

Dr. Ganesh hung his head and mumbled, "I think anywhere from a few months to a few weeks. Or less. Your father is actively dying, Ey-leah-nor."

"*Actively* dying?" I had my voice back now. "Is that like jumbo shrimp or freezer burn? You know what that's called, right? In English, it's an *oxymoron*, which I think translates to 'sharp' and 'dull,' but you'd have to check. Or don't check. You're a busy guy. Who has time for etymology, right? Did you know there are some languages that are going extinct? Mostly in Morocco. I always wondered, if there was only one person left who knew how to talk in some language, what if she said 'Help!' and no one else knew what it meant?"

Dr. Ganesh shook his head again. He looked like a little boy getting in trouble. Which reminded me that I had to apologize also.

"I'm sorry too," I whimpered. "I'm sorry I sent you those pictures. I didn't mean to. I mean, I did, but . . ."

"Yes, this was compromising." I waited for him to explain. "That phone number is just for patients, so I use it in the hospital, and unfortunately this is not a private area."

I had visions of Mariel and Saffi huddled around his cell phone, scrolling through my pucker series. I pulled the wine cooler to my lips and just kept guzzling until bottle number two was done.

"Thawassupposed to be your personal number," I whined.

"It is not," said Dr. Ganesh faintly. Everything was moving

too fast. I couldn't get my mouth to put together the words I wanted to say.

"Wait! Did somebody else see? Did you get in trouble because of what I sent?"

He made that tight line with his mouth again. "I will meet with Dr. Lowenstein and the patient advocacy board tomorrow and I will explain."

"Noooo," I moaned. "Can I come to the meeting? I'll be very respectful. Or I can just write a note on good stationery and tell them it was completely my fault."

"No," he said quickly. "Please. It will be okay, I hope."

"Yes it will. Of course it will. My mom is a judge, for what that's worth. But you don't need to be judged. It's all because of me. Really it's a testament to how great a practitioner you are, but I won't say that. I won't say anything unless you need me to, and then I can testify in court. But it's going to be okay. Yes, it is. Can you just let me know it's okay after the meeting? Somehow? You can text me . . . ugh. Sorry, I mean, maybe we can come up with some code. Or . . . ?"

Dr. Ganesh waited for me to talk myself into a sweat and then asked, "How will you get home now?" I shrugged spastically. "Can I get you a cab?"

"Sure."

We went downstairs and out into the world, where it was just edging toward evening. Dr. Ganesh put two fingers in his mouth and let out a piercing whistle. The first cab that stopped was playing the Beach Boys and the driver had on a turquoise Hawaiian shirt.

Dr. Ganesh leaned into the passenger window and said, "Please take this young lady to—" Then he looked back at me for a destination.

His face was long and soft and already so far away. I couldn't have this be goodbye. I couldn't end it all or watch it end through a cab window. The world getting snuffed out with his lips in the lamplight. I knew it was so wrong and too late and couldn't make anything better. But if we were all catapulting into oblivion on a rowboat of sour apples, I had to act now.

I held on to both of Dr. Radhakrishnan Ganesh's shoulders and pulled him in closer.

"I'm sorry," I murmured. Then I pressed my face into his, clenching his lips with mine. Squeezing everything that was about to disappear.

Alien Invasion

Compelling arguments for alien invasions:

1. There's now a panel at the United Nations investigating extraterrestrial intentions.
2. Stephen Hawking just paid millions for the CSIRO Parkes radio telescope so he can scan the 100 closest galaxies.
3. Emma's best friend lost her virginity while watching *E.T.*

Chapter 15

MOST LIKELY TO BE AN ALIEN

When the cab pulled up to Grand Central Station, I tried to give the driver my four leftover wine coolers, but he just shook his head and said, "Ramadan."

"Good luck with that," I said. "I don't know what I believe in anymore."

I got out on the corner of Vanderbilt Avenue and Forty-Second Street. It was Thursday night and the sidewalks were thick with people. Commuter pubs were shuffling cocktails and business suits. I was shaking so much from the talk and face-mashing with Dr. Ganesh, I felt like I needed to kick over all the newsstands or scale a tall building. Nobody would notice in this city. Everybody was so busy being rich or homeless, beautiful or crazy. In front of the entrance there was a sweaty couple making out, twisted around each other like vines. Also an Asian man playing the pan flute; a bunch of five o'clock shadows talking about the last time they saw Kirsten Dunst at the gym; and half of Holland, all looking for Radio City Music Hall. I wanted to smash them all together and scream, *Do you know how much time you're wasting?! This could be your last day on Earth!*

It wasn't my dad's last day on Earth. I was pretty sure of that just from the useless string of texts I'd been getting from Mom.

Pls B s8fe

Wanna talk?

Just got Emma can pick u up 2

Meet @ Kaling for sup?

Pls just write S for s8fe

I wrote back, **S. Spending pm w/Juln**, and elbowed my way into Grand Central. It was the first time I'd lied about where I was sleeping, and I felt my arm hairs lifting in shock. I didn't have a plan per se, I just knew I couldn't go back to the hospital and hear about Emma's coed trickle-down escapades and admit that even the Remover of All Obstacles conceded there were no more medical options.

I kept my head down and pretended I knew where I was going. There were hundreds of people so alive and loud in here—laughing, shouting, pushing, eating. Not one of them knew that I'd just been told my dad was going to die soon. Not one of them would know if he was dead right now.

I opened a third wine cooler—because why not?—then took a sip and wandered to the Grand Concourse. The next train to Mountainside didn't leave for another forty-nine minutes. It felt like it was two in the morning, but the big clock said it was only 8:25. Time stops flying by when you're miserable. So I leaned against the information booth in the middle of the room and tipped my head back and tried to get lost in the constellations painted on the ceiling. I'd read once that the stars were drawn out of order and that Orion was the only one in its proper place.

I used to look at these same stars with Dad on our date nights at Lincoln Center. He loved coming into the city to hear live jazz. I loved the smell of hot dog carts on every corner. After each concert, he'd buy me a big pretzel and I'd lick off the chunks of salt extra slowly. Or else we'd go to our favorite deli on Broadway and request a table by the window for optimal people watching. I always ordered a potato knish with an extra side of pickles—the first bowl was complimentary. Dad got a tuna melt with slaw, and we split a vanilla milkshake. Then we walked the twenty-five blocks down to Grand Central, picking out "best dressed," "best tourist," "best evangelist," and "most likely to be an alien sent here on a reconnaissance mission."

I had no idea if Dad and I could ever go on a date again. The last one we'd done was when I was twelve and I wore my first training bra, which gave me a rash. I'd wasted so much of that night complaining about how itchy I was and texting people who never really cared, like Becca and Sylvie. Now I wondered what pickles would taste like when Dad was gone. Or if I'd even be able to listen to jazz.

"Don't be stupid," said a curt voice.

"Sorry?" I answered. There was a thick police officer holding his belt and standing in front of me.

"Don't be sorry and don't be stupid. Just get rid of it before I write you up." He nodded at the wine cooler in my hand.

"Oh, this was just . . ." He didn't wait around for the explanation. I headed down one of the corridors because I knew Grand Central was teeming with thirsty people and I hated to throw away unopened drinks, even if they tasted like sour apple slop.

I circled the floor over and over again. "Best dressed" went to someone who could've been a man or a woman in a strapless sequined number and calf muscles that looked like rocks. "Best tourist" was a tie between this couple in matching Izods reading one of the plaques on the wall about how Grand Central was constructed. "Best evangelist" was easy—there was a woman with straight dark hair pulled back in a banana clip and a ruffled pink blouse belted into hip-hugger jeans. She also had an open cat carrier at her feet, which was stuffed with bright pamphlets.

"You can be saved!" she said chirpily. She was the only person who was excited to see me that day. According to her, Jesus was thrilled about my prospects too. He was going to love me unconditionally and wash away my sins and show me absolute truth. Until I told her I was a born-again Quaker and sort of drunk and felt very conflicted and horny for my dad's doctor. She handed me one of her paradise-colored pamphlets and said, "Time is running out."

"Duh!" I yelled at her. "That's what I've been saying all along!"

I was about to drop my syrupy wine coolers in the trash when I found my true comrade-in-arms. He was a droopy-looking man sitting with his saxophone by track 19. He had a sign on his lap that said PLEASE DON'T MAKE ME PLAY ALIEN MUSIC.

"Oooooh yeah!" he growled, followed by some atonal saxophone riff.

"Can I ask you a question?" I said. As I walked toward him I saw he had only three fingers on his left hand.

"Please," he answered.

"How do you know it's alien music?"

"Yup," he said. "They're out there. Kepler-62, Kepler-186. Who's getting the water onto Mars? Some supersonic telescope in Austria now."

"Australia," I said. I actually knew what he was talking about. The sixty-four-meter Parkes telescope that Hawking had just commissioned to look for extraterrestrial life.

"That's what I'm talking about!" said my new one-and-only friend. He started clapping his hands and rocking back and forth.

"Thank you," I said. I put a dollar twenty in change into his open saxophone case and the coolers next to his sign.

"Hoo ha!" he said. "You want me to play something for you?"

"No, that's okay. I have to get home." Then I turned back to tell him, "My dad's dying."

"Nooooo!" he howled.

"Yeah," I said. Saying and hearing it for the first time. "It's true."

The 9:14 train up the Hudson line was packed. Everyone pushing and yammering. Even the posters felt obnoxiously loud.

There was one for direct flights to Singapore and another for some high-speed monorail they were building in New Jersey. I hated everyone for wanting to be the fastest. As if we had somewhere better to be. I thought we'd already proven that if you were extraordinarily speedy you would either have to wait for everyone else to catch up or you'd get tested for steroids.

Just before the doors closed, a swarm of sweaty college-aged guys shoved each other into the row across from me. They each wore different versions of the same Michigan State T-shirt and they were playing "Would you rather?" in booming, slurry voices.

"Would you rather get caught masturbating or lose one of your balls?"

"Easy—I get caught all the time!"

"Would you rather sleep with Rosie O'Donnell or Rosie Perez?"

"O'Donnell's a dyke!"

"Exactly."

"Hot!"

"Would you rather eat a raw onion or a raw . . . something else."

"Dude, you're so drunk."

"I know!"

I thought about changing cars at the next station, but I really needed to sit near an emergency exit and I didn't know how crowded it was in the rest of the train. It was easier to stew in my fury than to get swallowed up by all the heartache, shame, and rapidly replicating tragedies of the past twelve hours.

I also really needed to find my house keys. I checked all the pockets of my backpack twice, but they weren't there. I checked my jeans pockets, the train seat, and the overhead rack. Not that I'd been climbing up there, but because at this point everything was hopeless and nothing was impossible.

"Would you rather lick an electric socket or your dad's—"

I plugged my ears and started chanting a new mantra for myself: *This is not happening. This is not happening.* If I didn't find my keys, I had no idea where I would sleep or how I'd see the next day. I'd lost our spare key over a year ago and never replaced it. If I tried sleeping on the train, I was sure this clan of cave idiots would get bored and try to molest me.

"Would you rather eat a shit sandwich or take a shit on a sandwich and then make . . ."

"But what if the sandwich isn't shit, it just tastes like shit, and then, would you rather . . ."

These guys were more stupid than scary, but I just wanted out. I bit the inside of my left bicep until I tasted blood and felt tears pooling. The sharp sting gave me somewhere to breathe at least. I thought of how pounding on my head used to do this for me, before Oscar Birnbaum made me stop.

Oscar. I could maybe call him. Except I didn't have his number. Or really anything to say except *Hellllllllllllp!*

I pulled out my phone and saw that I'd butt-dialed Julian

three times. I guess my body knew I was feeling desperate even if my brain couldn't admit it.

Julian had texted me after the third call: **You ok?**

I wrote back: **Never better. Out with Ganesh.** Followed by a screen full of heart emojis and smiley faces.

I had three nasty-looking self-inflicted arm welts by the time we got to the Mountainside station. The Would-You-Rather's didn't even look up when I left. Which should've given me relief but actually only made me feel lonelier. I walked directly to the Unicorn, just on the off chance that Julian was there waiting. Plus, I was starving and still had no idea where I was going to spend the night. I hadn't come here in four days—which was a record for me, though I'm sure nobody else noticed my absence. I stared at the rusty blue Dumpster in the parking lot with the spray-painted unicorn, feeling homesick, not for a place but for a time. Timesick.

Walking to the entrance, I knew something was wrong. There was a pot of fake roses on the second step and a bristly welcome mat that read FINE DINING in loopy letters. Then I opened the door, walked straight to our booth, and saw what was really going on.

Don Juan Crustaceo was gone.

The whole fish tank was gone too. All that was left was another plastic palm tree in the corner. Trying to fool us into thinking we were on some island where unicorns and lobsters could run free.

I marched over to the host station to ask for Dara. She wasn't working, though. I got a guy named Topher, who was one of our high school football prodigies until he'd gotten his third concussion last year. He couldn't be near bright lights anymore and Emma said he tried to feel her up at a party with his eyes closed.

"What can I get you?" Topher asked.

I had no time for small talking. I cleared my throat so he knew I meant business. "Where's the fish tank?"

"What fish tank?"

"The fish tank that was over here just a few days ago. It had a treasure chest, some pearls, and a very important lobster in it."

"Ha!" Topher laughed. "Did you just say a very important *lobster*?"

"Shut up! Where is it?"

"I have no idea. Nobody orders lobster here anyway."

"That's not the point. Is Dara around? She knows what I'm talking about."

Topher picked some wax out of his ear and started to walk away.

"Or Stephan," I said, standing up taller. "Where is Stephan?"

"I dunno," said Topher.

"What exactly *do* you know?" I pounced. "Do you know that by some counts there are over six hundred species of endangered crustaceans? Do you know that evolution started in the ocean and something like 80 percent of the different species on Earth live in the ocean but they won't be able to for much longer if we keep dumping crap in there and spilling oil barges and catching fish just to stick them in tanks until we get sick of them?"

"I think you should leave," said Topher. He did not look amused anymore.

I wanted to shine a flashlight through his concussed eyes up into his amygdala. "You killed him!" I said with flaring nostrils.

"What? Who?"

"Don. Juan. Crustaceo."

"What the hell?! You need to leave. *Now.*" He started doing a little sidestep toward the door, shooing me with his tray.

"*You* should leave. *Now.*"

Which I knew made no sense, but I'd never felt this kind of rage before. Like a fever of hate was taking over my whole body and I could choke him with my bare hands. I hated his smug little face and his self-righteous indignation. I hated that he could dim the lights or close his eyes and it would all feel better. I hated him. I hated Stephan too, and Dara, Julian, Lowenstein, parts of Dr. Ganesh, Linda's sweaters, Durvalumab, Pembrolizumab, and whoever first said, "Can I get a what what?" I hated extraterrestrials and Stephen Hawking and everyone who made eligibility requirements for drug trials just so they could get great results and publish them in thick medical journals that nobody read.

I stole as many jelly packets as I could and stormed out of the Unicorn. Past the spot where Don Juan had been. The same spot where nobody would know about him if they came in right now. Past the host station and potted plants and toothpick dispenser.

Once I was out, I kicked the door. Hard. Harder than I thought, actually. Hard enough to make a popping sound. The glass cracked. I watched in shock as sparkly tentacles shot out across the bottom pane.

This is not happening. This is not happening. This is not happening.

Only it was happening. I saw Topher's head whip around through a window and then he was pointing at me to one of the dishwashers and started toward the door. I sucked in a huge breath and took off running. Through the parking lot, behind the Dumpster, along the wooded side of the golf course, and in and out of side streets. Running, running like I was in one of those bad convict movies where maybe he escapes this time but he can't escape forever.

Running and ducking and hiding and unraveling.

Nobody was safe. Nothing lasted. Never, in the history of time, could we slow or stop ourselves from self-destruction.

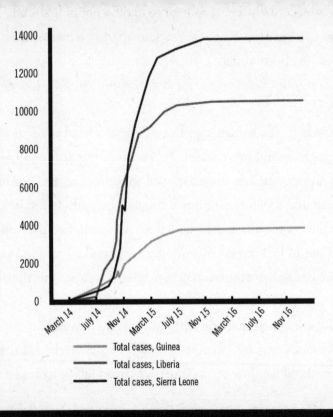

Total cases, Guinea
Total cases, Liberia
Total cases, Sierra Leone

Lingering questions about Ebola outbreak:

How do I know if I have it?

What are we doing to stop it?

Can you look at this rash and please tell me I don'

Chapter 16

PINKY AND WIZZLE

I spent forty-five minutes hiding and sniveling in our rhododendrons while I listened for sirens. Our block was eerily quiet. The dark was too dark and I shivered even though it was mid-May. I could've knocked on someone's door, I guess. But I wasn't really close with any of our neighbors after I overpromised and underdelivered Girl Scout cookies three years before. My attempts at a door-to-door anti-fracking scavenger hunt didn't make me very popular either. I'd never run from the law before. I wasn't actually sure I was doing it now. The saddest part of this whole crime spree was that I'd enraged and lied to so many people in the past few days that I had no idea who would bail me out if needed. That made me feel even sorrier for myself.

I kept checking my phone as if it had forgotten how to tell time. There was no way I'd make it through a whole night crouched in the bushes without either self-harming or getting eaten alive by squirrels. At 11:18 (my birthday numbers) I decided to at least check if any of our doors were unlocked, even though I knew they weren't. But it did make me circle my house and realize I could get into the bunker and go to sleep there.

"Thank you!" I whispered up at the sky, because whatever force was out there, it had spared me this once.

It was mildly exciting to open up one of the space blankets and fold myself into it on the floor. I ate three of my jam packets just to have something to do or taste besides this aching hollowness. Then I got jittery from all the sugar and had to distract myself by looking up facts on my phone about extraterrestrials, asteroids, Ebola outbreaks, and alternative water supplies until my battery died and my eyes started sagging.

When I woke up the next morning, Mom was sitting on the dirt floor next to me, stroking my hair. She acted like it was the most natural, cozy place to be—staring at the moon chart I'd drawn, singing the song she always sang to me before bed when I was little. It was about a little girl named Pinky and a horse named Wizzle. They went on lots of adventures together. I didn't know why it took me sixteen years to realize it, but right then and there I knew that every time Mom sang it, wherever they traveled, they always came back home.

I shut my eyes quickly and tried to go back to sleep. Only my head was so sore and my bladder was about to explode.

"Sorry," I whispered, tripping to the stack of chipped flowerpots I'd designated as the outhouse.

Mom just kept singing. When I was done, I dumped myself back onto the floor and curled into a lump.

"Mom?" I asked.

"Chicken?" she sang quietly.

I didn't have much to say. I just wanted to make sure she was really here and this was actually happening, because the past twenty-four hours had been so surreal and horrible.

"Lost my house key," I said. The fifth set of keys I'd lost in the past three years. Which usually led to a lecture from Mom about responsibility and trust. But things must've been bad because all she said was, "I figured." She kept stroking my head while I bobbed in and out of sleep. Then at some point, she lay down on the floor next to me and we were looking up at the flaky ceiling together.

"I thought I was going crazy when all my canned chickpeas started disappearing," she said, nudging me in the ribs.

"Sorry. When did you notice?"

"A few months ago, I guess." Mom kissed my left hand. "Every bunker needs access to good hummus." She laughed momentarily, propping us both up and making me take a sip from a bottle of warmish water she had.

Then her voice dropped an octave and she said, "At first, I didn't know what you were doing. But Dad reminded me about your research on extinction. I'm not sure what kind of supplies you need, but if I can give you anything . . ."

Instead of finishing her sentence, she wrapped her body around mine and I smushed my cheek into her gray silk blouse. She'd gotten dressed up for the Bad News meeting just yesterday morning. We both had. As if we could put a sassy beret on the truth and make it a party.

Swoosh swoosh swoosh swoosh. I heard her heart working so determinedly. Without her ever asking, it just pumped mightily. This was all that kept us on Earth. This was all we had. This tiny valve, clenching and releasing, clenching and releasing.

I burrowed into her chest farther and started bleating. It was such an ugly noise. Whiny and off-key.

"Oh, my sweet Chicken," Mom whispered into my hair. Her song was just scraps of words now, with long, wavering hums in between. And then she was moaning with me. I could feel her sorrow collecting in her lungs, hitching onto a little swell of breath and floating out in a low *huuuuuuuuuuuh.*

I hated her crying, but I was also so grateful to be collapsing together. There was no plan of attack anymore. There was no way to batten the hatches. There was this eye of the storm, where we sat. Just a moment of surrender, before the winds thrashed us again.

I buried my head in her armpit and said, "I did something bad. I mean, I did a lot of things bad, but one of them could be on a security camera."

"Oh yeah?" Mom asked. She peeled me away from her a little to find my eyes. "Do tell," she said.

I didn't want to go on. But I also didn't want to have any shards of yesterday wedged in my gut anymore. Linda's sweaters and the shit-sandwich boys on the train were all dancing to alien saxophone music, expanding like jumbo shrimp monsters to the edges of my brain.

I took a stick and dug into the dirt floor with it while I

confessed. "Well, first of all I sent some stupid, bad pictures to Dr. Ganesh and I didn't know it was a hospital phone so he might be in big trouble. I used the emergency credit card to buy a gas mask and wine coolers and some water for an endangered elephant named Clara. But I can pay it back, I swear." I felt the tears about to tip out and I didn't stop them. I just wailed and ranted while Mom sat listening.

"And then I did more stupid, bad things with Dr. Ganesh and then the fish tank was gone and it's not fair! They killed this beautiful lobster who had so much charisma and life and everything ahead of him. He could've had a family, you know? So I kicked the diner door, not even that hard but I guess hard enough to break the glass, which I can replace, but how much would that cost do you think? Two hundred? Two thousand? I can babysit every weekend. Three thousand?"

Mom shrugged. I don't think she understood I was really asking for a price estimate.

"Do you think . . . ?" I started. "Well, what do you think?"

"What do I think?" She sighed. "I think that's a lot to digest. First of all, what were those photos you sent to Dr. Ganesh?"

I'd never been so grateful for a dead phone battery in my life. I described the Ambrosia-inspired photo shoot without mentioning Ambrosia herself and then told Mom about all my pathetic follow-up texts and the patient-advocate meeting Dr. Ganesh mentioned. Mom said "Oy" a lot under her breath, but besides that, she let me do all the talking.

"I really don't want him to get in trouble and I told him I

could come to the meeting and explain how it's all my fault or at least write a note, but he said no. But maybe Dad could speak on his behalf? Or all of us could go in there together? They can't fire him, can they? Or suspend his license?"

The more I sounded out the possibilities, the more I wanted to lock the bunker door and never emerge again. Mom was drawing on the floor with a stick too now, as if she could map out a plan.

"Please say something," I begged her.

She put down the stick and cleared her throat. "Okay, my dear. It sounds to me like the best course of action is to let this go. I don't know the hospital protocol on this type of matter, but professionally speaking, if he didn't encourage it and you are not the one suggesting wrongdoing, he's probably in the clear."

"Okay," I said, willing myself to breathe. I was chewing my bottom lip so hard it was throbbing.

"I think you know this by now, but it bears repeating," Mom continued. "Posting any kind of compromising pictures is a really dangerous thing, Lenny."

"I know."

"I know you know. And if you haven't already, you need to erase those."

"Got it."

"C'mere." She pulled me back into her lap and started trying to tame my hair into some braidy updo. "It's going to be okay," she said. "First it's going to be really, really shitty. But then—slowly, surely—we will make it through." I nodded. "You have a lot of babysitting to do, huh?" She poked me in the side.

"I will. I swear. If I don't go to jail for vandalism."

"Bah!" Mom laughed. "My girl's not going to jail. But we do have to go talk to the manager of the diner. In our spare time, right?" She touched one palm to her chest and the other to mine. "Whatever you know, know this. You have an amazing heart, sweet girl."

I looked down at her hand, because I knew I couldn't gaze at her face-on without dissolving again.

When we got inside a few minutes later, Emma's backpack and duffel were emptied all over the den floor and it smelled like her rosemary conditioner, but she'd left a note about going out to get groceries. I felt oddly excited to see her hairbrush spilling out of her bag. I also wanted to sleep for a year before she came back and started grilling me with questions in typical Emma fashion. Mom said she had to make a few work calls to explain that she'd be taking some more time off and that I was welcome to the first shower. I stayed under that stream of scalding water until the fog was so thick in the bathroom I couldn't see my towel. I put my face into the stream and willed it to wash everything away.

As I stepped out into the hall, the cool air slapped me awake. So did the cabinet doors slamming shut and the angry stomping.

"Dried seaweed? Fiber crackers? This is what you should feed housecats, not *people*," Emma yelled. "Mom, you and Lenny need to be eating *real* food."

Mom's voice was much softer and mumbly. Something about not exactly having a lot of spare time to be Martha Stewart. Emma cut her off.

"I'm not talking about whipping up a roasted chicken with fingerling potatoes, Mom. I'm talking about fueling yourself. And is Lenny even taking lunch to school? This is *not* okay!"

I admired Emma's ability to fight. She was the only one in our family who knew how to put up her dukes. She almost thrived on conflict. Which wasn't so fun when I just wanted to hang out or go into town and instead she wanted to tell me what was wrong with my outfit or debate the new online music-sharing rules. But it was times like these that I felt very grateful for her fire.

"Go take your shower," I heard her order Mom. "I'm making eggs and toast with butter and you're going to eat it. We all are."

"Yes, ma'am," Mom said docilely. I got dressed quickly, waited for her to close her bathroom door, and then headed downstairs.

"What was that all about?" I asked Emma.

"Lenin!" Emma said. She rushed over while buttering a piece of toast and clinched me in an airtight hug. "SPF, SPF, SPF," she growled. SPF was Emma's term for *shit piss fuck*. It was only to be used for horrible events, which before now meant a missed concert or when Emma got caught drinking with her SAT tutor. Now we'd entered a whole new stratosphere of SPF-ness.

"Yeah, right?" I whispered back, getting a mouthful of her hair. I pulled away to get a better look at her. In the past two months she had definitely made some big changes. Her honey-colored mane was parted in the middle and had a turquoise streak on the left side. Her worn Rosie the Riveter T-shirt looked like it would split in half if she stretched her hands up.

"Are you like a D-cup all of a sudden?" I asked.

"E," Emma said proudly. "From taking the pill." She shimmied and hopped on one foot to show me how versatile her boobs were before shoving a piece of toast in my mouth. "Breakfast is served!" she hollered.

Emma and Mom were on one side of the kitchen table and I was on the other. Usually I had Dad next to me to make it a little more even. That's how we'd always sat. I had so many questions I wanted to ask that empty chair. Mom cleared her throat and nodded, as if she could hear my confusion.

"A lot to do today," she said.

The toast was buttery and thick. The eggs salty and hot. Emma poured us each coffee and had even sliced up some fresh tomatoes. I couldn't eat it fast enough, I was so hungry.

"I told Mom that you are no longer allowed to subsist on walnuts and sprouts," Emma said, pointing an eggy fork at me. "This is just not an option. We need to be here and be strong for Dad."

"It wasn't intentional," Mom said weakly. I looked at her plate, still piled high with eggs and three-quarters of a piece of toast.

"It doesn't matter, Mom. You can't starve yourself. You can't do this to me and Lenny." Emma twisted her hair back into a bun and stared at Mom's plate defiantly. Mom ate with her head bowed. I forgot too often that she was needy and scared too.

"How long are you staying?" I asked Emma.

"As long as . . . Well, that's what I wanted to ask you guys," she answered. "Is anyone giving us a timeline?"

Mom and I shrugged in sync. Then I added, "Dr. Ganesh said between a few weeks and a few months. He used the words *actively dying.*"

"What about Lowenfeld?" Emma asked.

"Lowenstein," I corrected, "is a putz."

We all went back to eating until there was literally nothing left. Mom pushed back her now-empty plate and said, "That was delicious, Emma, thank you. Now I need to ask you both a question and I don't want you to feel pressured to answer right away. I even made little ballots so you could write about your feelings and tell me truly your thoughts."

She passed out scraps of paper that I could tell from the other side were once an electricity bill. Then she explained that Dad had a choice. He could be transferred to a hospice in the Bronx or he could come home. Both options had their plusses and minuses. The hospice staff was really lovely—she'd spoken to them already and they were very skilled with end-of-life patients. Plus, they had planned activities, social workers, pain management.

"Yeah, but nobody comes out of hospice," said Emma.

"Well." Mom took another sip of coffee. "Yes, it's pretty

unusual for patients to leave there." If Dad came home, Mom continued, we would get a hospital bed and a visiting nurse. And we would do whatever we could to keep him comfortable.

"Just remember," Mom said. "I think it'd be nice to stay in this house after it's all over. But if that would be too hard for you. I mean, if Dad does pass away here, and, then, I know he wants us to be able to live here. So it's just . . . Well, just really think about it," Mom said, cutting herself off.

That was not a great idea. While Emma wrote a tome on her scrap of paper, I just sat there coming up with horror-movie scenarios—Dad clutching the walls in our sky-blue hallway and struggling for air; Dad coughing up blood in our paisley-plagued living room with a scythe above his head; TinyGinsberg coming up to Dad's sickbed and licking his oozing brain.

"Is it . . . messy?" I asked.

"You mean, death?" Mom said.

I nodded. Emma put down her pen.

"I don't know," Mom said thoughtfully. "I wasn't actually in the room when either of my parents died."

I constantly overlooked the fact that Mom was an orphan. She'd lost both her mom and dad just before Emma was born. Grandma had had a stroke while shopping at Marshalls. A saleslady found her at closing in a dressing room holding three coats. Grandma survived, but all she could do for the next year was sit in a dining room chair, talking to ghosts. My grandfather tended to her diligently and started emptying the liquor cabinet into his mouth while they watched *Jeopardy!* Mom was seven months pregnant when her parents' neighbor called to say she'd heard a large crashing sound from my grandparents' house and had gone over to see what was up, but there was no answer at the door.

"Death by coffee table" is how Mom sometimes joked about Grandpa. She was the only one allowed to say things like that. (He'd slipped in a puddle of mint schnapps, which made it even worse somehow.) Grandma lasted another few weeks in facilitated care, but she refused to eat. It was probably the worst year of Mom's life—losing both her parents in the space of two months. And then Emma was born.

To be honest, I never asked Mom about her parents. She only brought them up in passing and there was exactly one picture of them in our home—black and white and posed in stiff smiles that I didn't trust. The idea of Mom parentless took on a whole new texture now, though. Also, I was starting to connect why Emma was getting so worked up about Mom's poor eating habits.

"I'm sorry," I whispered. I was sorry that Mom was losing so much and that I never gave her credit for all that she'd lost already.

"It's okay, Chicken," she said.

"No, it's definitely not okay," said Emma. "It's suckier than all the suck in suckdom." She folded her piece of paper and handed it to Mom. I wrote *HOME* on mine and gave it to Mom too.

She read them both and smiled shyly.

"I have the best girls in the whole world," she murmured. With both arms extended, she pulled Emma and me into the middle of the table so our foreheads touched. Emma took the opportunity to lick my nose. It felt miraculous to laugh, even with a slimy nostril. I gave her a wet willy in return.

The three of us headed to a medical supply shop that Mom had looked up in the next town over. She rented a hospital bed that had so many features it could double as a spaceship. We also picked out a little portable speaker so Dad could listen to his jazz compilations, a new inflatable pillow for his butt, and a sitz bath. Emma and I were in agreement that the picture of an older woman giving a thumbs-up to her steaming sitz needed to be illegal.

Then Emma picked out a medical marijuana vaporizer. She said she'd brought home some "premium herbs." I thought she'd get a talk from Mom about being respectful of the law, but she just paid for the supplies and ushered us back to the car. The owner of the store followed us home in his delivery truck and wheeled Dad's bionic Posturepedic into the entryway of our house. We would have to do a lot of rearranging before there was even a big enough pathway to the den.

"Okay," Mom said once the man left. "So, that took a little longer than expected, and I wanted to pick up Dad and sign some release forms by three." She looked at the bed and tried to shove it at least to the other side of our upright piano, but the wheels on the bottom screeched angrily across the wood floor.

"Mom, you go," said Emma. "We'll handle this."

"Right," Mom said, unconvinced. "I do have that cleaning service coming soon and maybe when Julian stops by he can help too."

"Wait, you spoke to Julian?" I asked, trying not to squeak.

"Yes," Mom said. "Several times." Which meant she knew I wasn't with Julian last night. "He's the one who had the brilliant idea of looking for you in the toolshed," Mom explained. "Love that kid," she added, patting her heart to remind me of our talk.

Blood Moon Prophecy

Once upon a time there was a little girl named Eleanor who loved to talk to the moon at night. Then she read about the Blood Moon Prophecy and how it was going to mark the end of the world and she got anxiety attacks for a month straight after sundown.

The Blood Moon Prophecy is something that sounds like it should be a hoax because why would a lunar eclipse that makes the moon glow red be the universal "time's up" signal?

But then I found some footage online of this guy in Omaha who zoomed his camera in on the moon at its "bloodiest," and even Julian admitted it was creepy. There are too many scientists perplexed by this phenomenon too. The next blood moon tetrad—four total lunar eclipses with no partial lunar eclipses in between—is scheduled for 2032–2033.

Party at my house.

Chapter 17

JUST A DAY

I knew it was humanly possible, but I found it really hard to giggle and be incensed at the same time.

Julian pulled into our driveway just a few minutes after the Pinch Hitters Cleaning Crew did. I was all prepared to tell him something like, "Thank you for coming by and for your years of support and friendship, but I don't need you to move my couch or for anything else."

Julian wasn't interested in my speech, though. He leapt out of the driver's seat before the Jetta had fully coughed to a stop and said, "Ta da!"

He was wearing the most ludicrous powder-blue tuxedo with a matching ruffled shirt underneath. He did a little clickety-clackety dance step and I saw he had on patent-leather shoes that were at least three sizes too big.

"Maestro?" he said, snapping his fingers. A derby hat flew out from the passenger seat and just missed clocking him in the face. Julian let it fall and switched gears quickly to scoop me into his arms instead.

"Never did like sports," he muttered. I didn't realize until that moment how much I missed his coffee breath.

Someone in the car was playing the twinkly ballerina music from my showcase solo. I tried to peek in and see who it was, but Julian held me to him tightly.

"Hey, concentrate," he said in a sharp but playful tone. He whirled me around the car in a wide, lilting waltz. Even with the huge shoes and nylon ensemble, he was the epitome of elegance.

"How did you know I was in my bunker?" I asked. Julian smiled, but didn't say a word.

"Okay," I continued. "And where did you get this cheesy outfit and why does it smell like mildew and how much did my mom tell you and who is that watching us in the front seat of your vehicle?"

"Shhhhh," whispered Julian. He led me through a few more loops of the driveway before depositing me in front of the passenger-side door.

"Hiya," came a gravelly but now familiar voice from inside the car.

"Oscar?!" I sounded much more eager than I meant to.

"Yeah, hey."

Julian pulled us away from the Jetta and did a little ceremonial bow. "May I present to you . . . Mister Meowsome!"

Oscar stepped out with a more restrained, "Ta da?"

He had on a green T-shirt with a calico cat ironed on and neon yellow lettering on top that said MISTER MEOWSOME. He was also wearing lavender-and-navy checkered bell-bottoms and a rainbow sweatband on either wrist. His mop top was flecked with wood shavings.

"Meowsome is my wingman," Julian explained. Then Julian got on one knee and cleared his throat a good half dozen times before saying, "Eleanor Miriam Rosenthal-Hermann, will you please go to the prom with me?" He reached into his suit coat pocket and produced two tickets that he fluttered in front of his face.

This had to be a joke.

"Um . . . wait, why?" I asked.

Oscar started laughing. It was the first time I'd ever seen him enjoying himself. He had a long dimple on his left cheek and a handprint of dirt just below it.

"I told you she wouldn't make this easy for me," Julian said, getting up and dusting off his knee. "Thanks for the moral support, Meowsome. I'll take it from here. Keys are in the car. Ignore the oil-change light."

"You sure?" asked Oscar. He looked from Julian to me uncertainly. Then he pulled his backpack out of the car and started digging through pockets, looking for something. He pulled out a ball of newspaper and handed it to me.

"You don't have to open it now. Or ever for that matter. I just thought you might . . ." He let that sentence end in a shrug and got in the driver's seat, closing the door. Julian and I just stood there watching him until the Jetta disappeared over the hill.

"He's definitely a strange one," Julian said. "But I have to say he's smart as shit and really kind." He pointed to the crumpled newspaper in my hand. "Sorry. He was with me when your mom told me what was going on and he saw how . . . Well, he saw me shaken up."

Inside the newspaper was the crystal that had been hanging from Marty's first-aid kit. Now that it was in my hand I could see all the wild golden veins inside.

"He said it was for inner compassion and healing. Or something like that," said Julian.

"He did?" I chirped. I thought Oscar was such a snob just a few days ago. But I guess a few days ago I thought I could cure cancer with sheer devotion and a bunch of hand sanitizers. I had never heard of Kepler-62 or alien saxophone music or spent a night under a space blanket, too hurt to hurt more.

I held the stone up toward the light and inspected it. "Do you believe in that stuff?" I asked Julian.

"I believe in love, honesty, and caffeine." Julian took the amber from me and passed it back and forth from hand to hand. "Yeah, that guy's sweet. If you won't go to prom with me, I'll give him the tickets and you should go with him. Though I think he's scared of high heels."

There was too much new information being thrown at me. I took the amber back and tucked it into my jeans pocket for safekeeping, then tried to start from the beginning of my confusion. "Wait, you were serious about the prom?"

Julian scanned the tickets in his hand. "I think they're real. Paid good money for them." He shoved them under my nose. "Well, maybe not *good* money," he said. "Katya already moved half her office into my bedroom, so I helped myself to a few of her checks. Let the games begin!"

"Did you spend her money on this tuxedo too?" I asked. Up close I could see the blue ruffled shirt was ripping at the shoulder seam.

"Nah, Oscar and I went to this awesome secondhand store up in Poughkeepsie because Marty wanted us to get twenty-two burlap sacks for the show. Five bucks for these sweet threads." He ran his hands up and down his body and did a wormy dance move that made me want to crack up, but I bit my cheek to stop myself.

"There's actually a few strapless dresses there too, but I couldn't tell what you'd like," Julian continued. "I was going to get this flowery number, but Oscar said you were cooler than that."

That time a smile escaped before I could stop it. Julian caught me and started hopping up and down.

"There she is! My Lenny's back! I missed you, girl."

I shut back down into a frown. I knew it was childish, but I didn't want him to think he could get me back so easily.

"Hey, what happened?" he asked. "Where'd you go?" He gripped both of my wrists and shook my arms a little. "Listen, I don't think you believe me when I tell you how much you mean to me. But it's true." I bored my eyes into the ground while he went on. "I'm sorry. I really am. I didn't want to tell you about San Francisco because I didn't want to upset you, but then there was no way not to upset you because your dad . . ."

His voice started wobbling. I looked up without meaning to and saw there were tears in his eyes. "I just really love him," he moaned. "He's the kind of dad I wish I could be." He dove into me and I could feel his tears tickling my right collarbone. I didn't dare move. I wanted to cry too, but I couldn't. So we stayed there in the driveway for I don't know how long as Julian sniffled into my neck.

Eventually, Emma called from the front steps, "You guys re-enacting that penguin movie?"

Julian popped his head up and she must've seen his pink tear splotches. She ran out in bare feet and joined our hug.

"Whoa," said Julian. "Double D?"

"E," whispered Emma. We both took turns using her new and inflated boobs as a headrest until she made us get off. "What about you?" she asked, pulling on Julian's ruffled collar. "Is this a new look or a special occasion, Monsieur le Freak?"

Julian winked at me. "I had to find some way to get my girl back and tell her that I love her." He held out his elbow for me to loop my arm through his. "Would you be willing to stroll with me to the Unicorn Diner, m'lady?"

My skin prickled and I shook my head involuntarily. Until that moment, I'd forgotten about my possible vandalism charge. Plus, I had yet to tell Julian about Don Juan, the Ambrosia sel-fies, and Dr. Ganesh's lips on mine.

"I think we have a lot to do around here to get ready for my dad coming home," I said.

"It's all good," said Emma. "The cleaning crew is great. And

I'm just gonna put my stuff away and do a few loads of wash. Get out of here."

Julian poked me with his elbow again.

"Okay . . ." I didn't know where to begin though. "Can we do Carvel instead?" I squeaked.

"Carvel it is," Julian answered.

We walked slowly, deliberately. Most of the time we were silent, which was such a gift. We got to Carvel just as they were closing. Julian paid for a sleeve of flying saucers and we decided to take a walk around the little pond behind our public ice-skating rink. Julian told me about Katya's fights with the construction company and the two dog beds that had been hand-stitched specifically for Daphne and sent back because they were too rough for her sensitive skin.

After eating so much ice cream my lips felt numb, I blurted out, "I kissed him."

"What?" Julian stopped. "Who?"

I told him about the horrible meeting and the wine coolers and how I wanted to be Sheena the cashier's midwife and I might've lost Dr. Ganesh a job but my mom didn't think so because it was really my fault.

"Listen to Nutbags," Julian assured me. "She knows the law. And hey"—he pulled me in so tight I could almost count his nose hairs—"I'm really proud of you for smooching that man. That was ballsy."

We circled the pond another three or four times—I stopped keeping track. There were new leaves sprouting everywhere and we saw a family of turtles playing something like hide-and-seek. I heard the train coming into our station downtown and thought about how it would keep running no matter who was getting on or off.

"Hey," said Julian, pointing up at something blinking through the darkening sky. "I think tonight is supposed to be that partial eclipse. Didn't you say the nineteenth?"

"Did I?" I went to check the moon tracker on my phone and saw I'd left it at home. "Honestly, I don't know what the date is. Is it the nineteenth today?"

"Who cares?" said Julian. He took my hand and swung it back and forth. "Today is just a day."

Supervolcanoes

My whole
family went to
Yellowstone National
Park when I was nine.

Emma got a cowgirl hat and
I got homemade moccasins and
Mom got this weird bug bite that
made her whole knee hot. But it was
amazing to see the geysers and we drank
as much soda as we wanted on the plane.

What I didn't know then, and wish
I didn't know now, is that Yellowstone
is on top of a supervolcano.

The last three super-eruptions in recorded
history were right there. The most recent one
(640,000 years ago) had 100,000-foot-tall pillars of ash
and lethally hot fogs that were about 1,470 degrees Fahrenheit.

There is something strangely beautiful about
Earth sort of turning itself inside out like that.
And that trip to Yellowstone is one of my favorite
memories of us all together.

Chapter 18

FINDING FINIAN

Dad looked pretty much the same as the last time I'd seen him. Which was only about twenty-eight hours before. Or a lifetime. Depending on how I was counting. I actually thought he'd grown back a few more eyelashes and had the beginnings of stubble on his gaunt cheeks. The top of his head was a patchwork of peach fuzz. He walked up our path, hanging on Mom like a piece of loose scaffolding.

Julian hummed the theme song from *Rocky* as Dad reached our front door. We all cheered as Dad stopped to flex what was once a hefty biceps muscle. I was so glad Julian had decided to hang out with us. It made this homecoming a little less intimate and terrifying. I tried to get him to stay for supper too, but we'd each had three flying saucers from Carvel and couldn't pretend to be hungry. Also, Julian had to refocus some lights with Marty and it was obvious Dad was exhausted from the car ride home.

"Really glad you're back," Julian said. "I'll see you this week for sure." He leaned in and gave Dad a hug easily. Yet another talent I was lacking. I was sure I'd snap Dad's skeletal frame. Or I'd open my arms and he'd be a pile of dust.

"You're a good man, J," Dad said, watching Julian go. I couldn't help thinking that might be the last time they saw each other.

I thought that about everything, actually. *This could be the last time I hand Dad the remote. This could be the last time he asks for a glass of water.* I knew I was supposed to be treasuring every moment of us all being together, but that first night of Dad being back felt so treacherous. I couldn't be alone in the same room as Dad. Everything felt too fragile and I was sure he'd die in the middle of his next sentence. Emma looked at me running in and out of the den, opening windows and fetching unsolicited snacks, and found it hysterical.

"We should get Lenny and TinyGinsberg matching chew toys. Or do they make human-size wheels so she could just jog in one spot?" She giggled.

"C'mon now," Dad said. They were stretched out on his new deluxe aerodynamic mattress side by side, staring out the picture window at the backyard. Emma was rubbing some arnica cream into the bruises on his hands and arms from all the needles he'd had in the hospital. I hated that she could hold and soothe him so effortlessly. As opposed to the last time I tried to be his caregiver, which led to incredible anguish and an almost fatal fever. I didn't dare look at his chest for lingering signs of that recent tragedy.

"Seriously," said Emma the next time I dropped off a bowl of crackers, "can you slow down for just a sec?"

"Why?" I shot back bitterly. Then I saw the look of surprise on Dad's face and tried to reword. "I mean, there's just a lot to do right now. Mom's interviewing another home nurse and I'm about to make supper." I went to the kitchen and put some water in a pot to boil, just in case Emma wanted to verify my story.

Mom's interviews took forever—mostly because she kept asking each candidate about their hobbies and aspirations. She was a firm believer in rapport. Again, a gene I admired but couldn't seem to access the way Emma could. I made a feast of the blandest boiled foods I knew—noodles, broth, oatmeal, hard-boiled eggs. I didn't know if Dad could eat any of it. It was just something to do besides watch Emma and Dad snuggle and snicker while she scrolled through pictures of her dorm-mates.

I came in one more time to deliver Dad's seven o'clock pain meds.

"Come join us, Len," he said. "We just got to the Night of a Thousand Genders." He patted the little margin of bed space next to him. "I'm getting a real lesson in anatomy here."

"Just a minute. Something's burning or boiling I think." I retreated back to the kitchen for another half hour until I heard Mom close the door on the last home health-care applicant.

The supper I concocted was borderline inedible. "You don't have to," I said every time Dad tried to sip more oversalted broth. Emma and Mom poured themselves each a glass of white wine and I was ready to join them, but even sniffing the bottle brought back too many Grand Central memories.

I did all the dishes—twice—before curling up on the couch next to Mom to watch some double-agent spy movie from the eighties that she and Dad loved. Emma popped a big bowl of popcorn and again climbed into bed with Dad. I was worried he couldn't digest popcorn or a kernel would make him cough up whatever was left of his insides. Nobody else shared this concern. I stared at his jaw, opening and shutting, opening, shutting. And at Dad and Emma, chuckling as their hands fished through the popcorn bowl, sometimes grazing each other.

By the closing credits, Dad and Emma both had their eyes closed. Mom tried to get her up to go to her own bed, but Emma just burrowed her nose into Dad's pillow. He was oblivious.

"Oh well," Mom said. "I guess that's fine." She looked at me as if she was asking for my approval. Or maybe she was asking for permission to collapse in her own bed. She hadn't slept there for more than a cumulative eight hours over the past week. The gray circles under her eyes just kept dipping lower and lower.

"This is fine," I told her, though I had no idea if it was.

When I was sure her light was out and the house was quiet, I started a little chart of Dad's nutritional intake. And how much fresh air he got. And whether or not he started talking in gibberish (something I'd read about people who were approaching death). Really, in my head it was my "Is This It?" chart. But I'd never say that out loud. Or even close to my consciousness.

Action	Friday	Saturday	Sunday
Drink water	Yes—three glasses (filtered)		
Eat	½ bowl of broth Five penne noodles Popcorn		
Get fresh air	Yes		
Good spirits	Yes		
Lose consciousness suddenly	No		
Speak in gibberish	No		
Froth at the mouth	No		
Uncontrollable screaming	No		
Rattling sound in back of throat	No		

I made the chart in one of those computer programs that just keeps generating more columns, so there was no visible end.

I couldn't get my eyes to close until almost four, and when I did, my nightmares were epic. First, I was picking out peaches at our grocery store and I spied my dad sneaking to the checkout. He was totally healthy but obviously avoiding me. When I asked him where he was going, he said, "Sorry. I have to go home to my real family now." I watched as he got into a station wagon with Chelsea Diamond at the wheel.

The second one was gristlier physically. He looked bone thin and could barely stand up. He kept knocking on the door, but Julian told me not to let him in. I didn't know who to listen to. Then we all went to Yellowstone again, but we had to run from the volcano because it was spitting fire at us. When we got back to the hotel, I couldn't find my room key. I turned my jeans pockets inside out and there was my dad. He was just a stick-figure drawing now. When I woke up from that one, I'd wet my bed.

The sky was just turning lavender and I thought I was the first one up. I changed my clothes, pulled all my sheets off, and carried the wet bundle downstairs to drop it in the washing machine. I stopped off for a cup of coffee since the pot was already gurgling. That's when I noticed the open box of Cheerios on the counter and the dish towel stuffed under the basement door.

Emma didn't even notice me heading down the creaky basement steps. All the lights were on and she was tearing through the big Tupperware of paper plates and Halloween decorations, with a pink tiara on her head that said BIRTHDAY PRINCESS. There was a laptop computer open next to her, perched on a shelf next to Mom's case binders. A studly-looking guy with olive skin and a long nose was on the screen, singing something in Spanish.

"Hello?" I asked.

Emma yelped in surprise. Then she rushed over to me as if I'd just come home from the war and we were long-lost lovers.

"Lennylennylennyloo! Oh my darling, I love youuuuu!" She tried to pick me up but I was carrying a load of wet bedding, so she could barely get her arms around me and she fell backward on her butt, cackling. She reeked of pot. The guy on the screen lifted up a blue speckled bong and started cackling too.

"Owwww!" Emma howled. "That was my coccyx!"

"You have a cock sex?" the screen-stud asked.

"Coccyx," I corrected him. "It's a vital part of your spinal anatomy."

The guy looked shocked. Then he craned his head around seemingly to look at his spine and make sure he had a coccyx too.

Emma was rolling on the cement floor of the basement saying, "Manuel, meet Lenny. Lenny, Manuel. I can't believe you two haven't met yet. You're both so important to me and you both have coccyxes. Coccyx? Cocci?"

Manuel blew me a kiss and said, "It is an honor to meet you."

"Thanks," I mumbled. "You too." I wasn't a teetotaler or anything, but I really didn't want to be around the two of them while they discussed the plural form of coccyx and floated into some altered state of reality.

"Aren't you supposed to be with Dad?" I asked sternly.

"Am I?" she said, ignoring my pout.

"Forget it." I pushed past her and pretended to be fascinated with the process of getting my sheets into the washing machine and pouring the detergent.

"Lenny, how long do you think I should take off from

school?" Emma whined. She was on the floor, now pedaling an imaginary bicycle above her. "Manuel thinks I should come back now and finish out the semester, but I told him Dad isn't gonna make it 'til summer break."

Her words hit me like a belly flop off the high dive. I spun around as fast as I could and tried to harpoon her with my icy glare. "Emma," I said in my lowest voice, "stop. Now."

"I know you don't like talking about it, but you never like talking about anything and we have to talk about it because it's really happening and things don't not happen because you don't talk about them. Plus, Manuel had this great idea that we could get out all the holiday decorations and we could celebrate all the holidays with Dad one last time or he could pick his favorite holiday and we could make it Halloween or Christmas or even Passover. I don't know why he likes matzo so much, do you?" Emma was rummaging again through the strings of lights and wrapping her arms with streamers.

"No!" I screamed. "No, Emma, this is not—no!" I walked over to the computer, where Manuel was watching us both while he pulled out a hair from his tongue piercing. "Goodbye, Manuel," I said, slamming the computer shut. Emma's head snapped at the sound, but she kept decorating herself, adding ornaments to her ears now too.

"It's not Manuel's fault," she said.

"I know," I spat back. "It's *yours*."

"How is it my fault?"

"You can't say things like that out loud. You're putting that energy out in the world and you're making it like a done deal. We don't know if—we just don't know!"

I was so outraged and indignant and outraged again. Emma had no right to proclaim the end was here and then flaunt her fearlessness while I cowered.

"Hey," she said. "I'm sorry." She came over to me and tied some tinsel around my shoulders like a shawl. Then she pulled me down next to her, our backs against the washing machine, letting the whirr and swish rock us back and forth. "You're right," Emma said. "We just don't know."

I couldn't remember a single time in Rosenthal-Hermann history when Emma had told me I was right.

"Did you really just say that?" I asked. "You *must* be high."

"Nah," she said wearily. "I wish. I only smoked a little because Manuel wanted to."

"Do you really like him?" I asked.

"I don't know. The sex is okay, I guess. We only have fun together when we're smoking things, though. It's certainly not love, but I guess it's my coping mechanism of the moment." I didn't say anything. "What about you?" she asked. "How are you dealing, besides cleaning out all the cabinets and hiding in the shed?"

I shrugged.

"Mom said you had a little private meeting with Dr. Hottie. Is that true?"

"No!" I jumped up defensively. "And even if it was true, it's none of your beeswax."

"Whoa whoa whoa." Emma stood up to look at me straight on. "You realize that you cannot say the words *none of your beeswax* after you hit puberty, right?"

"I don't say it to anybody except you!" I squawked, throwing the tinsel back in her face. This was us in a soggy nutshell. Trying to find our way to a new connection, then clicking back into our old roles of bickering. I felt like I had this choice to make—stalk off, as usual, or see what would happen if I stayed.

Emma heard my inner debate without me saying anything more. "Before you leave, can I just show you something funny I found?" she asked.

"I guess."

She sifted through the streamers and party hats to unfurl a big, fuzzy picture of a Yangtze finless porpoise taped to some worn-out poster board.

"Finian!" I yelped. Emma handed me the sad-looking artifact with a smile. For my seventh birthday party, Mom had gotten pin-the-tail-on-the-donkey, but I'd just watched a nature program about endangered porpoises. (Their close relatives the Baiji dolphins were the first species of dolphin to be wiped out by human activity.) I told Mom that we needed to do pin-the-fin-on-the-finless-porpoise instead and she said, "If we have time," which I knew was a fancy way of saying, "No."

So Emma walked me downtown to the library to get a

picture book of porpoises. We enlarged it on the copy machine until it was so big it just looked like a sea of gray with two black holes for eyes. And then, because Emma loved adventure, she copied her bare butt and gave the image to the librarian. I was so sure we'd get carted away by the police or at least banned from the library for life that I took off running without paying for my copies. Really, that grainy porpoise mug shot marked the beginning of my life of crime.

"What else did Mom tell you?" I asked Emma now, holding Finian to my chest. I didn't wait for her to answer. "Vandalism, riding the train while intoxicated, and jeopardizing Ganesh's job. Also I almost starved the guinea pig to death. Not bad for a young felon, huh?"

"She didn't tell me any of that," Emma said. "She just said she was worried about you. And so am I." She yanked me into a tight bear hug. It was so warm and quiet folded into her chest.

I didn't want to blubber all over her hair, so I whispered, "Thank you for finding Finian."

"I would do anything for you. If you let me," Emma said.

RADHAKRISHNAN GANESH, M.D., Ph.D.

Medical Oncology Resident   917-555-0198

PATIENT'S NAME _____ AGE _____

ADDRESS _____ DATE _____

R⟨

It is all good.

_____
SIGNATURE

☐ LABEL

REFILL   0   1   2   3   4   PRN   NR

Chapter 19

WHAT TO EXPECT

Mom handed me the prescription from Dr. Ganesh while we were cooking a big Sunday breakfast. I burst into tears in the middle of the kitchen, giddy with relief.

"What is it?" Emma asked over and over again while I clutched the note, trying to form sentences.

"He's a very gracious man," explained Mom. "I'm glad no Ganeshes were harmed in the making of this story."

Emma helped me craft a farewell text to him. I already had a few drafts that I hadn't sent yet—luckily.

Thank you for your time, patience, and wisdom. I'm sorry if I made you feel . . .

"Violated" sounded too harsh, but "uncomfortable" didn't cut it.

Thank you for your kindness. I wish you peace and light.

"That sounds like you're joining a nunnery," Emma said.

We settled on **Be well.** The response was silence, of course. If I was Dr. Ganesh, I would've traded that phone in or blocked incoming texts long ago. But it still felt good to do. I also deleted his number along with the Ambrosia selfie series from my phone and fist-bumped myself with my reflection in the oven.

On Monday morning, I heard a honk from our driveway a half hour earlier than usual.

Just out of shower, I texted Julian.

Congrats. Just out of bed, he wrote back.

It wasn't his Jetta outside our house. It was the Batmobile, with my mom at the wheel. When she saw me at the bathroom window she waved wildly and revved the engine.

"Sarge, you're nuts!" I heard Dad call from the den down-stairs.

"This is the one, right?" she yelled back.

"Exactly," Dad said. "Nuts," he repeated.

It wasn't really the real Batmobile, of course. It was some sleek half-electric, half-french-fry-oil sports car that I guess Dad had always wanted to try. He couldn't drive it because his legs were so weak and sitting for long periods of time was no longer an option. But Mom came in and told us she'd leased it for a month and even rigged it up with a fancy new doughnut pil-low in the passenger seat. She also had a map of the Hudson Valley and she and Dad started plotting out day trips.

I wondered how Mom had decided on a month.

I caught her by the coffeemaker and whispered, "What hap-pens after a month?"

"We have the option to lease it again," she whispered back.

"That's it?"

"Or buy it, I guess. Might not be such a bad idea since it's gonna come down in price soon."

It was a relief to go back to school. At least there I had to pretend to think about other things, like how to preserve my nerd status after getting a 72 percent on my Cold War midterm. Final labs were being assigned in physics, our Spanish teacher announced she was seven months *embarazada* (as if we couldn't tell), and there were posters for *I Have But One Desire* all over the school. They were collages of iris buds and female protest marchers. By midday, every single poster I saw had genitalia-based graffiti on it. The most imaginative was *I Have But One ~~Desire~~ICK, YO!*

The show itself was in turmoil. Marty passed out the burlap sacks and there was a swift uprising.

"Um, excuse me?" asked a horrified Becca. "I'm supposed to sing the most meaningful song I've ever written in this?"

"Georgia celebrated the simplicity of each shape and nuance," answered Marty. "This way we get to see how you extract her vision."

"Such bullshit," Becca muttered in the locker room. "I worked hard for this body."

"Right?" someone agreed.

I was happy to wear something big and formless, except it was incredibly itchy and smelled like hay and dry-cleaning chemicals. That made me think again about who would wear all of my dad's stored suits after he was gone. And if he knew which one he wanted to be buried in. Or maybe he wanted to be cremated. These were just a few of the questions I was too timid to ask.

I'd been watching carefully and taking notes on Dad's behavior—four glasses of water and an Italian ice. Still no gibberish or rattling. The closest I got to a "sign" that this was really the end was when Barry—Dad's best friend from law school—came over for a visit. He held me by both shoulders and shook me a little. "Damnit," he said. "Damnit, damnit, damnit." Then he pulled me in for a hug so strong it lifted me off the ground. I could feel a sob rising through his chest.

That night, I filled in a few more boxes on my "Is This It?" chart, but I wasn't sure what to track anymore. Dad seemed to be doing everything living people did, just more thoughtfully. He still bit his lower lip when he was thinking hard or about to break out into a smile. His teeth looked extra large to me. Maybe because the rest of him was shrinking. I was so sick of trying to figure out what was happening and nobody giving me answers. Not that I knew what to ask. And I felt guilty that I kept on wanting to know when Dad was going to die. I didn't want to come downstairs each morning and say, "Hey, Dad. How you doing? You think today's the day?"

I did some more research about timelines for terminal illness, which was not only depressing but also totally inconclusive. I needed more information about how this was all going to happen and how long we were going to be suspended in this horrible limbo.

"Let's try this!" yelled Julian, breaking through my reverie from the back row of the theater.

We now had a total of three monologues and four dance pieces, plus Becca's ballad of devotion. Only nobody could remember the words or the choreography. We had to keep stopping and starting. Julian was shouting out everyone's cues and Marty was making us take emotional inventory. By nightfall, they both looked frazzled. Julian had now inserted himself into every dance so at least there was someone onstage to follow. Our turkey-baster piece was the finale at this point because it was at least well-rehearsed and concise. Marty looked pretty distraught about the rest of the acts. She kept lunging around the auditorium doing a sort of word association—"Freedom. Femininity. Fury. For all future."

I felt bad for her. She had poured so much of herself into this fiasco. I thought of telling her that no one in the end-of-life data I'd read had valued work over family. She knew that, though. Every time we were on break, I saw her sharing coconut water with Oscar or going over chord progressions on the piano. I had to thank him for that healing amber he'd given me. Nobody in my family had noticed it yet, which made me really happy for some reason. I wanted to tell Oscar that every day around five it turned the den into this warm sunbath. I was sort of saving that conversation for a reward once rehearsal was over.

Except Marty kept us there until eleven on Monday night. At which point Julian said he was getting in his car and either I came now or he'd see me in Georgia's vajayjay. I was exhausted too, but more than that I was scared to go home and see how much was left of my dad.

When I walked through the door, he and Mom cheered. They were so excited to see me and tell me all about their Batmobile adventures. They'd gone all the way up to a beach in Connecticut where the seagulls had wingspans a yard long. Then on the way back, they'd stopped at some petting zoo and fed a blind elephant. Mom kept on trying to tell me something about the elephant's trunk breath, but she dissolved into giggles.

"Guess it's working," said Emma, holding up Dad's pot vaporizer. I realized the whole house had a skunky funk to it now, and I was jealous and hungry, but all I could do was plop myself on the couch and close my eyes.

So my dad did not die on Monday. Or Tuesday, Wednesday, or Thursday, for that matter. He actually had a fabulous week, zipping up and down the Hudson Valley with Mom and sometimes Emma. I was worried they were getting high all the time, but Emma assured me she'd only brought home a little and Mom and Dad were ridiculous lightweights and never drove while under the influence. Dad was high on life, though. Tuesday night he told me about getting a watermelon ice pop that touched every one of his senses. Wednesday, it was the view from West Point that took his breath away. Thursday morning, while I was saying goodbye before school, Dad saw a squirrel carrying a hoagie roll back from the deli on our corner and laughed so loudly I thought he was choking. But he wasn't. He was just thoroughly amused.

Thursday's *VaGeorgia* escapades were extra ridiculous. With twenty-four hours until curtain time, Becca announced in the locker room that she was quitting because Marty was trying to make us all look like fools. Four of her minions threw down their burlap ensembles and said they'd go too. Then a ninth grader named Nikki said she'd never felt like she had female role models or a group before this and if the show didn't happen, she didn't know what she'd do. A lot of tears and accusations after that. Marty said we could all take a ten-minute break while she tried to sort through our options.

I sent Dad a message: **Still at rehearsal. U up?**

He wrote back: **Take your time. Watching Honeymooners.**

Marty was dancing out her aggression onstage. There were clutches of girls in different levels of hysteria all around the auditorium. I thought of taking a moment to thank Oscar for his present, but he was all the way on the other side of the room listening to Julian rant. So I took my notebook and went to sit on the hill outside the auditorium.

I'd never been cool enough for sitting on this hill before. At lunchtime, it was reserved for the stoners and the kids who belonged to yacht clubs. At ten thirty at night it was completely empty, of course. I could see all the way out to the little forest preserve a few miles away where Emma and I once caught a turtle. We put it in a metal soup pot and fed it Apple Jacks, but it ran away.

It ran away, and I never went looking. I never went back to the preserve and checked to see if it found its way home to the marshy inlet. Or maybe we'd caused it to get horribly sick with sugared cereal. I never thought about how slow it all could be— life and death and waiting. I opened my notebook and tried to get back to the research I'd been working on all week. Some of it was from what I'd read. The rest was kind of just what I hoped could be true.

"Packing list?" I heard behind me. This time I knew it was Oscar's voice right away. I felt a tear catch the page and automatically slammed my notebook shut. "Sorry," he said. "I didn't see anything."

Turning around to face him, I felt shy but also so grateful he was here. He had a bandana holding back his hair and it looked like a cartoon halo, glittering in the security lights from the parking lot.

"That's okay," I said. "You can look if you want."

So he sat down next to me and read what I'd written. I didn't try to explain which was fact or fear or wish or wonder.

I closed my eyes as Oscar read, hearing his breath get slower, and then the tiniest *pwaa* as his lips parted into a smile.

What to Expect When You're Expecting (to Die)

Long, shallow breaths with pauses in between
    Rattling sound
    Yellowish film over the irises
    Tunnel vision with mysterious "light"
    Hallucinatory tastes, smells, touches
    Gasping, choking, bleeding from mouth

    There is no day or night
    There is just loud or soft or itchy or cool
    You love peanut butter for the first (and last) time
    You feel music under your fingernails
    You fall in love with Italian ices, squirrels, and the color turquoise
    You know it will continue. Somehow.

Probability:
    100 percent

Preventive measures:
    none

Chapter 20

AND SO IT BEGINS

"And so it begins!" called Marty. She charged through the backstage area and had us form a lopsided circle. We held hands, eyes closed, and listened to the packed auditorium. Becca's mom was always the loudest in a crowd. I heard her gushing over Emma's new hair color and talking about how "our girls weren't just girls anymore." Mom wasn't much quieter. I'd made my family vow they'd sit toward the back so I didn't have to look any of them in the eye or hear Mom yell, "Delicious!" when she liked something. I also really wanted Dad seated near an exit sign in case he was too uncomfortable in one of those ancient auditorium folding chairs.

"Okay, now let's bring our focus inward for a moment," Marty said. She chanted something really eerily beautiful in Sanskrit.

"I just asked our foremothers to bless the energy of this group and to thank the universe for this incredible night," she said. She looked around the circle, catching each of us with her swirly gray eyes. "You have all gone above and beyond my wildest dreams for this production. Saying yes to this astounding artist. Yes to this groundless space of fruition. Yes to yourselves."

Becca got a special wink after that statement. The nth-hour truce between her and Marty had involved a lot of cathartic venting and both of them admitting they had issues with their moms and felt stifled in their youths. Marty then asked the cast if she could perform a "kinesthetic poem" based on the life of O'Keeffe instead of people trying to memorize monologues. There was a resounding *yes* to that one. The burlap sacks were trashed and people were allowed to wear whatever they wanted. Becca had on a spandex one-piece that opened in the back and was a little see-through. Most of the other girls had on variations in Lycra.

I'd been planning to just stick to my scratchy hay-infused shift, but Emma said that was unacceptable. She took a few hours yesterday to find me a billowy green shift and awesome orange tights. She even got me a black leotard to wear underneath that had some boob padding in it for "shelf life." I could tell she was getting pretty restless being home and also that she was not used to doing things like waking up before ten on the weekends or listening to music below DEFCON levels. I was so grateful to have her back, though.

I was also in awe of how incredible she was with Dad—giving him long scalp massages and reading through the newspaper to him so he didn't have to strain his eyes. Most impressive to me was watching her gently ease his body into a new position when he was feeling nauseous or uncomfortable. Sometimes he just needed to stretch his legs and she helped lift him up and sort of swayed with him like they were slow dancing. It was so gorgeously sad I had to turn away.

I peeked out the side of the curtains one last time before the show started. Emma was leading Dad through the aisle while Mom cleared a path. Then Oscar opened the lighting-booth door and wheeled out a rolly chair with a pillow propped up on the backrest. The three of them helped Dad into the seat and he said something that made everyone around him crack up. I watched them sharing that hilarious moment, my skin tingling.

A few minutes later, the curtains parted and we launched into our opening dance number. It went fairly well, considering we had twenty-three people on stage and only one (Julian) who knew what he was doing. Just the fact that I didn't run into any light poles or hanging murals felt pretty momentous. I heard Mom whisper, "Delicious!" after it ended, which made me giggle.

We were supposed to stay on stage for the whole show, so it could feel more "organically collective." Originally I thought that was dumb and an invitation to have serious bladder issues. But now I saw how it helped bring these unfinished pieces together, even if there was a lot of fidgeting and picking at sports-bra stitching.

Marty's poetry was actually pretty coherent and definitely fascinating. She talked about how Georgia O'Keeffe grew up in Wisconsin and drew her inspiration from nature. She segued into a treatise on how all of us were animals, often too scared to respond to our primal urges. She impersonated rams and undulating cattle, contorting herself around Oscar's canvases. It was humbling to watch how fluidly she could move and to hear how much O'Keeffe had been a sort of artistic mother figure to her. She finished with a loud roar and the audience clapped a little nervously.

Then there was a long, gaping pause.

Becca was supposed to be singing her ballad to Kevin Kripps. The spotlight was on and her backup singers were arranged in their signature horseshoe behind her. But Becca looked stricken with sudden muteness. And nobody would dare start the song without her lead.

"I have . . . I have . . ." she stammered. Followed by some vicious throat clearing. "I have . . ."

The end of that sentence was obviously "no idea what to do." She looked miserable, especially because she was surrounded by all these people who looked like they needed her to breathe.

I knew all of her lines, of course, but I didn't want to make her look stupid. Maybe if it was an "organically collective" effort it wouldn't be quite as noticeable. So I snatched up Nikki the ninth grader's hand and started chanting, "I have . . . I have . . . I have but one desire."

The mantra spread slowly across the stage. Everyone taking a hand and repeating the words, "I have . . . I have . . . I have but one desire."

We threaded ourselves in a zigzag formation around Becca, saying it over and over again. Julian even picked up a bongo and slapped out a tribal beat. And I had to admit, when Becca did find her voice, it was bright and stunning. She sang those two lines in a gorgeous, velvety croon that I'd never heard before.

There was no pretension or posing either. The audience cheered loudly, and I heard Kevin give a guttural, "Yessss!"

The best part of the show for me was waltzing with nothingness. I knew I wasn't the epitome of grace, but I loved feeling like my only responsibility was to follow this set rhythm and glide. I loved that Julian had asked Oscar to play a little oompah tune on the piano instead of the canned ballerina music. It still sounded a little bit like *Star Wars* to me, but in a familiar way.

Oscar made the waltz go longer than usual, and when he stopped it was so abrupt that I was honestly surprised. I did my dramatic fall and heard a bunch of audience gasps, followed by Mom murmuring, "It's an artistic choice. She warned me about that." Embarrassing, but to be expected. Julian's entrance had blossomed from a slow walk to a dazzling little solo for himself. I loved lying on the stage, watching him pounce, leap, and lunge. He was so agile and buoyant, the floor barely registered his feet touching down. I felt like a lake below him, absorbing his energy and rippling outward.

The audience reaction was pretty spectacular. There was even a standing ovation, which I blamed on my sister. It was a little absurd, but fantastic at the same time. After the final bows, Marty gave a tearful thank-you speech and invited everyone to come onto the stage and look at Oscar's collages up close. I chose to hightail it to the locker room.

The push of sweaty shoulders and post-show trembles in there was intense. People were too jittery to change back into street clothes and there was a lot of running back and forth and swooning over bouquets. Kevin planted a kiss on Becca that made everyone squirm before we shut the door and let out a group shriek.

As I got changed, I heard Becca talking about how emotional she'd felt on stage and the momentousness paralyzing her.

"You were phenomenal," Leigh assured her.

"Seriously," added Madison.

Becca never recognized that I'd helped her out. The closest I got to a thank-you was Sylvie shyly turning toward me and giving me a half smile. I didn't care. I already knew I'd done something great.

"Bravo! Bravissimo! Bravalavadingdong!" Dad yelled when I got up to the auditorium again. He was leaning against one of the big windows in the back, almost as narrow as the molding. When he opened his toothpick arms for a hug I stepped in, gingerly.

"Was that chair okay?" I whispered in his ear.

"Stop thinking about my ass and enjoy this night, will ya?" he answered.

Emma clutched me from behind and lifted me by the armpits. "You totally saved that girl's ass," she whispered. "And you were hot!" Her voice was so close and fierce that my ear got wet and ticklish.

Mom announced to whoever was listening, "My little

Eleanor is delicious!" over and over again. She started hopping up and down. "Where's the cast party? What's happening now?" she panted. She smelled like Rice Krispies treats and I knew the sugar rush was making her extra loopy.

"I'm not exactly sure," I said warily.

"Don't get scared." Mom slapped me playfully with her program. "I'm not crashing your good times. I just want to make sure you're going out and celebrating."

"We will." I looked around for confirmation, but didn't know exactly what I was looking for. Julian was ensconced with some friends from his old performing arts private school who'd shown up unexpectedly. It was fun to watch him out of the corner of my eye, especially as he talked animatedly to a lanky guy with long sideburns. They were standing really close together too. I always thought it'd sting to see Julian be affectionate with a guy, but it didn't. It was kind of thrilling.

"Party at the Ditmas house!" Sylvie yelled.

"Party!"

"Ditmas!" came the echoes.

I couldn't commit to anything without checking in with Julian first. Also, in my secret pocket of secrets, I was wondering what Oscar was planning for the rest of the night.

"Oh Lenny, it's so good to see you!" That was from Sylvie's mom. I hadn't seen Mrs. Ditmas in at least five years. She had thick gray curls and even thicker bags under her eyes. She was twisting a tissue between her fingers and seemed very scared of looking at Dad, but she also couldn't stop talking. She was saying how this summer she hoped to grow sweet potatoes in their backyard but there had been a lot of rain so maybe the ground was too moist but when she lived in Arizona the air felt so arid and yet the vegetation was extraordinary. She loved Arizona; had we ever been? she wondered.

Mom was now chatting with Mrs. Ditmas. Emma had cornered Marty to talk about gender identities. Dad said he'd driven cross-country once, but he had yet to visit a few key states. "Always wanted to see the sun set over the Grand Tetons."

"Oh yes, you *have* to!" said Mrs. Ditmas. Then there was a giant cloud of silence as she realized there was no way he could. Dad's wish just sat there in the middle of the auditorium with the leftover programs and candy wrappers. Untouched.

I felt like it was my job to say something.

"How about Wahonsett Bay instead?" I mustered.

"You got it," Dad said. "Excuse me for a minute." He stepped out of the circle of conversation and turned toward the window, breathing out through puckered lips. I noticed he was shifting his weight back and forth too.

"Dad? You okay?" I asked him quietly.

"Oh, ya know."

"No, I don't know. Can you tell me?" I asked.

"Nothing to tell. It's just really painful sometimes."

"Where?" I held his hand.

"All over." He gave me one of those grimacey smiles.

"Let's go home," I said.

Dad stood up as straight as I'd seen him in weeks. "*I'm* going home. *You* are going out with your friends to have fun. That's an order." He didn't even let me get out the word *but* before he clamped onto my other hand and looked me straight on. "Listen, I promise I'll tell you if anything is happening. I will tell you everything I know. And you have to do something for me in return. Actually, two things."

I nodded because I didn't trust my voice not to croak. It was the first time I'd actually looked at him directly all week. I didn't mean to. But when I did, I saw his eyes were still chocolatey and warm.

"One—go enjoy this awesome night," he said. "And two, give me a hug like you mean it." I did as I was told. His arms were shaking and so were mine. Mom told me again how proud she was of me and Emma gave me a hip bump. Then they each took one of Dad's arms looped in theirs and shuffled out.

I couldn't find Oscar anywhere. Everyone was deciding who was going in which car and what flavor chips to pick up at the store. Julian motioned for me to come over and meet his friends, but at the same moment Marty spun me around and held my face in her hands.

"You. Were. Astounding," she said. She looked at me so deeply I thought I'd fall into her eye sockets. There was so much more in her brain than I'd ever given her credit for.

"*You* were," I said softly.

"We both were," she corrected.

"Sorry to interrupt," Julian said, bringing his posse with

him. "I just wanted to introduce you to some people who are big fans of your work, ladies." There was Astrid, Paul, Katinka, and Mateo with the sideburns. They were all really affected by the show and talked about how much they missed Julian. Mateo put his hand on the small of Julian's back and I shuddered a little for him.

"We were thinking of getting some food all together. Unless you really want to go to the party." Julian looked at me.

"Yeah," I said. "I mean no. Or I mean, whatever is fine." I didn't know how to telepathically relay the message that I needed help locating Oscar. Marty had already disappeared too.

"I don't mean to be rude," said Paul, "but I'm gonna eat my own foot soon. What's the name of that diner you mentioned?"

"The Unicorn," said Julian.

My breath caught. I wasn't ready to go in there.

"Hooray!" said Astrid. "I love unicorns!"

There was a loud thud as one of the hanging canvases fell to the stage floor. "Sorry about that," said Oscar, leaning off the catwalk near the ceiling. I was so excited to see his face.

"Thanks for everything," I said. No response.

"Yeah, thanks, Oscar!" shouted Julian. He nodded at me, which I knew was his way of saying, *Speak up*.

"Sure," Oscar called back. "Came out okay after all."

"Yeah." Julian, Mateo, and the gang were already almost at the door. If I walked out too, the conversation would end right there. I felt my chest tightening. Then I saw the rolly chair from

Marty's office by the exit sign. "Oh! And thanks for helping my dad out with the chair. That was really sweet. I mean—generous. Or. Yeah."

"No problem. Hope it helped."

He wasn't making this any easier. But I couldn't leave. If I left now I could possibly never see him again. There was no reason for him to come to our high school since the show was done, which meant he'd be gone. It would all be over. There were so many things that I couldn't stop from ending. Life was too short and this night was only here once and he had laughed with my dad, which was the most romantic or at least hopeful thing in the world. So I sucked in some foolish courage and said, "Hey! A bunch of us are going to the Unicorn Diner just FYI if you want to come you don't have to but I just thought I'd say it in case."

"I'm in!" he called. Then I heard his feet tramping down the metal ladder and he was next to me, wiping dust out of his eyes with his T-shirt. I tried not to smile too widely.

"There's just one thing . . ." I said as we started walking. If we were going to the Unicorn, I needed to prepare myself. Or get a disguise. I pulled out my trusty Groucho glasses from my backpack and put them on.

"Too much?" I asked.

"Not enough," Oscar answered.

Black Holes Colliding

Black hole 36 times
as big as the sun

Gravitational waves in
an unseen apocalypse

Energy equivalent to the brightness
of a billion trillion suns

Proof that Einstein's theory of relativity
is true and that every movement
we make affects the universe

Even this breath

Black hole 29 times
as big as the sun

Chapter 21

IK BELOOF

Dara was thrilled to see us. She was sporting a platinum-blond beehive and had a suspicious new beauty mark just below her left nostril. She led us to one of the big tables in the party room and tugged me lightly by my elbow.

"What's up, Grouch?" Dara asked. "Don't I get a hello?"

My Groucho glasses slid down my nose and I accidentally slapped myself trying to get them back on. I smiled politely but couldn't say anything. I didn't know what she'd heard about the taped-up front door, and my voice would give me away if Topher was still looking for the culprit.

"She's on the lam," Julian told her. "Dara, meet our friends." He went around making introductions. Mateo told her about how life hadn't been the same since Julian moved back to Mountainside and how he'd just beheld true art on stage. Julian stuffed a dinner roll in Mateo's mouth to stop him from going on. Astrid stood up with her water glass and said she'd been sober exactly three years to the day and she owed it all to this incredible network of artists. Everyone raised a glass and started hooting. I really wanted to join in the festive mood. I just kept envisioning the cops popping out from behind a potted ficus and quizzing me about my whereabouts last Friday night.

"You okay?" asked Oscar. I felt bad. He didn't know anybody at the table except for Julian and the silent black hole known as me.

"Yeah, what's making you so quiet, Eleanor Rigby?" Dara asked, giving the top of my head a little scratch. Maybe that spot on my scalp had special nerve endings or something, because I could feel my head tingling and my throat got all tight like I was about to cry. I didn't want Oscar to hear the whole story about Don Juan and the shattered door, but I couldn't stay mute all night and I really wanted to sit next to him. It would be a little awkward to make him plug his ears. Maybe it would make me look like a badass animal activist.

"I was having a really rough day last Friday," I began. "Really rough. We got some bad news about my dad and then I was locked out of my house and I thought maybe I could come here and get some toast, but you weren't here. And neither was Don Juan the lobster."

Dara bit her lip and smoothed back my hair. She knew from all my early-morning coffee sessions with Julian how bad the bad news could be.

"So I asked the guy who was here what happened to the lobster tank. And he was a little snooty about it, like a why-does-it-matter-anyway kind of thing. I went a little ballistic because, as you know, I thought that lobster was pretty fabulous." Now

Dara scooted me halfway off my chair and wedged her butt in next to me. She nodded solemnly, but it also looked like she was stifling a smile.

"Wait, you think this is funny?" I asked.

"No!" Dara said. "I just—I knew it was you."

I hunched down so Dara's profile blocked me from the line cooks. "You knew? How?"

Oscar was switching between our faces, watching us like a tennis match. He raised his hand, then jumped into the fray. "Can I ask a question? Are we talking about a real lobster? And did you say his name was Don Juan?"

"Yes," I said, feeling my call to arms. "It was a real lobster. A real, live lobster, and someone flushed him down the toilet, or threw him in a Dumpster."

Dara kissed the top of my head and told me, "Not a Dumpster. But certainly not the burial he deserved."

"Wait!" I squeaked. "So he did . . . ?"

Dara nodded somberly. It wasn't exactly a shock, but I also had counted on her telling me Don Juan had just been moved to a sunnier locale or thrown back into the Hudson. I could hear myself panting. Dara handed me my ice water and I gulped it greedily. Meanwhile, she turned to Oscar and explained, "This little lady has some big balls. She went on some rampage about endangered crustaceans that they caught on security camera."

"What? No!"

"Kidding." She snorted. "You think that thing actually works?

Damn, girl, you need to breathe. The door's getting replaced Sunday. Stephan's cousin is a glass expert or something; it is not a big deal."

"Yeah but what if . . . ? What if . . . ?" I wanted to trust her that I was in the clear, but it didn't seem fair or possible that I could get off scot-free.

Dara took out her gum and welded it behind her ear to show me she meant business. "Listen. I am not condoning what you did, but it's over now. I feel kind of responsible, too, because I was pretty sure Stephan was set on dumping that thing and I didn't stop him. Turns out there was some bad algae in there and someone had the brilliant idea to clean it with ammonia, which as you probably know is not fun for sea creatures. I'm sorry, my friend. I think I let you down."

Now I really wanted to cry, but so far Oscar had witnessed every horrible side of me possible. Luckily, Dara had more to say.

"Nobody actually saw you lose your shit except that Topher kid and he's not exactly well liked around here. He was so caught up in being the hero that night that he ran out after you and left the place unattended and we had two tables leave without paying and he got fired. So really, there were a lot of crappy decisions made, which doesn't mean two wrongs equal a right, but you know all this."

She removed my glasses and wiped away the rings of sweat around my eyes.

"So what if?" Dara continued. "That's what we have to live

with every day, dear Lenny. What. If." And with that, she stood up, walked to the other side of the table, and started taking everyone's orders.

"Hey, I don't know exactly what you did, but if you're running from the law, that's cool," said Oscar. "I love that you stood up for a lobster."

"Thanks," I said. I wished I still had my Groucho glasses on so he couldn't see the way my whole face was turning a silly pink.

Oscar took his napkin, folded it into an airplane, and shot it over my head. It made it all the way to the bowl of creamers. "You have a lot of friends who live underwater?"

"Just Don Juan. Although, I guess I haven't really connected with too many other crustaceans."

"I hear ya," Oscar said. "I once hung out with a mollusk. Very aloof." I tried to make an airplane with my napkin too, but my hands were too fumbly and shaky to do much.

"Seriously, though," he continued, "there's this awesome boat called *Lobster Tales*. It goes up and down the Atlantic coast, testing the acidity levels and doing these kids' shows about the environment. My mom took me to see them once. I actually applied to be on their crew next year."

"Oh," I said. Now my hands were really trembling. Yes, I barely knew this guy and I had no right to expect him to stay here. But it was so hard to keep hearing about everyone moving away or planning the next place that they were going to go and the next horizon they were going to see. I took another swig of water and counted the basket of jelly packets under my breath, trying not to act too sulky.

"Who knows, though," Oscar went on. "I like what your friend said about *what if*. Like, what if we didn't spend so much time trying to prepare for the next gust of wind, you know? It's more fun to just . . . see where things go."

"Right," I said. "You don't like getting attached to anything. *Cut the cord so the sainted bird can fly?* Or something like that."

Oscar shook his head. "Sorry. I can be a real asshole sometimes."

"I didn't think you were an asshole. Just lonely. And possibly a Catholic missionary." Oscar had a really warm laugh.

"Lonely, yes. Catholic, no." He sighed. "And I like to use quotes instead of Groucho glasses when I'm hiding."

I felt my ears getting hot. I deposited my glasses on the salt and pepper shakers and smoothed back the ferocious eyebrow. Then I tried to get interested in everyone else's conversation even though I just wanted to talk to Oscar all night.

"Can I ask you a weird question?" I mustered.

"Please," answered Oscar.

"Could you maybe tell me something yucky about yourself? I mean, you've kind of seen me at my worst a few times now."

"That's hard," he said. "First of all, I don't think I've seen you at your worst, but more importantly, I have no faults. I'm perfect in every way." He poked a finger up his nose to show me he was kidding.

"Thank you, that was charming."

"Yeah, I like to piss people off so there's no chance of them missing me." His face got somber and he said quietly, "The truth is, I've tried to keep so many relationships, but it's hard when you're always saying goodbye."

"Relationships" sounded like a euphemism for "girlfriends." But I didn't dare follow up on that.

"Where are you off to next?" I asked. Not that I wanted to know that either, but I felt like I had to brace myself.

"I honestly don't know," answered Oscar. "My mom's between gigs and I finished all my credits for high school graduation but I have no desire to go to college right away. A few possible job opportunities. A lot of *what if.*" He wiped a line through the condensation on his water glass and I did the same on mine. Then we watched the sweat drops form again. "I've spent so many years living out of a suitcase, you know? This past school year is the longest my mom and I have spent in one town since I was eight. Moving around so much really sucks sometimes."

"I've been in the same house my whole life," I admitted. "But all my taxes go to Unicorn renovations."

Oscar smiled and I tried not to notice. "I'm really glad we came in here, because we tried to get my grandma interested in the retirement community just around the corner but she said it was for old people," he said. "I'm actually thinking of living with her in the Bronx next year."

I was sure he could hear me screaming inside, *Yes! Please. Stay.*

Dara started bringing around plates of French fries and mozzarella sticks. Julian snuck up behind me with some burnt toast and said, "Pat of butter?"

It was actually our code for *Do you need to leave this situation because if so I'll make a distraction.*

"No thanks," I said. "You?"

"Please no."

It was very fun to watch Julian sashay back to the other end of the table and lean into Mateo's shoulder, laughing.

"I thought of a few more," Oscar said.

"A few more?"

"A few more crappy things about me. I have never flossed in my life. I once got detained on the way back from a trip to Tijuana because I was trying to smuggle in a bag of papayas. And I get really dark sometimes."

"Thank you." I looked into his gray eyes so he knew I meant it. "I want to hear more about all of those things, please. Except for the flossing."

It definitely was the best night I'd ever spent at the Unicorn. Even though I was starving, I tried to take dainty bites so each one would last longer. The best part of the meal was when Oscar and I reached for the catsup at the same time and brushed forearms. Of course I acted like the Empress of Spazland and took my hand off the bottle too quickly so it crashed down on a plate and flipped a fork into the air, but nothing broke.

"You really want to destroy this place, don't you?" kidded Oscar.

"To Lenny and her burgeoning career in petty crime!" Julian cheered. Everyone raised a glass.

"To Julian!" I yelled back. I wanted to come up with something funny, but I had too much else to say first. "And his magnificent new world on the West Coast. His new home, his new studies, his new life."

"Here here!" boomed Mateo. The glasses went up again. Julian looked at me and crossed his eyes so the moment wouldn't get too sentimental. Then he mouthed the words *I love you*.

After everyone had eaten enough fried food to anchor us for a week, Dara came over and pinched me in the rib. "Hey, you. I want you to swear that even if Julian the Great is out in San Francisco, you're going to keep coming back to see me. Otherwise, how am I going to survive?"

"Thanks, Dara. I will."

"Remember, I got your back, girlfriend." She hugged me so hard that her beehive started to tip.

"Accept the updos you cannot change," I told her as she scurried to the bathroom with one hand on her head.

Meanwhile, everyone else at the table was getting ready to head out.

"What's the plan?" I asked Julian.

"Well, there was talk about going into the city and seeing one of Astrid's friends do some stand-up." Mateo hooked one arm around Julian and offered me his other. I wanted to go wherever the group was going, but the thought of being on a train late at night again made me queasy. Also, it was already almost eleven and I didn't want to sleep half the day away tomorrow. Dad and I had firm plans to do a *Star Wars* marathon.

Julian could tell I wasn't hot on the idea of going out. He always could read my mind. "Maybe you can get a ride home from someone else. Oscar, which way do you go?" he asked.

"Whichever way you need," Oscar answered.

"It's okay. I can totally walk."

"Of course you can, but it's late and I'd like to drive you home," said Oscar. "Is that okay?"

It was more than okay. It was dreamy and sort of otherworldly. We each left a huge tip for Dara and then ambled out to the Unicorn parking lot. Oscar pointed to a crotchety pickup truck that was listing to the left because one tire was clearly smaller than the others. There were bumper stickers all over the back of the bed. My favorites were MY OTHER CAR IS MY FEET and WHAT WOULD MALALA DO?

I decided I wanted to get both of those to stick in my suitcase under my bed. In fact, I wanted to put this whole night in there for safekeeping.

As Oscar drove, the truck creaked and bounced over every divot or loose piece of gravel in the road. We didn't talk except for my saying, "Right at the fork," and "Just a few blocks up." Oscar seemed perfectly content being silent, though. A week ago I thought that meant he was disabled or smug. Now I was holding on to that quiet like a flotation device.

Then we were in front of my house and the light was on in the den, which meant that Dad was still awake and alive and I hated to use him or his illness as a way to get close to Oscar, but I needed to say something to keep us both there for a moment longer.

"Thanks again for getting that chair for my dad."

"Sure," said Oscar. "He's a really sweet guy. I'm sorry that he's . . . that you're all . . ."

I nodded into the silence. "Yeah. It's okay. I'm just really glad that you got to meet him."

"Me too. Me too."

We stared out the windshield a few eons more. Then Oscar said, "Oh!"

He pulled out a piece of paper from his sweatshirt pocket that had been folded so many times it was as small as a quarter. "I started this last week, but it's not really done. It's a list. Because you had a list and I thought, I like lists. Which, yeah. I mean, everyone likes lists. But whatever. Don't read it now. Just when you have a minute. If you want."

He handed me the note. On the outside, it said in small block letters, IK BELOOF.

"In Dutch it means *I promise*," he said, yanking at a few curls so they covered his eyes more. "I just thought. I don't know if you remembered that I made you promise in the lighting booth to stop doing that punching thing to yourself, and you wanted me to promise to stop being a pompous ass."

"I didn't say that, did I?"

"No, but it was implied," he said. "And well deserved."

"I don't know about that. But I really appreciate that you be-loofed me. Or I beloofed you? That sounds weird."

"Yeah." He laughed. "I like it."

I wanted Oscar to lean over and grab me and kiss me and marry me and vow to never leave me. But he didn't. And I'd already mashed my face into an unwilling partner's too recently and wrongly. So I settled for a lurchy hug that was more like a collision of my forehead and his shoulder, and then I opened the truck's door and blurted, "I had a really fun time and I didn't think I would or I didn't know what to think but I did and I hope you don't move away unless you want to in which case goodbye and thank you so much."

"Thank *you*," he said slowly. "And *what if* we hung out again soon?"

"Yes please!" I chirped, closing the door. Then he waited in the idling truck while I went inside my house.

"Hello?" I whispered. The den light was on, and the TV. But Dad was actually asleep in his rocket-ship bed. So was Mom, on the couch next to him.

It was both beautiful and horrible to watch them drifting in some other state. There was something distinctly different about how they were breathing. Mom's inhales and exhales were steady and efficient, like a steam engine. Dad, on the other hand, sucked in air erratically. As if he'd forgotten he needed more air. Then he let it out so slowly while he sank back into his pillow.

On the TV, a late-night talk-show host was laughing about a wild turkey that walked into a strip club in Indiana and started dancing. True story.

Also true: everything was ending and beginning at the same time.

Mysteries of the Universe (and I Like Them That Way)

by Oscar Birnbaum

The meaning of life

Is time an illusion, a dimension, or an invention?

Gladiator shoes

How some people are born in Westchester, NY, and some people are born in Katmandu and the kid in Westchester thinks he *needs* more

Skunk spray

Unconditional love—does it really exist?

That weird explosion in Siberia in 1908 that was maybe a meteor but also could've been a UFO

Grand Unification Theory: Newton, Einstein, Heisenberg—can't we find a way that they fit together?

The lure of Justin Bieber

What exactly is a soul and how does it continue after our bodies die?

Seriously. Bieber?

Chapter 22

WADING

Usually when we went up to Wahonsett Bay, we stayed with Dad's sister, Aunt Josie, about twenty minutes away from the beach. She was a few years younger than Dad and single, unless I counted her five shih tzus. She did. She always said "we" when she talked about herself. As in, "We can't believe you're not staying with us this time."

Mom's colleague had offered us her cabin right on the water. No one was using it the first week in June and it had a ramp leading down to her dock, so we could bring Dad's newly rented wheelchair. We'd never gone this early in the season. The water would probably be freezing. It actually wasn't officially summer yet—at least not by anyone else's calendar. Emma had taken off the end of her semester, Mom had gotten a leave of absence, and I was bringing two essays and a take-home quiz on this little trip.

Still, the timing felt right. We really didn't know if Dad would be here through the whole summer, though no one would say that out loud.

Usually when we went up to Wahonsett Bay, the car ride

took three and a half hours at most. Emma and I loaded up on watermelon-flavored gum and we played celebrity trivia games since the radio was busted in the station wagon. But this time, Emma was at the steering wheel so Mom could nap and we had to make a bunch of stops. Dad kept on saying he needed to stretch, which meant we were pulling over and Mom lifted him out of the front seat like a grocery bag full of eggs. Once he got up, he felt better, but he was so winded that they just sort of huddled on the road's shoulder. Then Mom rotated his doughnut pillow and put him back in the Jolly Roger for another twenty miles or so.

(The Batmobile sat in our driveway, collecting bird poop. A month lease was a lot longer than it seemed when Mom first brought it home.)

Usually when we went up to Wahonsett Bay, all four of us stripped down to our bathing suits before our feet even touched the hot sand. We slogged through the tangles of seaweed and splashed wildly. Then raced out to the floating waterslide by the line of green buoys, teeth chattering, goose bumping, yodeling loud enough for our voices to bounce off the lighthouse down the shoreline.

"Suits on?" Dad said as we rolled into the gravelly driveway of the strange-looking cabin.

"Maybe once we're settled in," Emma answered.

We couldn't pretend this was just another visit to Wahonsett Bay.

By the time we got in, it was late afternoon. Mom eased Dad from the passenger seat to the wheelchair and zoomed him straight onto the screened-in back porch, facing the water. The house was built on stilts and inside it smelled like firewood and wet dog. Mom, Emma, and I started opening up all the doors and windows. There were bowls of sand dollars and seashells on every shelf and a clock that ticked loudly, marking the time and also the tides. Someone in their family was obviously into surfing because there were three boards propped up in the basement and lots of framed photographs of waves. I was grateful it was all so unfamiliar. I also loved the wooden sign over the screen door that read A DISASTER AT SEA CAN RUIN YOUR WHOLE DAY.

Dad sat so close to the screen that his nose nearly touched it. He closed his eyes and the rest of his face opened into a huge smile. He looked so relieved. I watched him for a few minutes while I tried to take in big whiffs of saltwater and dune grass. Just past the first sandbar was where I went clamming with Dad when I was ten years old. It was supposed to be just a little stroll, but Dad pointed out all the little bubbles rising up below us and we started digging with our bare hands. It was so rough and exciting; seizing those scratchy shells and feeling the clams burrow inside. Dad went back for a big pot and we stayed out there for hours scavenging. In the end, I couldn't stomach the idea of boiling them and dipping their meaty insides in melted butter, so Dad helped me toss them back into the water. All we brought home from our expedition was a pot caked in seaweed and two wild sunburns.

"You want something to drink? How about a cracker? You feel cold? Too hot?" Emma kept tossing questions at Dad while we bustled around the house. It was small and busy, with thick wooden slabs for walls. There was a half-finished jigsaw puzzle set out on the coffee table, a stack of island maps on the kitchen counter, and lots of shag carpeting that smelled faintly moldy.

Dad said, "I don't need a thing, but I am heading out to the dock. Who's coming with me?"

Emma and Mom were setting up the daybed for Dad and adding a special contoured mattress pad. Mom said, "Join you in a sec. Lenny, you want to head down? The brake is just over the left wheel."

"That's okay," said Dad. "I think I can walk."

"You don't need to," said Emma.

Dad nodded at me. "Lenny and I got this." I was honored and terrified at once. I watched carefully as Emma cupped her hands under his armpits like we'd been taught by Frances, the nurse who came to our house once a week.

"Who's a rock star?" Emma murmured.

"I'm a rock star," Dad answered. She transferred him to me one pit at a time and I couldn't believe how flimsy his arms were. It felt like I was trying to hold up a marionette with no strings. His feet did a little shuffly dance before finding their place on the ground. I swallowed hard.

"You ready?" I asked, more for myself than him. Instead of speaking, Dad threaded his arm through mine and I felt his skin, warm and soft. The screen door slammed behind us as we started down the ramp.

"Maybe I'll follow you with the chair in case you decide for the way back . . ." Mom called after us. I didn't answer and neither did Dad. We were focusing on our feet next to each other. Lifting and stepping. Lifting and stepping. We had no shoes on. Nothing separating our toes from the dock's planks except a sliver of air as we inched forward.

It took 238 steps to get to the edge of the dock. We were just three houses away from the beach entrance and the floating slide. I saw a few youngish families there. Tiny bodies zipping down with a splash and sand castles being stomped by a pudgy toddler. One guy with a beard and a loud hairy laugh cracking himself up with stories in between swigs of Pabst. He's the one who looked up and waved at us.

"Ahoy!" he called.

Dad waved back. I knew he couldn't summon that big a voice so I called, "Thar she blows!"

Pabstman thought that was hilarious. I was glad we weren't totally alone anymore. "See? You make friends wherever you go," said Dad.

Emma came down to the dock with two glasses of ginger ale and a long, flat pillow. Together we lowered Dad down onto it. I sat next to him.

Our feet just touched the water; that first moment of skin contact so cold I hiccupped. Dad jolted too, then laughed a little.

"Gets me every time," he said. The words "every time" felt purposeful and poetic. I'd been in that salty water each summer for as long as I could remember. I'd peed in that water, cried in that water, learned how to hold my breath and dunk in that water. It was a third of a mile from the edge of the red rocks to the lighthouse, and Dad swam all the way across and back at least once a day. Dad's strokes were long and deliberate. He never rushed when he was in the water. He scooped out palmfuls of water as he glided through, his mouth opening for air in small, efficient sips. His head, his heart, his arms all moving nimbly in the same direction.

When I was six, I started trailing behind him in my pink inflatable seahorse. Then I upgraded to an inner tube when I was eight. Just before I turned eleven, I swam the whole way with him. He lifted me over his head and carried me like a trophy down the street all the way to the snack shack, where we got onion rings and push pops to celebrate.

The water was cool and quiet today. Strands of seaweed branching out like capillaries. Our toes bobbed, white and willowy.

Mom said, "Emma and I were going to just run down to Westerly's and get some eggs, salad stuff, you know. Any requests?"

Dad shook his head, then looked at me so I could do the same. I still had the urge to say, *Please don't leave us alone. This could be his last afternoon on the dock. His last sip of ginger ale. His last breath.*

I let the words dissolve on my tongue without voicing them, though. I didn't want to ruin the calm we had, at least in this moment.

"Okay, then," said Mom. "Don't stay out past curfew."

Dad winked at her, patted my knee, and tipped his head up toward the hazy sun. I heard Mom retreating to the house, then the Jolly Roger pulling out of the driveway.

"Hey, Madam Osprey got here before us," Dad said.

The snack shack had a small platform on its roof and every summer a family of ospreys made a huge nest there. The mama was standing up large and in charge, with her bright white chest puffed out as she sounded her whistley alarm. The kids in the beer-club day care on the beach were playing tag and shrieking. And in the distance, a motorboat skidded and snorted, churning up sea foam. There was so much life and noise all around us that I'd never appreciated before.

We sat there. Watching, listening. The water lapping at our heels and slowly receding. Leaving our toes out in the breeze.

"I guess this takes longer than we thought, huh?" Dad said.

"What does?"

"Dying."

I sucked in my breath so fast. I didn't dare let it out.

"You're going to want to exhale at some point," said Dad with a little laugh. I didn't know what to say. It felt so raw and tender sitting here, like we were both covered in new skin.

"Lenny," said Dad, "it hurts a lot less when we can go through this together."

"Yeah?" I squeaked.

"Yeah." He patted my knee again. "Do you want to ask me any questions?" I was panting and chewing my bottom lip so hard. I didn't know if I could make my way to forming complete sentences.

"Um, I guess . . . is there anything you want to do? Or see?"

"I'm doing it," he said.

I nodded, letting a tear fall.

"How about you?" he asked. "Is there stuff you want to do?"

"So much. Go to college. Fall in love. Take a kickboxing class. Or maybe pottery. Do some sort of backpacking thing through Israel or India or I guess any place that starts with an *I*."

"Sounds like a plan," said Dad.

"Yeah, but I want to do them with you *here*."

"Well, I'll be *here*." He tapped lightly with one finger just below my clavicle. "Also *here*." This time, tapping on my head. "And most of all, *here*." Three taps on my nose, because I used to blame him for it being so big.

"I guess I have a question." I gulped. "What does it feel like?"

My father smiled. And swallowed. And breathed. And then he said, "It feels like wading."

"Waiting?"

"Yeah. That too."

So we waited. For the osprey to gather all her chicks and the Pabstman to open another can and the sun to start melting into its orange evening gown. We waited, sitting on the edge of the dock. On the edge of whatever was next.

"I think the tide's going out," I said at some point.

"I think you're right," answered Dad. I leaned forward instinctually, as if trying to get it to roll back in.

Dad put his right palm on top of my left hand. "Don't worry, Len," he said. "It'll come back."

All the Ways We're Just Beginning

Azuay stubfoot toad (labeled extinct in 2002) just found
in Ecuador
the mayor two towns over announced she used to be a
guy
new species of giant clam identified off Canadian coast
three "super earths" spotted circling a dwarf star
humanized yeast
gravitational wave chirps
Emma passed her freshman humanities course
ocean thermal energy conversion
lab-grown vagina (no joke)
this new wheel drum they're trying in South Africa that
holds 13 gallons of clean water

today is here
tomorrow is pretty likely
besides that it's all just
What.
If.

THANK YOU

There are so many people to thank.

Thank you thank you to my brilliant frienditor, Joy Peskin. I truly cannot thank you enough for finding this story with me and bringing it here to today. Thank you to Simon Boughton, Angie Chen, Grace Kendall, and Nicholas Henderson, who make FSG a beautiful place. Thank you to the distinguished Franck Goldberg, Nathaniel, and Madame Ginger. Thank you to my incredible agent, Mollie Glick, along with Joy Fowlkes, Heidi Gall, and all the awesome people at Foundry Media. Thank you to Andrew Arnold for the best cover art in the history of covers or art.

But wait, there's more.

Thank you to all of my inspiring muses: Al Gore, Stephen Hawking, Dr. Samantha Karpel, Dr. Bhuvanesh Singh, Joselin Linder and the Tigers, Molly Lyons, Kimmi Auerbach Berlin, Nicole Bokat, Merideth Finn, Susan Shapiro, V.C. "Boom Boom" Chickering, Susanna Eisenstein, Marvi Lacar, Gabra Zackman, Sara Moss, Martha Barylick, and the great minds of Studio B and Village Coffee.

Thank you to my mom, Joan Lear Sher, and my dad, Roger Evan Sher, for giving me a song to sing each day and making me believe in what if's. Thank you to my dear sister, Elisabeth, and brother, Jon, and the cast of Kinesthesia, circa 1990.

Thank you again and always to my delicious husband, Jason, and our three ridiculously awesome kids—Sonya, Zev, and Samson.

And to you, dear reader, for going along for this ride.

Wheeeeeeeee!

Thank you.

GO**FISH**

ABBY SHER

How did you craft the character of Lenny? What inspired her personality?
Lenny is me at sixteen—only with a better sense of fashion. I was obsessed with so many catastrophic ideas and in love with my best friend, who was openly homosexual. I lost my dad when I was eleven, though, so in that way, I guess we differ. I never had Lenny's sense of awareness or responsibility as I watched him fade.

You infuse such wonderful and dark humor into moments of great seriousness and sadness. How do you maintain that balance in your writing?
Thank you! I guess that's just how I see this magical, mysterious, terrifying, hilarious world. I always feel like laughing and crying are two of the greatest things we get to do while we're here on earth. Also, if I take myself too seriously, I'll melt.

If you could give advice to a teen whose parent also had a terminal illness, what would you say? What would you want them to know?
Wow. That's a hard question. First of all, I'd tell that teen: *You are NOT alone. This sucks in every which way, and whatever*

you are feeling is real and true. I'd also love to give that teen a copy of Harold Kushner's book *When Bad Things Happen To Good People.* It's one of the only things that made sense to me when I lost my dad.

In creating great teen romances, what's your trick for encouraging not only the protagonist to fall for the love interest, but also the reader?
I guess the most important thing to me is that the love interest is never too good to be true. She or he has to be geeky and awkward or have anger issues and acne. This person can't ride in on a stallion and save the day. There's got to be some risk in feeling this attraction.

What kind of message do you want readers to take away from this story, if any?
I want readers to feel less alone. Whether they are struggling with a family member dying, an unrequited love, obsessive thoughts about the end of the world, or losing a best friend—or even none of the above. I want this to be a story of connection between lost souls—and a hope that we continue somehow even after death.

What challenges did you face while writing this book, and how did you overcome them?
None. It was incredibly easy.

Kidding!

I had trouble showing that Lenny's mom, aka Sergeant Nutbags, is not being heartless or inattentive. She's just struggling to cope and accept that her husband is dying. I did feel better when I could channel my own frenetic energy into that mom character—so I felt like I was making fun of myself more than her.

What is your favorite scene or moment in *All the Ways the World Can End?*

I am so grateful for the last scene with Lenny and her dad on the dock. I had a much-abbreviated scene about this moment, and my awesome writing group said, "Why don't you let us see Lenny and her dad connect?" I thought that was impossible since it hadn't ever happened in my real life. But then when I accepted the challenge, I really felt like I got to visit my dad again and have the conversation I'd always longed to have with him.

What's the best advice you ever received about writing?

Write down a grateful list every day. Or three pages of the worst garbage you can imagine. Or everything you remember about the summer of 1991. Don't let your pen stop moving for twenty minutes. Now, go!

What would your readers be most surprised to learn about you?

I still don't know what I want to be when I grow up.

TURN THE PAGE FOR AN EXCERPT OF
ABBY SHER'S NEXT NOVEL,
MISS YOU LOVE YOU HATE YOU BYE.

CHAPTER 1
pepe le meowsers

I STILL DON'T CONSIDER MYSELF A CRUEL PERSON. BUT I DID HAVE a moment—or really, several—when I was ready to strangle that cat.

Zoe says that Pepe le Meowsers *chose* her. Her mom joined some mega-gym-spa that had just landed in our town. Zoe went for a tour and on the bulletin board she saw a note about a litter of newborn kittens that were available for adoption. It said if they didn't find homes soon, they'd most likely be put to sleep. By the end of one fateful Zumba class, Zoe was caught in a herd of women, all doing cool-down squats around a plastic crate with five squirming tabbies. As she said, maybe it was just from over-exertion, but when she saw how tiny and fuzzy and malleable these small creatures were, she felt faint. She literally *swooned*.

"I mean, what the what? I'm not even a cat person," she reported to me twenty-four hours later as I sat in her basement. Actually, Zoe wasn't talking just to me. She was declaring her newfound feline love to the world—perched on a metal stool in front of a sky-blue fitted sheet. I was holding her phone, filming her testimonial and trying desperately to stifle a sneeze.

"There was just something so *primal* and yet indescribable connecting us in that moment," Zoe recounted. "I don't know. All of a sudden, I was lying on my back and the whole gym was sort of turning this peachy-sunset color and fading away. And then . . ."

It was as if Pepe knew she was in distress. Apparently, he leaped over the side of the crate and risked his life tripping on a StairMaster machine, then scrambled up Zoe's arm, gumming her face, pawing at her eyes. She still had the tiny pink scratches to prove it. Three jagged lines etched into her left cheek. She also had a splotch of blush on her nose and whiskers drawn on her face in what looked like navy eyeliner.

Zoe Grace Hammer and I had been best friends since our moms bumped into each other while pushing us in strollers. Or at least that's how Zoe always relayed our past. She also claimed that we hid in the bathroom at nursery school and ate blue Play-Doh, but I have no recollection of that. I think that was either told to her or she made it up. Which I guess is the definition of anyone's history, really.

I do not remember how Zoe and I met. Only that she was there, with her sparkling green eyes, already laughing. Waving her hands at me from across the room as the morning bell rang on our first day of kindergarten. She had already dumped out all the wooden blocks onto the carpet for circle time and was using the empty toy bin as a boat. Her first-day-of-school dress was a patchwork pattern of every color in the rainbow. It was also tiny enough to fit a doll.

"Come here!" Zoe beckoned. "I'll save you from the storm!"

Even though I had no idea what she was talking about, I heeded her call.

Our friendship didn't grow or evolve. It was instantaneous. While the rest of our kindergarten class made their introductions, Zoe nested me in her lap, trying to tame my curly hair into a semidecent braid. Two hours later, she presented me with a pact of undying bestfriendhood. Of course, I said yes.

I learned how to sing from Zoe.

I learned how to do a cartwheel from Zoe.

I learned how to melt broken crayons and sneak jelly beans in the sides of my cheeks from Zoe.

All vital skills that made my life feel more colorful and vibrant than ever before.

When Zoe came to play at my house, my mom liked to say that she "brought the party with her." She always had matching Froot Loops necklaces or glitter tattoos that we had to put on right away. She would kick off her shoes and twirl me around and before I knew it, we were mixing ingredients for slime or having a naked dance party in my room or both at the same time. Zoe was pure electricity—darting and leaping everywhere, because walking was too predictable and slow.

To be honest, I preferred going to Zoe's house—with a drawer just for Fruit Roll-Ups and framed Disney pictures everywhere. Her bedroom had so many pillows and ruffles, I felt like we would both float away on a unicorn sneeze or tumble into a vat of cotton candy. Everything was enchanted. Especially Zoe. She was an Irish firecracker, with stick-straight ebony hair that shimmered and huge eyes that took in everything. Her nose was barely bigger than a thimble. As an infant, she'd been the cherubic face of BabyFresh Ultra Diapers and made a buttload of money in some car commercial about antilock brakes. Also, she got to sing the jingle for IPopUPop microwave popcorn and traveled to fifteen states with the national touring company of *Annie 2*.

There was a whole photo album of her commercial work in her living room, but Zoe didn't like to talk about it much. She once told me that the day she met me was the day she decided she was done running off to auditions and memorizing tap dance routines. She just wanted to stay home and be *a plain ol' kid, like you*.

Which I chose to take as a compliment.

I'd always wanted to be Zoe's twin, though I was far from it. Zoe came up to my shoulder—if I was slouching. Where she was petite and wiry, I was a mess of loose limbs. If I had to describe myself, I'd say I was mildly awkward with grand intentions. Mud-brown hair to my chin that was somewhere between wavy and unmanageable, a nose that took up too much face real estate, and a unibrow that was hazardous. I did like that my eyes were the same sea-glass turquoise as my mom's. Also, that I wore mismatched socks on purpose. I was an avid recycler, and one of my teachers called my punctuation "exemplary!?,;"

But I longed to be more like Zoe. From the moment I met her, I did basically anything Zoe told me to do—sit, stand, lie down, roll over. At night, I tried to train my nose to slope up like hers at the very end. I practiced walking with my feet turned out to match her ballet strides and joined the track team briefly to literally chase after her. When we had sleepovers, I memorized the stripy patterns in her mint-green wallpaper, as if they could lead me closer inside. She started calling me *Hank* instead of Hannah, because she said it gave me more personality. I had to agree. Zoe was the sun, and I would gladly orbit her in whichever direction she chose.

Here's a pathetic secret that I have no interest in holding on to anymore: In seventh grade, when I was developing faster than Zoe, I even shaved my lady parts, so we'd look the same *down there*. Which turned out to be the itchiest, most unrewarding experience ever.

Until maybe this moment.

It was the day before our first day of junior year at Meadowlake High. I hadn't seen Zoe in practically two months. And now I'd walked into some situation that felt a little bit like cat porn. Zoe had on a loose gray tank top and what looked like the hotpink polka-dotted short shorts that she wore for our first-grade ballet recital. Once upon a pirouette, I had matching ones too. (Just to clarify—I wasn't in the recital, because it was by audition and I sucked at ballet. But my mom knew how much I wanted to be like Zoe and sewed me some facsimile short shorts out of retired bedsheets.)

"I just felt so alone and misunderstood until I met you, sweet Pepe," Zoe declared now. "I really didn't know how or if I'd even make it through this horror. You are my *hero*."

Zoe tipped her head back and started kissing the animal all over his body. He squirmed and wriggled, and his hind legs looked as if he were trying to run a marathon. Then she cradled him like a baby and hummed a lullaby until his ears sagged. "Ooh, you see? He loves me too. He really does," she cooed.

I know it wasn't the cat's fault. That thing was probably just as stunned as I was by all this smoochy-faced madness. I just felt allergic to everything inside this basement—the dander, the drama, the long watery gaze that Zoe fixed on this multicolored hairball.

To be fair, Zoe had a lot going on. She had been away basically all summer. First, she spent a month by the Jersey Shore with her grandparents, who were awesome, but they ate dinner at 5:00 P.M. and didn't have a great Internet connection. While Zoe was wandering the coastline, her dad, Travis, moved out of their family house. I didn't know much about his new place, other than it was twenty minutes away and next to a car wash. Zoe described it as "a beige coffin." Then she went to performing arts camp, where she was cast as the scarecrow in *The Wiz* and made out with three different Munchkins. Alli (her mom) picked Zoe up on the last day of camp—the night after an "epic" cast party—and took her straight to a weeklong mother-daughter self-empowerment retreat in the Catskills that involved a lot of sage and a ginger juice cleanse that was "energizing, but in an angry way."

I only knew all this because Zoe posted pics on a special secret Tumblr called Zoozoo4u. She was documenting all of her feelings about life, her parents' separation, and those sexy Munchkins. It was supposed to be password protected so Alli and Travis couldn't see it. Only, the password was zoozoo4u too, so that wasn't much protection.

Zoe loved putting it all out there on social media. She'd even made an Insta account for the two of us called ZoenHank, where she put up pictures of us cheek to cheek or trying on granny glasses at the drugstore. I loved that she did this for us, but I never got into it as much as she did. Maybe I'd watched one too many scary movies about private eyes or online trolls. Something ooked me out about dumping all my thoughts into the ether for some interweb audience to behold. Yes, I was the last holdout from my grade, or my hemisphere really. And the only teenager I knew who owned a dollhouse. But still.

Even though we were less than an hour apart for most of the summer, Zoe and I had communicated mainly through photo captions and hashtags. She said talking would be "too intense," and I wanted to respect that. Also, I didn't have much to report from the home front. I'd been home doing my usual summer job for the past six weeks: arts and crafts counselor at the Y. The most excitement I had was one day when a camper almost choked on some googly eyes. Also, I went to the pool, and learned how to finger knit, which is just slightly less thrilling than it sounds.

Yeah, it was a typical boring summer until I got a text message from Zoe a half hour ago that said:

we're home! wanna come by and meet my new lover?

The first thing I saw when I came over was a hulking green dumpster in the driveway and a lopsided stack of cardboard boxes next to it. Someone had scrawled TRAVIS on the sides of each box in brazen red Sharpie. The *T*s looked so ferocious, as if they might eat all the other letters. Alli was humming while bent over a milk crate of cassette tapes, and I knew I should say *Hi* and *How ya doing* but I didn't have all the words ready yet, so I stole into the basement through the side door.

All I could see was what was missing. The gray beat-up couch where we'd made forts was gone. So was the wooden coffee table where we'd spilled nail polish remover and taken off a blob of finish. And the red easel where I'd painted such childhood masterpieces as *Upside-Down Rainbow*, *Upside-Down Rainbow 2*, and *Today, with Rainbow*.

Of course, Zoe was the only one with any real talent in drawing. She drew me these hilarious stick figures with huge eyes, saying silly things like, *Welcome to planet Marzoompf, may I take your coat?* or *Hey! You look like a fish I once dated.* Together, we had plans to start an art gallery that also served potato pancakes. Or else we were going to write a book called *Have You Seen My Nosehair Named Larry?* (based on a true story). I was in charge of the writing and I still had all the pages in a purple folder in the top drawer of my desk at home. Zoe was in charge of the illustrations. Which— from the looks of it—were now in a dumpster.

Everything that had been in here was gone. There were no plastic bins of markers, Play-Doh, and decapitated Barbies. There was no Leaning Tower of Board Games on the shelves above the washing machine. What I missed most of all was the Powerpuff Girls drum kit and the disco ball . . . catching those last slips of streetlamp light when we convinced her parents to let us stay up just one more hour.

"What happened to the—?" I started to ask.

"I know, right?" Zoe said. "It's just too sad."

"Did he take everything with him?"

"Who? Travis? Ha!" Zoe coughed out a bitter laugh. "No. He has nothing in his new place." She looked around the shadowy basement with a frown. "This is just Alli's whole purging idea. *Start over with simplicity* or whatever that decluttering self-help guru she bought into on that retreat said."

I felt like I'd just been purged of most of my vocabulary.

"Wow," I said again. "That sounds . . ." I didn't want to end my sentence with *dismal*, *horrible*, or *scarring*. But those were the only adjectives I could dig up at the moment.

"Ooh! But I did save one thing for you!" Zoe said. She ran to the basement stairs and brought back a lavender-colored journal with a glittery unicorn on the cover.

"My nana actually gave this to me a while ago, but you're the real writer, so . . ." She pushed it into my hands. I felt bad that I hadn't brought her anything.

"Thank you. I tried to make you one of those tie-dyed head-bands, but it came out supersplotchy. But maybe we could . . . I mean, would it help if you stayed at my place for a few nights?" I offered.

"Oh, you're the bestest, Hank. No, that wouldn't help anything." My face must have registered as insulted because she followed that up quickly with, "I mean, thank you. It would *help*, but there's just too much going on here right now, including—bah!"

Apparently, Pepe had plenty to say. He was purring and batting at Zoe's dark bangs like they were catnip. It looked like a horrible game to me, but Zoe had now transformed from sullen back into camera-ready pep. "I'm sorry," she gushed. "I really do want to catch up about everything and hear about your summer, but can you just press PLAY while he's letting me hold him? I mean, can you even believe the cuteness happening right this very second?"

She held up Pepe in front of me, so I could see his terrified, unextraordinary face. He yelped wildly, clawing at the wisp of air between us. "I mean, the stripes and the whiskers," she explained.

"Yup," I got out before sneezing three times in rapid succession. Zoe tucked the cat back into her chest and wrapped her arms around him protectively. "I swear I'd breastfeed him if I could. Did you know hundreds of thousands of animals go starving every day?"

I shook my head and rubbed my eyes.

"It's so sad. The woman who brought the litter in is from the

Ukraine and she was telling us these horror stories about how cats are abused there and left to roam . . . and while she was telling us all this, Pepe was just clinging to me, yowling. Like he could hear what she was saying. It was just so *tragic*." Zoe's eyes puddled.

"Got it," I said with a cough. Not that I didn't care. I just felt too short of breath and displaced. Zoe knew I couldn't stand to be around cats. We'd even once promised that if we didn't find respectable partners by the time we turned thirty, we'd move in together and adopt a Labradoodle, a ferret, or a baby—really anything but a cat. I guess that deal meant a lot more to me than to her.

"Ugh, you really are allergic." She sighed. More annoyed than remorseful though. "Okay, we'll be quick. Are you ready for your close-up, Monsieur Meowsers?"

Zoe backed herself up onto the stool and shook out her dark mane while I wiped my drippy nose on the bottom of my T-shirt. Pepe got busy climbing up her neck and gnawing on her nose. Then draping himself around her milky-white throat and tickling her with his fur until she shook with giggles.

"Are you getting all this?" Zoe squealed. "Come closer! Make sure you can see his tiny tongue. It's just beyond."

"Uh-huh," I wheezed.

"I really feel like this amazing little creature *chose* me," she began. As she mused, I shut my eyes tight. Partly because they were burning and partly because I thought if I could just listen I'd hear my old friend. My sister-from-another-mother. My rock.

Zoe's voice was always so husky and clipped. She said what she meant and she meant what she said. She dared me to be bigger and wilder too. That's why I'd admired and adored her for most of our lives.

But even her voice sounded false now. It dipped and swirled as if she were following some melody I'd never heard before.

"Pepe le Meowsers," she serenaded. "In a world full of pain and uncertainty, will you be my *pussyyyyy . . . cat?*"

Pepe loved this line. He meowed on cue.

"Meeeooow!" Zoe chimed in, cackling with glee. The two of them sang over each other, louder and louder. As the cat licked Zoe's mouth, her nostrils, her dark silky hair. The cat was perfectly in tune with her too. Something I could never pull off when we sang together.

Which is why maybe I might have sort of fantasized about wrapping my itchy palms around that feline neck and squeezing until it all just stopped.

Now it's 9:55.

(Cuz, of course, had to stop writing for

"Morning Musings" Group.)

Okay, maybe <u>hate</u> is too harsh a word.

 <u>Despise</u>? <u>Abhor</u>? <u>Fiercely repelled by</u>?

 (I know, a preposition at the end of the sentence is a no-no, right? You were always the greater grammarian, Hanky-Panky.)

 Speaking of your superior brain . . .

 Pop quiz!

 When did you decide to abandon me like that?

          a. Yesterday.

          b. Today, with a side of tomorrow.

          c. It's been so long I don't remember.

          d. I still love you more than life itself.

          e. Sorry, I think you have the wrong Hank.

 But seriously, betrayal takes a long time to plan. Was it a gradual realization or more of a sudden epiphany?

 Speaking of epiphanies, there are three girls on my floor here who blacked out from starvation. Lucky ducks.

 Coulda.

 Woulda.

 Shoulda.

 I know that sounds horrific to you, but the way they describe it sounds absolutely dreamy to me. They are pitifully small and covered

in that malnourished-person body fur and here's the honest truth
(even though you don't deserve truth from me): I'm so freaken
jealous.

They hit that glorious rock-bottom moment.
That clear and definitive sign in the road that says
DO NOT ENTER.

That's all I wanted, really. I just wanted to faint or qualify as
a crisis in some way. I really still fantasize about all the lights
going out and maybe some thick straps pinning me down by
the wrists.
Especially in the middle of a BodybyBernardo class.
With all those ladies clucking and sweating around me. Alli would
probably shit herself.
Ha!

But you couldn't even let me have that moment, Hank.
You just _had_ to step in and "save the day," huh?

None of this is pretty, Hank.
You are not pretty.
I am not pretty.
Fuck _pretty_.
Even the word sounds airbrushed and unattainable. Isn't it hilarious
that right by the checkout counter with all the hangry impulse-buy
candy bars, you can get those tabloids with the horrifying pictures of

Lady Gaga's boobs falling or some Moroccan princess caught on film in a bikini with <u>stretch marks</u>?

Because it's so scandalous and unacceptable to grow.

I didn't do all this to be pretty, by the way.

It was never about being pretty.

<u>Well, then what was it about?</u> you ask.

A fine question, my fair ex-friend. And one that every doctor, nurse, and counselor keeps lining up to ask. If I ever have an answer, I'll let you know.

Actually, that's another lie. I don't feel like I'll be telling you anything anytime soon.

But if you have something to say to me—maybe something that rhymes with

<u>I'm florry</u>, or

<u>I'm snorry</u> . . . ?

Well, you know where I'll be for the next eon.

Seriously, they don't even let us know how many pounds we have to gain or how many self-affirmations we have to chant before we can get out.

This place SUCKS MY NOT-EVEN-THAT-SKINNY WHITE ASSSSSSS.

Yours till the kitchen sinks!

Xoxo,

Zoe